Praise for
Elvis Cole Novels

"The dialogue's clever, and the action's lean and pictorial, with gunshots pinging like mad pinballs."
—*Voice Literary Supplement*

"Cole delivers the goods in the kind of bravura performance only a pro can give." —*Kirkus Reviews*

"This novel shows why the Elvis Cole series has become one of crime fiction's best."
—*Detroit Free Press*

"Sue Grafton's Kinsey Milhone has become a fixture in the genre [and] Robert Crais's Elvis Cole ought to become one, too. Cole is fast replacing Spenser as the best of the intelligent but sensitive tough guys." —*Detroit Free Press*

"Elvis Cole is lean, mean and completely lovable."
—*People*

"Crais . . . flips a quick, cutting wit at Hollywood hucksters, and shows a keen ear for their inane industry prattle."
—*The New York Times Book Review*

"The ghostly influence is Robert B. Parker, including the wisecracks and the incessant attention to food. . . . But once Crais gets past the mandatory wise-mouthing and sets his story in motion, forget influences; he is his own man."
—*Los Angeles Times Book Review*

STALKING THE ANGEL

BY ROBERT CRAIS

STALKING THE ANGEL

AN ELVIS COLE AND JOE PIKE NOVEL

ROBERT CRAIS

BALLANTINE BOOKS
NEW YORK

Stalking the Angel is a work of fiction. Names, characters,
places, and incidents are the products of the author's imagination
or are used fictitiously. Any resemblance to actual events,
locales, or persons, living or dead, is entirely coincidental.

2020 Ballantine Books Mass Market Edition

Copyright © 1989 by Robert Crais
Excerpt from *A Dangerous Man* by Robert Crais
copyright © 2019 by Robert Crais

Published in the United States by Ballantine Books,
an imprint of Random House, a division of
Penguin Random House LLC, New York.

BALLANTINE and the HOUSE colophon are registered trademarks of
Penguin Random House LLC.

Originally published in hardcover in the United States
by Bantam Books, an imprint of Random House, a division of
Penguin Random House LLC, in 1989.

Grateful acknowledgment is made for permission to reprint the
following: "Somebody to Love," on page ix, Lyrics and Music
by Darby Slick, copyright © 1967 IRVING MUSIC, INC. (BMI).
All rights reserved. International copyright secured.
"Old Time Rock & Roll," on page 63, copyright © 1977.
Muscle Shoals Sound Publishing Co. Inc.
"Cruel Summer," on page 42, copyright © 1984
IN A BUNCH MUSIC LTD. & RED BUS MUSIC, LTD.
All rights on behalf of IN A BUNCH MUSIC LTD. Administered by
WARNER-TAMERLANE PUBLISHING CORP. All rights reserved.
Used by permission.

ISBN 978-0-593-15716-9
Ebook ISBN 978-0-307-78996-9

Cover design: Kaitlin Hall
Cover image: Greg Esparaza/EyeEm/Getty Images

Printed in the United States of America

randomhousebooks.com

2 4 6 8 9 7 5 3

Ballantine Books mass market edition: January 2020

For Lauren,
whose parents will always love her,
& for Carol and Bill,
who have made me larger
by sharing their lives.

I love to hear the story
which angel voices tell.
—EMILY MILLER,
   The Little Corporal

When the truth is found to be lies,
and all the joy within you dies,
don't you want somebody to love?
—JEFFERSON AIRPLANE

STALKING THE ANGEL

1

I was standing on my head in the middle of my office when the door opened and the best looking woman I'd seen in three weeks walked in. She stopped in the door to stare, then remembered herself and moved aside for a grim-faced man who frowned when he saw me. A sure sign of disapproval. The woman said, "Mr. Cole, I'm Jillian Becker. This is Bradley Warren. May we speak with you?"

Jillian Becker was in her early thirties, slender in gray pants and a white ruffled shirt with a fluffy bow at the neck and a gray jacket. She held a cordovan Gucci briefcase that complemented the gray nicely, and had very blond hair and eyes that I would call amber but she would call green. Good eyes. There was an intelligent humor in them that the Serious Businesswoman look didn't diminish.

I said, "You should try this. Invigorates the scalp. Retards the aging process. Makes for embarrassing moments when prospective clients walk in." Upside down, my face was the color of beef liver.

Jillian Becker smiled politely. "Mr. Warren and I don't have very much time," she said. "Mr. Warren and I have to catch the noon flight to Kyoto, Japan." Mr. Warren.

"Of course."

I dropped down from the headstand, held one of the two director's chairs opposite my desk for Jillian Becker, shook hands with Mr. Warren, then tucked in my shirt and took a seat at my desk. I had taken off the shoulder holster earlier so it wouldn't flop into my face when I was upside down. "What can I do for you?" I said. Clever opening lines are my forte.

Bradley Warren looked around the office and frowned again. He was ten years older than Jillian, and had the manicured, no-hair-out-of-place look that serious corporate types go for. There was an $8000 gold Rolex watch on his left wrist and a $3000 Wesley Barron pinstripe suit on the rest of him and he didn't seem too worried that I'd slug him and steal the Rolex. Probably had another just like it at home. "Are you in business by yourself, Mr. Cole?" He'd have been more comfortable if I'd been in a suit and had a couple of wanted posters lying around.

"I have a partner named Joe Pike. Mr. Pike is not a licensed private investigator. He is a former Los Angeles police officer. I hold the license." I pointed out the framed pink license that the Bureau of Collections of the State of California had issued to me. "You see. Elvis Cole." The license hangs beside this animation cel I've got of the Blue Fairy and Pinocchio. Pinocchio is as close as I come to a wanted poster.

Bradley Warren stared at the Blue Fairy and looked

doubtful. He said, "Something very valuable was stolen from my home four days ago. I need someone to find it."

"Okay."

"Do you know anything about the Japanese culture?"

"I read *Shōgun*."

Warren made a quick hand gesture and said, "Jillian." His manner was brusque and I didn't like it much. Jillian Becker didn't seem to mind, but she was probably used to it.

Jillian said, "The Japanese culture was once predicated on a very specific code of behavior and personal conduct developed by the samurai during Japan's feudal period."

Samurai. Better buckle the old seat belt for this one.

"In the eighteenth century, a man named Jōchō Yamamoto outlined every aspect of proper behavior for the samurai in manuscript form. It was called 'Recorded Words of the Hagakure Master,' or, simply, the Hagakure, and only a few of the original editions survive. Mr. Warren had arranged the loan of one of these from the Tashiro family in Kyoto, with whom his company has extensive business dealings. The manuscript was in his home safe when it was stolen."

As Jillian spoke, Bradley Warren looked around the office again and did some more frowning. He frowned at the Mickey Mouse phone. He frowned at the little figurines of Jiminy Cricket. He frowned at the SpiderMan mug. I considered taking out my gun and letting him frown at that, too, but thought it might seem peevish. "How much is the Hagakure worth?"

Jillian Becker said, "A little over three million dollars."

"Insured?"

"Yes. But the policy won't begin to cover the millions our company will lose in business with the Tashiros unless their manuscript is recovered."

"The police are pretty good. Why not go to them?"

Bradley Warren sighed loudly, letting us know he was bored, then frowned at the gold Rolex. Time equals money.

Jillian said, "The police are involved, Mr. Cole, but we'd like things to proceed faster than they seem able to manage. That's why we came to you."

"Oh," I said. "I thought you came to me so Bradley could practice frowning."

Bradley looked at me. Pointedly. "I'm the president of Warren Investments Corporation. We form real estate partnerships with Japanese investors." He leaned forward and raised his eyebrows. "I have a big operation. I'm in Hawaii. I'm in L.A., San Diego, Seattle." He made an opera out of looking around my office. "Try to imagine the money involved."

Jillian Becker said, "Mr. Warren's newest hotel has just opened downtown in Little Tokyo."

Bradley said, "Thirty-two stories. Eight million square feet."

I nodded. "Big."

He nodded back at me.

Jillian said, "We wanted to have the Hagakure on display there next week when the Pacific Men's Club names Bradley Man of the Month."

Bradley gave me more of the eyebrows. "I'm the first Caucasian they've honored this way. You know why? I've pumped three hundred million dollars into the local Asian community in the last thirty-six months. You got any idea how much money that is?"

"Excuse me," I said. I pushed away from my desk, pitched myself out of my chair onto the floor, then got up, brushed myself off, and sat again. "There. I'm finished being impressed. We can go on."

Jillian Becker's face went white. Bradley Warren's face went dark red. His nostrils flared and his lips tightened and he stood up. It was lovely. He said, "I don't like your attitude."

"That's okay. I'm not selling it." I opened the drawer in the center of my desk and tossed a cream-colored card toward him. He looked at it. "What's this?"

"Pinkerton's. They're large. They're good. They're who you want. But they probably won't like your attitude any more than I do." I stood up with him.

Jillian Becker stood up, too, and held out her hand the way you do when you want things to settle down. "Mr. Cole, I think we've started on the wrong foot here."

I leaned forward. "One of us did."

She turned toward Warren. "It's a small firm, Bradley, but it's a quality firm. Two attorneys in the prosecutor's office recommended him. He's been an investigator for eight years and the police think highly of him. His references are impeccable." Impeccable. I liked that.

Bradley Warren held the Pink's card and flexed it back and forth, breathing hard. He looked the way a

man looks when he doesn't have any other choice and
the choice he has is lousy. There's a Pinocchio clock
on the wall beside the door that leads to Joe Pike's
office. It has eyes that move from side to side. You go
to the Pinkerton's, they don't have a clock like that.
Jillian Becker said, "Bradley, he's who you want to
hire."

After a while the heavy breathing passed and
Bradley nodded. "All right, Cole. I'll go along with
Jillian on this and hire you."

"No," I said. "You won't."

Jillian Becker stiffened. Bradley Warren looked at
Jillian Becker, then looked back at me. "What do you
mean, I won't?"

"I don't want to work for you."

"Why not?"

"I don't like you."

Bradley Warren started to say something, then
stopped. His mouth opened, then closed. Jillian
Becker looked confused. Maybe no one had ever before said no to Bradley Warren. Maybe it was against
the law. Maybe Bradley Warren's personal police were
about to crash through the door and arrest me for
defying the One True Way. Jillian shook her head.
"They said you could be difficult."

I shrugged. "They should've said that when I'm
pushed, I push back. They also should've said that
when I do things, I do them my way." I looked at
Bradley. "The check rents. It does not buy."

Bradley Warren stared at me as if I had just
beamed down from the *Enterprise*. He stood very
still. So did Jillian Becker. They stood like that until a
tic started beneath his left eye and he said, "Jillian."

Jillian Becker said, "Mr. Cole, we need the Hagakure found, and we want you to find it. If we in some way offended you, we apologize."

We.

"Will you help us?"

Her makeup was understated and appropriate, and there was a tasteful gold chain around her right wrist. She was bright and attractive and I wondered how many times she'd had to apologize for him and how it made her feel.

I gave her the Jack Nicholson smile and made a big deal out of sitting down again. "For you, babe, anything." Can you stand it?

Bradley Warren's face was red and purple and splotched, and the tic was a mad flicker. He made the hand gesture as quick as a cracking whip, and said, "Write him a check and leave it blank. I'll be down in the limo."

He left without looking at me and without offering his hand and without waiting for Jillian. When he was gone I said, "My, my. Man of the Month."

Jillian Becker took a deep breath, let it out, then sat in one of the director's chairs and opened the Gucci briefcase in her lap. She took out a corporate checkbook and spoke while she wrote. "Mr. Cole, please understand that Bradley's under enormous pressure. We're on our way to Kyoto to tell the Tashiros what has happened. That will be neither pleasant nor easy."

"Sorry," I said. "I should be more sensitive."

She glanced up from the check with cool eyes. "Maybe you should."

So much for humor.

After a while, she put the check and a 3 × 5 index card on my desk. I didn't look at the check. She said, "The card has Bradley's home and office addresses and phone numbers. It also has mine. You may call me at any time, day or night, for anything that pertains to this case."

"Okay."

"Will you need anything else?"

"Access to the house. I want to see where the book was and talk to anyone who knew that the book was there. Also, if there's a photograph or description of the manuscript, I'll need it."

"Bradley's wife can supply that. At the house."

"What's her name?"

"Sheila. Their daughter Mimi lives at the house, also, along with two housekeepers. I'll call Sheila and tell her to expect you."

"Fine."

"Fine."

We were getting along just great.

Jillian Becker closed the Gucci briefcase, snapped its latch, stood, and went to the door. Maybe she hadn't always been this serious. Maybe working for Bradley brought it out in her.

"You do that well," I said.

She looked back. "What?"

"Walk."

She gave me the cool eyes again. "This is a business relationship, Mr. Cole. Let's leave it at that."

"Sure."

She opened the door.

"One more thing."

She turned back to me.

"You always look this good, or is today a special occasion?"

She stood like that for a while, not moving, and then she shook her head. "You really are something, aren't you?"

I made a gun out of my hand, pointed it at her, and gave her another dose of the Nicholson. "I hope he pays you well."

She went out and slammed the door.

2

When the door closed I looked at the check. Blank. She hadn't dated it 1889 or April 1. It had been signed by Bradley Warren and, as far as I could tell, in ink that wouldn't vanish. Maybe a better detective would have known for sure about the ink, but I'd have to risk it. Son of a gun. My big chance. I could nick him for a hundred thousand dollars, but that was probably playing it small. Maybe I should put a one and write zeros until my arm fell off and endorse it Elvis Cole, Yachtsman.

I folded the check in half, put it in my wallet, and took a Dan Wesson .38 in a shoulder rig out of my top right-hand drawer. I pulled a white cotton jacket on to cover the Dan Wesson, then went down to my car. The car is a Jamaica-yellow 1966 Corvette convertible that looks pretty snazzy. Maybe with the white jacket and the convertible and the blank check in my pocket, someone would think I was Donald Trump.

I put the Corvette out onto Santa Monica and

cruised west through Beverly Hills and the upper rim of Century City, then north up Beverly Glen past rows of palm trees and stuccoed apartment houses and Persian-owned construction projects. L.A. in late June is bright. With the smog pressed down by an inversion layer, the sky turns white and the sun glares brilliantly from signs and awnings and reflective building glass and deep-waxed fenders and miles and miles of molten chrome bumpers. There were shirtless kids with skateboards on their way into Westwood and older women with big hats coming back from markets and construction workers tearing up the streets and Hispanic women waiting for buses and everybody wore sunglasses. It looked like a Ray Ban commercial.

I stayed with Beverly Glen up past the Los Angeles Country Club golf course until I got to Sunset Boulevard, then hung a right and a quick left into upper Holmby Hills. Holmby is a smaller, more expensive version of the very best part of Beverly Hills to the east. It is old and elegant, and the streets are wide and neat with proper curbs and large homes hidden behind hedgerows and mortar walls and black wrought iron gates. Many of the houses are near the street, but a few are set back and quite a few you can't see at all.

The Warrens' home was the one with the guard. He was sitting in a light blue Thunderbird with a sticker on its side that said TITAN SECURITIES. He got out when he saw me slow down and stood with his hands on his hips. Late forties, big across the back, in a brown off-the-rack Sears suit. Wrinkled. He'd taken a couple of hard ones on the bridge of his nose, but that had been a long time ago. I turned into the drive, and showed him the license. "Cole. They're expecting me."

He nodded at the license and leaned against the door. "She sent the kid down to tell me you were on the way. I'm Hatcher." He didn't offer to shake my hand.

I said, "Anyone try storming the house?"

He looked back at the house, then shook his head. "Shit. I been out here since they got hit and I ain't seen dick." He shot me a wink. "Leastways, not what you're talking about."

I said, "Are you tipping me off or is something in your eye?"

He smirked. "You been out before?"

"Uh-uh."

He gave me some more of the smirk, then ambled back to the Thunderbird. "You'll see."

Bradley Warren lived in a French Normandy mansion just about the size of Kansas. A large Spanish oak in the center of the motor court put filigreed shadows on the Normandy's steep roof, and three or four thousand snapdragons spilled out of the beds that bordered the drive and the perimeter of the house. There was a porchlike overhang at the front of the house with the front door recessed in a wide alcove. It was a single door, but it was a good nine feet high and four feet wide. Maybe Bradley Warren had bought the place from the Munsters.

I parked under the big oak, walked over to the door, and rang the bell. Hatcher was twisted around in his T-bird, watching. I rang the bell two more times before the door opened and a woman wearing a white Love tennis outfit and holding a tall glass with something clear in it looked up at me. She said, "Are you the detective?"

"Usually I wear a deerstalker cap," I said, "but today it's at the cleaners."

She laughed too loud and put out her hand. "Sheila Warren," she said. "You're a good-looking devil, aren't you." Twenty minutes before noon and she was drunk.

I looked back at Hatcher. He was grinning.

Sheila Warren was in her forties, with tanned skin and a sharp nose and bright blue eyes and auburn hair. She had the sort of deep lines you get when you play a lot of tennis or golf or otherwise hang out in the sun. The hair was pulled back in a pony tail and she wore a white headband. She looked good in the tennis outfit, but not athletic. Probably did more hanging out than playing.

She opened the door wider and gestured with the glass for me to come in. Ice tinkled. "I suppose you want to see where he had the damn book." She said it like we were talking about an eighth-grade history book.

"Sure."

She gestured with the glass again. "I always like to have something cool when I come in off the court. All that sweat. Can I get you something?"

"Maybe later."

We walked back through about six thousand miles of entry and a living room they could rent out as an airplane hangar and a dining room with seating for Congress. She stayed a step in front of me and swayed as she walked. I said, "Was anyone home the night it was stolen?"

"We were in Canada. Bradley's building a hotel in Edmonton so we flew up. Bradley usually flies alone, but the kid and I wanted to go so we went." The kid.

"How about the help?"

"They've all got family living down in Little Tokyo. They beat it down there as soon as we're out of the house." She looked back at me. "The police asked all this, you know."

"I like to check up on them."

She said, "Oh, you."

We went down a long hall with a tile floor and into a cavern that turned out to be the master bedroom. At the end of the hall there was an open marble atrium with a lot of green leafy plants in it, and to the left of the atrium there were glass doors looking out to the back lawn and the pool. Where one of the glass doors had been, there was now a 4 × 8 sheet of plywood as if the glass had been broken and the plywood put there until the glass could be replaced. Opposite the atrium, there was a black lacquer platform bed and a lot of black lacquer furniture. We went past the bed and through a doorway into a *his* dressing room. The *hers* had a separate entrance.

The *his* held a full-length three-way dressing mirror and a black granite dressing table and about a mile and a half of coats and slacks and suits and enough shoes to shod a small American city. At the foot of the dressing mirror the carpet had been rolled back and there was a Citabria-Wilcox floor safe large enough for a man to squat in.

Sheila Warren gestured toward it with the glass and made a face. "The big shot's safe."

The top was lying open like a manhole cover

swung over on a hinge. It was quarter-inch plate steel with two tumblers and three half-inch shear pins. There was black powder on everything from when the crime scene guys dusted for prints. Nothing else seemed disturbed. The ice tinkled behind me. "Was the safe like this when you found it?"

"It was closed. The police left it open."

"How about the alarm?"

"The police said they must've known how to turn it off. Or maybe we forgot to turn it on." She gave a little shrug when she said it, like it didn't matter very much in the first place and she was tired of talking about it. She was leaning against the door-jamb with her arms crossed, watching me. Maybe she thought that when detectives flew into action it was something you didn't want to miss. "You should've seen the glass," she said. "He brings the damn book here and look what happens. I walk barefoot on the carpet and I still pick up slivers. Mr. Big Shot Businessman." She didn't say the last part to me.

"Has anyone called, or delivered a ransom note?"

"For what?"

"The book. When something rare and easily identifiable is stolen, it's usually stolen to sell it back to the owner or his insurance company."

She made another face. "That's silly."

I guess that meant no. I stood up. "Your husband said there were pictures of the book."

She finished the drink and said, "I wish he'd take care of these things himself." Then she left. Maybe I could go out and Hatcher could come in and question her for me. Maybe Hatcher already had. Maybe I should call the airport and catch Bradley's plane and tell him he could keep his check and his job. Nah. What would Donald Trump think?

When Sheila Warren came back, she had gotten rid of the glass and was carrying a color 8 × 10 showing Bradley accepting something that looked like a photo album from a dignified white-haired Japanese gentleman. There were other men around, all Japanese, but not all of them looked dignified. The book was a dark rich brown, probably leather-covered board, and would probably crumble if you sneered at it. Jillian Becker was in the picture.

Sheila Warren said, "I hope this is what you want." The top three buttons on her tennis outfit had been undone.

"This will be fine," I said. I folded the picture and put it in my pocket.

She wet her lips. "Are you sure I can't get you something to drink?"

"Positive, thanks."

She looked down at her shoes, said, "Ooo, these darn laces," then turned her back and bent over from the hip. The laces hadn't looked untied to me, but I miss a lot. She played with one lace and then she played with the other, and while she was playing with them I walked out. I wandered back through to the kitchen and from there to the rear yard. There was a dichondra lawn that sloped gently away from the house toward a fifty-foot Greek Revival swimming pool and a small pool house with a sunken conversation pit around a circular grill. I stood at the deep end of the pool and looked around and shook my head. Man. First him. Now her. What a pair.

Whoever had gone into the house had probably

known the combination or known where to find it. Combinations are easy to get. One day when no one's around, a gardener slips in, finds the scrap of paper on which people like Bradley Warren always write their combinations, then sells it to the right guy for the right price. Or maybe one day Sheila flexed a little too much upper-class muscle with the hundred-buck-a-week housekeeper, and the housekeeper says, Okay, bitch, here's one for you, and feeds the numbers to her out-of-work boyfriend. You could go on.

I walked along the pool deck past the tennis court and along the edge of the property and then back toward the house. There were no guard dogs and no closed-circuit cameras and no fancy surveillance equipment. The wall around the perimeter wasn't electrified, and if there was a guard tower it was disguised as a palm tree. Half the kids on Hollywood Boulevard could loot the place blind. Maybe I'd go down there and question them. Only take me three or four years.

When I got back to the house, a teenage girl was sitting on one of four couches in the den. She was cross-legged, staring down into the oversized pages of a book that could've been titled *Andrew Wyeth's Bleakest Landscapes*.

I said, "Hi, my name's Elvis. Are you Mimi?"

She looked up at me the way you look at someone when you open your front door and see it's a Jehovah's Witness. She was maybe sixteen and had close-cropped brown hair that framed her face like a small inner tube. It made her face rounder than it was. I would have suggested something upswept or shag-cut to give her face some length, but she hadn't asked me.

There was no makeup and no nail polish and some would have been in order. She wasn't pretty. She rubbed at her nose and said, "Are you the detective?"

"Uh-huh. You got any clues about the big theft?"

She rubbed at her nose again.

"Clues," I said. "Did you see a shadow skulk across the lawn? Did you overhear a snatch of mysterious conversation? That kind of thing."

Maybe she was looking at me. Maybe she wasn't. There was sort of a cockeyed grin on her face that made me wonder if she was high.

"Would you like to get back to your book?"

She didn't nod or blink or run screaming from the room. She just stared.

I went back through the dining room and the entry and out to my Corvette and cranked it up and eased down the drive. When I got to the street, Hatcher grinned over from his T-bird, and said, "How'd you like it?"

"Up yours," I said.

He laughed and I drove away.

3

Three years ago I'd done some work for a man named Berke Feldstein who owns a very nice art gallery in Venice on the beach below Santa Monica. It's one of those converted industrial spaces where they slap on a coat of stark white paint to maintain the industrial look and all the art is white boxes with colored paper inside. For Christmas that year, Berke had given me a large mug with the words MONSTER FIGHTER emblazoned on its side. I like it a lot.

I dropped down out of Holmby Hills into Westwood, parked at a falafel stand, and used their pay phone to call Berke's gallery. A woman's voice answered, "ArtWerks Gallery."

I said, "This is Michael Delacroix's representative calling. Is Mr. Feldman receiving?" A black kid in a UCLA tee shirt was slumped at one of the picnic tables they have out there, reading a sociology text.

Her voice came back hesitant. "You mean Mr. Feldstein?"

I gave her imperious. "Is *that* his name?"

She asked me to hold. There were the sounds of something or someone moving around in the background, and then Berke Feldstein said, "Who is this, please?"

"The King of Rock 'n' Roll."

A dry, sardonic laugh. Berke Feldstein does sardonic better than anyone else I know. "Don't tell me. You're trying to decide between the Monet and the Degas and you need my advice."

I said, "Something very rare from eighteenth-century Japan has been stolen. Who might have some ideas about that?" The black kid closed the book and looked at me.

Berke Feldstein put me on hold. After a minute, he was on the line again. His voice was flat and serious. "I won't be connected with this?"

"Berke." I gave him miffed.

He said, "There's a Gallery on Cañon Drive in Beverly Hills. The Sun Tree Gallery. It's owned by a guy named Malcolm Denning. I can't *swear* by this, but I've heard that Denning's occasionally a conduit for less than honest transactions."

" 'Less than honest.' I like that. Do we mean 'criminal'?" The black kid got up and walked away.

"Don't be smug," Berke said.

"How come you hear about these less than honest transactions, Berke? You got something going on the side?"

He hung up.

There were several ways to locate the Sun Tree Gallery. I could call one of the contacts I maintain in the police department and have them search through their secret files. I could drive about aimlessly, stopping at every gallery I passed until I found someone who knew the location, then force the information from him. Or I could look in the Yellow Pages. I looked in the Yellow Pages.

The Sun Tree Gallery of Beverly Hills rested atop a jewelry store two blocks over from Rodeo Drive amidst some of the world's most exclusive shopping. There were plenty of boutiques with Arabic or Italian names, and small plaques that said BY APPOINTMENT ONLY. The shoppers were rich, the cars were German, and the doormen were mostly young and handsome and looking to land a lead in an action-adventure series. You could smell the crime in the air.

I passed the gallery twice without finding a parking spot, continued north up Cañon above Santa Monica Boulevard to the residential part of the Beverly Hills flats, parked there, and walked back. A heavy glass door was next to the jewelry store with a small, tasteful brass sign that said SUN TREE GALLERY, HOURS 10:00 A.M. UNTIL 5:00 P.M., TUESDAY THROUGH SATURDAY; DARK, SUNDAY AND MONDAY. I went through the door and climbed a flight of plush stairs that led up to a landing where there was a much heavier door with another brass sign that said RING BELL. Maybe when you rang the bell, a guy in a beret with a long scar beside his nose slithered out and asked if you wanted to buy some stolen art. I rang the bell.

A very attractive brunette in a claret-colored pants suit appeared in the door, buzzed me in, and said brightly, "I hope you're having a good day." These criminals will do anything to gain your confidence.

"I could take it or leave it until you said that. Is Mr. Denning in?"

"Yes, but I'm afraid he's on long distance just now. If you could wait a moment, I'd love to help you." There was an older, balding man and a silver-haired woman standing at the front of the place by a long glass wall that faced down on the street. The man was looking at a shiny black helmet not unlike that worn by Darth Vader. It was sitting on a sleek red pedestal and was covered by a glass dome.

"Sure," I said. "Mind if I browse?"

She handed me a price catalog and another big smile. "Not at all." These crooks.

The gallery was one large room that had been sectioned off by three false walls to form little viewing alcoves. There weren't many pieces on display, but what was there seemed authentic. Vases and bowls sat on pedestals beneath elegant watercolors done on thin cloth that had been stretched over a bamboo frame. The cloth was yellow with age. There were quite a few wood-block prints that I liked, including a very nice double print that was two separate prints mounted side by side. Each was of the same man in a bamboo house overlooking a river as a storm raged at the horizon and lightning flashed. Each man held a bit of blue cloth that trailed away out of the picture. The pictures were mounted so that the cloth trailed from one picture to the other, connecting the men. It was a lovely piece and would be a fine addition to my home. I looked up the price. $14,000. Maybe I could find something more appropriate to my decor.

At the rear of the gallery there was a sleek Elliot Ryerson desk, three beige corduroy chairs for sitting down and discussing the financing of your purchase, and a good stand of the indoor palms I am always trying to grow in my office but which are always dying. These were thriving. Behind the palms was a door. It opened, and a man in a pink Lacoste shirt and khaki slacks came out and began looking for something on the desk. Mid-forties. Short hair with a sprinkling of gray. The brunette looked over and said, "Mr. Denning, this gentleman would like to see you."

Malcolm Denning gave me a friendly smile and put out his hand. He had sad eyes. "Can you give me a minute? I'm on the phone with a client in Paris." Good handshake.

"Sure."

"Thanks. I won't be any longer than necessary." He gave me another smile, found what he was looking for, then disappeared back through the door. Malcolm Denning, Considerate Crook.

The brunette resumed talking to the older couple and I resumed browsing and when everything was back the way it had been, I went through the door. There was a short hall with a bathroom on the left, what looked like a storage and packing area at the rear, and a small office on the right. Malcolm Denning was in the office, seated at a cluttered rolltop desk, speaking French into the phone. He looked up when he saw me, cupped the receiver, and said, "I'm sorry. This will take another minute or so."

I took out my license and held it for him to see. I could've showed him a card, but the license looked more official. "Elvis Cole's the name, private detecting's the game." One of those things you always want to say. "I've got a few questions about feudal Japanese art and I'm told you're the man to ask."

Without taking his eyes from me, he spoke more

French into the phone, nodded at something I couldn't hear, then hung up. There were four photographs along the top of the desk, one of an overweight woman with a pleasant smile, and another of three teenage boys. One of the pictures was of a Little League team with Malcolm Denning and another man both wearing shirts that said COACH. "May I ask who referred you to me?"

"You can ask, but I'm afraid I couldn't tell you. Somebody tells me something, I try to protect the source. Especially if what they've told me can be incriminating. You see?"

"Incriminating?"

"*Especially* if it's incriminating."

He nodded.

"You know what the Hagakure is, Mr. Denning?"

Nervous. "Well, the Hagakure isn't really a piece of what we might call art. It's a book, you know." He put one hand on his desk and the other in his lap. There was a red mug on the desk that said DAD.

"But it's fair to say that whoever might have an interest in early Japanese art might also have an interest in the Hagakure, wouldn't it?"

"I guess."

"One of the original copies of the Hagakure was stolen a few days ago. Would you have heard anything about that?"

"Why on earth would I hear anything about it?"

"Because you've been known to broker a rip-off or two."

He pushed back his chair and stood up. The two of us in the little office was like being in a phone booth. "I think you should leave," he said.

"Come on, Malcolm. Give us both a break. You don't want to be hassled and I can hassle you."

The outer door opened and the pretty brunette came back into the little hall. She saw us standing there, broke into the smile, said, "Oh, I wondered where you'd gone." Then she saw the look on Denning's face. "Mr. Denning?"

He looked at me and I looked back. Then he glanced at her. "Yes, Barbara?"

Nervousness is contagious. She looked from Denning to me and back to Denning. She said, "The Kendals want to purchase the Myori."

I said, "Maybe the Kendals can help me."

Malcolm Denning stared at me for a long time and then he sat down. He said, "I'll be right out."

When she was gone, he said, "I can sue you for this. I can get an injunction to bar you from the premises. I can have you arrested." His voice was hoarse. An I-always-thought-this-would-happen-and-now-it-has voice.

"Sure," I said.

He stared at me, breathing hard, thinking it through, wondering how far he'd have to go if he picked up the ball, and how much it would cost him.

I said, "If someone wanted the Hagakure, who might arrange for its theft? If the Hagakure were for sale, who might buy it?"

His eyes flicked over the pictures on the desk. The wife, the sons. The Little League. I watched the sad eyes. He was a nice man. Maybe even a good man. Sometimes, in this job, you wonder how someone managed to take the wrong turn. You wonder where it happened and when and why. But you don't really want to know. If you knew, it would break your heart.

He said, "There's a man in Little Tokyo. He has some sort of import business. Nobu Ishida." He told me where I could find Ishida. He stared at the pictures as he told me.

After a while I went out through the gallery and down the stairs and along Cañon to my car. It was past three and traffic was starting to build, so it took the better part of an hour to move back along Sunset and climb the mountain to the little A-frame I have off Woodrow Wilson Drive above Hollywood. When I got inside, I took two cold Falstaff beers out of the fridge, pulled off my shirt, and went out onto my deck.

There was a black cat crouched under a Weber charcoal grill that I keep out there. He's big and he's mean and he's black all over except for the white scars that lace his fur like spider webs. He keeps one ear up and one ear sort of cocked to the side because someone once shot him. Head shot. He hasn't been right since.

"You want some beer?"

He growled.

"Forget it, then."

The growling stopped.

I took out the center section of the railing that runs around the deck, sat on the edge, and opened the first Falstaff. From my deck you can see across a long twisting canyon that widens and spreads into Hollywood. I like to sit there with my feet hanging down and drink and think about things. It's about thirty feet from the deck to the slope below, but that's okay.

I like the height. Sometimes the hawks come and float above the canyon and above the smog. They like the height, too.

I drank some of the beer and thought about Bradley and Sheila and Jillian Becker and Malcolm Denning. Bradley would be sitting comfortably in first class, dictating important business notes to Jillian Becker, who would be writing them down and nodding. Sheila would be out on her tennis court, bending over to show Hatcher her rear end, and squealing, *Ooo, these darn laces!* Malcolm Denning would be staring at the pictures of his wife and his boys and his Little League team and wondering when it would all go to hell.

"You ever notice," I said to the cat, "that sometimes the bad guys are better people than the good guys?"

The cat crept out from beneath the Weber, walked over, and sniffed at my beer. I poured a little out onto the deck for him and touched his back as he drank. It was soft.

Sometimes he bites, but not always.

4

The next morning it was warm and bright in my loft, with the summer sun slanting in through the big glass A that is the back of my house. The cat was curled on the bed next to me, bits of leaf and dust in his fur, smelling of eucalyptus.

I rolled out of bed and pulled on some shorts and went downstairs. I opened the glass sliding doors for the breeze, then went back into the living room and turned on the TV. News. I changed channels. Rocky and Bullwinkle. There was a thump upstairs and then the cat came down. Bullwinkle said, "Nothing up my sleeve!" and ripped off his sleeve to prove it. Rocky said, "Oh, no, not again!" and flew around in a circle. The cat hopped up on the couch and stared at them. *The Adventures of Rocky and Bullwinkle* is his favorite show.

I went back out onto the deck and did twelve sun salutes to stretch out the kinks. I did neck rolls and shoulder rolls and the spine rock and the cobra and the locust, and I began to sweat. Inside, Mr. Peabody and Sherman were setting the Way Back Machine for the Early Mesopotamian Age. I put myself into the peacock posture with my legs straight out behind me and I held it like that until my back screamed and the sweat left dark splatters on the deck, and then I went into the Dragon *kata* from the tae kwon do, and then the Crane *kata,* driving myself until the sweat ran in my eyes and my muscles failed and my nerves refused to carry another signal and I sat on the deck and felt like a million bucks. Endorphin heaven. So clients weren't perfect. So being a private cop wasn't perfect. So life wasn't perfect. I could always get new cards printed up. They would say: *Elvis Cole, Perfect Detective.*

Forty minutes later I was on the Hollywood Freeway heading southeast toward downtown Los Angeles and Little Tokyo and feeling pretty good about myself. Ah, perfection. It lends comfort in troubled times.

I stayed with the Hollywood past the Pasadena interchange, then took the Broadway exit into downtown L.A. Downtown Los Angeles features dirty inner-city streets, close-packed inner-city skyscrapers, and aromatic inner-city street life. The men who work there wear suits and the women wear heels and you see people carrying umbrellas as if it might rain. Downtown Los Angeles does not feel like Los Angeles. It is Boston or Chicago or Detroit or Manhattan. It feels like someplace else that had come out to visit and decided to stay. Maybe one day they'll put a dome over it and charge admission. They could call it Banal-land.

I took Broadway down to First Street, hung a left, and two blocks later I was in Little Tokyo.

The buildings were old, mostly brick or stone facade, but they had been kept up and the streets were clean. Paper lanterns hung in front of some of the shops, and red and green and yellow and blue wind socks in front of others, and all the signs were in Japanese. The sidewalks were crowded. Summer is tourist season, and most of the white faces and many of the yellow ones had Nikons or Pentaxes slung under them. A knot of sailors in Italian navy uniforms stood at a street corner, grinning at a couple of girls in a Camaro who grinned back at them. One of the sailors carried a Disneyland bag with Mickey Mouse on the side. Souvenirs from distant lands.

Nobu Ishida's import business was exactly where Malcolm Denning said it would be, in an older building on Ki Street between a fish market and a Japanese-language bookstore, with a yakitori grill across the street.

I rolled past Ishida's place, found a parking spot in front of one of the souvenir shops they have for people from Cleveland, and walked back. There was a little bell on the door that rang as I went in and three men sitting around two tables at the rear of the place. It looked more like a warehouse than a retail outlet, with boxes stacked floor to ceiling and lots of free-standing metal shelves. A few things were on display, mostly garish lacquered boxes and miniature pagodas and dragons that looked like Barkley from *Sesame Street*. I smiled at the three men. "Nice stuff."

One of them said, "What do you want?" He was a lot younger than the other two, maybe in his early twenties. No accent. Born and raised in Southern California with a surfer's tan to prove it. He was big for someone of Japanese extraction, just over six feet, with muscular arms and lean jaws and the sort of wildly overdeveloped trapezius muscles you get when you spend a lot of time with the weights. He wore a tight knit shirt with a crew neck and three-quarter sleeves even though it was ninety degrees outside. The other two guys were both in their thirties. One of them had a bad left eye as if he had taken a hard one there and it had never healed, and the other had the pinkie missing from his right hand. I made the young one for Ishida's advertising manager and the other two for buyers from Neiman-Marcus.

"My name's Elvis Cole," I said. "Are you Nobu Ishida?" I put one of my cards on the second table.

The one with the missing finger grinned at the big kid and said, "Hey, Eddie, are you Nobu Ishida?"

Eddie said, "You have business with Mr. Ishida?"

"Well, it's what we might call personal."

The one with the bad eye said something in Japanese.

"Sorry," I said. "Japanese is one of the four known languages I don't speak."

Eddie said, "Maybe you'll understand this, dude. Fuck off."

They probably weren't from Neiman-Marcus. I said, "You'd better ask Mr. Ishida. Tell him it's about eighteenth-century Japan."

Eddie thought about it for a while, then picked up my card, and said, "Wait here." He disappeared behind stacks of what looked like sushi trays and bamboo steamers.

The guy with the bad eye and the guy with no finger stared at me. I said, "I guess Mr. Ishida keeps you guys around to take inventory."

The guy with no finger smiled, but I don't think he was being friendly.

A little bit later Eddie came back without the card and said, "Time for you to go."

I said, "Ask him again. I won't take much of his time."

"You're leaving."

I looked from Eddie to the other two and back to Eddie. "Nope. I'm going to stay and I'm going to talk to Ishida or I'm going to tip the cops that you guys deal stolen goods." Mr. Threat.

The guy with the bad eye mumbled something else and they all laughed. Eddie pulled his sleeves up to his elbows and flexed his arms. Big, all right. Elaborate, multicolored tattoos started about an inch below his elbows and continued up beneath the sleeves. They looked like fish scales. His hands were square and blocky and his knuckles were thick. He said something in Japanese and the guy with the missing finger came around the tables like he was going to show me the door. When he reached to take my arm I pushed his hand away. He stopped smiling and threw a pretty fast backfist. I pushed the fist past me and hit him in the neck with my left hand. He made the sound a drunk in a cheap restaurant makes with a piece of meat caught in his throat and went down. The guy with the bad eye was coming around the tables when an older man came out from behind the bamboo steamers and spoke sharply and the guy with the bad eye stopped.

Nobu Ishida was in his early fifties with short gray hair and hard black eyes and a paunch for a belly. Even with the paunch, the other guys seemed to straighten up and pay attention. Those who could stand.

He looked at me the way you look at a disappearing menu, then shook his head. The guy on the floor was making small coughing noises but Nobu Ishida didn't look at him and neither did anyone else. Ishida was carrying my card. "What are you, crazy? You know I could have you arrested for this?" Nobu Ishida didn't have an accent, either.

I gave him a little shrug. "Go ahead."

He said, "What do you want?"

I told him about the Hagakure.

Nobu Ishida listened without moving and then he tried to give me good-natured confusion. "I don't get it. Why come to me?"

The guy with the missing finger stopped making noises and pushed himself up to his knees. He was holding his throat. I said, "You're interested in samurai artifacts. The Hagakure was stolen. You've purchased stolen artworks in the past. You see how this works?"

The good-natured confusion went away. Ishida's mouth tightened and something dark washed his face. Telltale signs of guilt. "Who says I've bought stolen art?"

"Akira Kurosawa gave me a call."

Ishida stared at me a very long time. "Oh, we've got a funny one here, Eddie."

Eddie said, "I don't like him." Eddie.

I said, "I think you might have the Hagakure. If

you don't, I think you might know the people who stole it or who have it."

Ishida gave me the stare a little more, thinking, and then the tension went out of his face and his shoulders relaxed and he smiled. This time the smile was real, as if in all the thinking he had seen something and what he had seen had been funny as hell. He glanced at Eddie and then at the other two guys and then back at me. "You got no idea how stupid you are," he said.

"People hint."

He laughed and Eddie laughed, too. Eddie crossed his arms and made the huge trapezius muscles swell like a couple of demented air bladders. You could see that the tattoos climbed over his elbows and up his biceps. Pretty soon, everybody was laughing but me and the guy on the floor.

Ishida held up my card and looked at it, then crumpled it up and tossed it toward an open crate of little plastic pagodas. He said, "Your problem is, you don't look like a private detective."

"What's a private detective look like?"

"Like Mickey Spillane. You see those Lite beer commercials? Mickey Spillane looks tough."

I hooked a glance at the guy with the crushed neck. "Ask him."

Nobu Ishida nodded, but it didn't seem to matter much. The smile went away and the serious eyes came back. Hard. "Don't come down here anymore, boy. You don't know what you're messing with down here."

I said, "What about the Hagakure?"

Nobu Ishida gave me what I guess was supposed

to be an enigmatic look, then he turned and melted away behind the bamboo steamers.

I looked at Eddie. "Is the interview over?"

Eddie made the tattoos disappear, then sat down behind the tables again and stared at me. The guy with the bad eye sat down beside him, put his feet up, and laced his hands behind his head. The guy with the missing finger pulled one foot beneath himself, then the other, then shoved himself up into sort of a hunched crouch. If I stood around much longer, they'd probably send me out for Chinese.

"Some days are the pits," I said. "Drive all the way down here and don't get so much as one clue."

The guy with the bad eye nodded, agreeing.

Eddie nodded, too. "Watch those Lite beer commercials," he said. "If you looked more like a detective, people might be more cooperative."

5

I walked back along Ki to the first cross street, turned north, then turned again into an alley that ran along behind Ishida's shop. There were delivery vans and trash cans and dumpsters and lots of very old, very small people who did not look at me. An ice truck was parked behind the fish market. At the back of Ishida's place there was a metal loading dock for deliveries and another door about six feet to the right for people and a small, dirty window with a steel grid over it between the doors. An anonymous tan delivery van was parked by the people door. Nobu Ishida probably did not use the van as his personal car. He probably drove a Lincoln or a Mercedes into the parking garage down the block, then walked back to the office. It was either that or matter transference.

I continued along the alley to the next street, then went south back to Ki and into the yakitori grill across the street.

I sat at the counter near the front so I could keep an eye on Ishida's and ordered two skewers of chicken and two of giant clam and a pot of green tea. The cook was an x-ray thin guy in his fifties who wore a pristine white apron and a little white cap and had gold worked into his front teeth like Mike Tyson. He said, "You want spicy?"

I said sure.

He said, "It hot."

I said I was tough.

He brought over the tea in a little metal pot with a heavy white teacup and set a fork and a spoon and a paper napkin in front of me. No-frills service. He opened the little metal refrigerator and took out two strips of chicken breast and a fresh geoduck clam that looked like a bull's penis. He forced each strip of chicken lengthways onto a long wooden skewer, then skinned the geoduck and sliced two strips of the long muscle with a cleaver that could take a man's arm. When the geoduck was skewered he looked doubtfully back at me. "Spicy very hot," he said. He pronounced the *r* fine.

"Double spicy," I said.

The gold in his teeth flashed and he took a blue bowl off a shelf and poured a thick powder of crushed chili peppers onto his work surface. He pressed each skewer of meat down into the powder, first one side, then the other, then arranged all four skewers on the grill. Other side of the counter, I could still feel the heat. "We see," he said. Then he went into the back.

I sipped tea and watched Ishida's. After a few minutes, Eddie and the guy with no finger came out, got in a dark green Alfa Romeo parked at the curb, and drove away. Eddie didn't look happy. I sipped more tea and did more watching, but nobody went in, and nobody else came out. Real going concern, that place.

The cook came back and flipped the skewers. He put a little white saucer of red chili paste in front of me. It was the real stuff, the kind they make in Asia, not the junk you buy at the supermarket. Real chili paste will eat through porcelain. He gave me a big smile. "In case not hot enough." Don't you love a wiseass?

When the edges of the chicken and clam were blackened, he took the skewers off the grill. He dipped them in a pan of yakitori sauce, put them in a paper-lined plastic basket, put the basket beside the chili paste, then leaned back against his grill and watched me.

I took a mouthful of the chicken, chewed, swallowed. Not bad. I dipped some of the chicken in the chili paste, took another bite. "Could be hotter," I said.

He looked disappointed and went into the back.

I sipped more tea, finished the first chicken, then started on the first geoduck. The clam was tough and hard and chewy, but I like that. The tea was good. While I was chewing, a Japanese guy wearing a Grateful Dead tee shirt came in and went up to the counter. He looked at the chalkboard where the daily menu was written, then looked at what was left of the geoduck lying beside the grill and made a face. He turned away and walked back to a pay phone they had in the rear. Some guys you can never please.

Twenty minutes later I was on my second pot of tea when Nobu Ishida came out and started up the street toward the parking garage. I paid, left a nice tip, then went out onto the sidewalk. When Ishida disappeared into the garage, I trotted back down to my car, got in, and waited. Maybe Ishida had a secret vault dug into the core of a mountain where he kept stolen treasure. Maybe he called this secret place The Fortress of Solitude. Maybe he was going there now and I could follow him and find the Hagakure and solve several heretofore unsolved art thefts. Then again, maybe not. I was three cars behind him when he pulled out in a black Cadillac Eldorado and turned right toward downtown.

We left Little Tokyo and went past Union Station and Olvera Street with its gaudy Mexican colors and food booths and souvenir shops. There were about nine million tourists, all desperately snapping pictures of how "the Mexicans" lived, and buying sombreros and ponchos and stuffed iguanas that would start to ripen about a week after they got home. We swung around the Civic Center and were sitting in traffic at Pershing Square, me now four cars behind and counting the homeless bag ladies around the Square, when I spotted the guy in the Grateful Dead tee shirt from the yakitori grill. He was sitting behind the wheel of a maroon Ford Taurus two cars in back of me and one lane over. There was another Asian guy with him. Hmmmm. When the light changed and Ishida went straight, I hung a left onto Sixth. Two cars later, the Taurus followed. I stayed on Sixth to San Pedro and went south. The Taurus came south, too. I took the Dan Wesson out of the glove box and put it between my legs. Freud would've loved that.

At a spotlight on the corner of Fourteenth Street and Commerce, the Taurus pulled up on my left. I looked over. The guy in the Grateful Dead shirt and the other guy were staring at me and they were not smiling. I gripped the Dan Wesson in my right hand and said, "Sony makes a fine TV."

The guy on the passenger side said something to the driver, then turned back to me and flipped open a small black leather case with a silver and gold L.A.P.D. badge in it. "Put it over to the curb, asshole."

"*Moi?*"

The Taurus bucked out ahead under the red light and jerked to the right, blocking me. They were out and coming before the Taurus stopped rocking. I put both hands on the top of the steering wheel and left them there.

The guy who had shown me the badge came directly at me. The other guy walked the long way around the car and came up from behind. The car behind us blew its horn. I said, "I swear to God, Officer. I came to a full stop."

The one with the badge had the sort of face they hand out to bantamweights, all flat planes and busted nose, and a knotty build to go with it. I made him for forty but he could've been younger. He said, "Get out of the car."

I kept my hands on the wheel. "There's a Dan Wesson .38 sitting here between my legs."

Grateful Dead had a gun under my ear before I finished the sentence. The other cop brought his gun out, too, and put it in my face and reached through the window and lifted out the Dan Wesson. Grateful Dead pulled me out of the Corvette and shoved me against the fender and frisked me and took my wallet.

Other horns were blowing but nobody seemed to give a damn.

I said, "Why are you guys watching Nobu Ishida?"

The bantamweight saw the license and said, "PI."

Grateful Dead said, "Shit." He put away his gun.

The boxer tossed my wallet into the Corvette and dropped the Dan Wesson into the roof bay behind the driver's seat. I said, "How about those search and seizure laws, huh?"

They got back in their Taurus and left, and pretty soon the horns stopped blowing and traffic began to move. Well, well, well.

I drove back to my office and called the cops. A voice said, "North Hollywood detectives."

"Lou Poitras, please."

I got put on hold and had to wait and then somebody said, "Poitras."

"There's an importer down on Ki Street in Little Tokyo named Nobu Ishida." I spelled it for him. "I was on him today when two Asian cops come out of my trunk and take me off the board."

Lou Poitras said, "You got that four bucks you owe me?" These cops.

"Don't be small, Lou. I call up with a matter of great import and you bring up a paltry four dollars."

"Great import. Shit."

"They took me out just long enough to lose Ishida. They don't say three words. They flash their guns all over Pershing Square and they don't even rub my nose in it the way you cops like to do. Maybe they're cops. Maybe they're just two guys pretending to be cops."

He thought about that. I could hear him breathe over the phone. "You see a badge?"

"Not long enough to get a number."

"How about a tag?"

"Maroon Ford Taurus. Three-W-W-L-seven-eight-eight."

Poitras said, "Stick around. I'll get back to you," and hung up.

I got up, opened the glass doors that lead out to the little balcony, went back to my desk, and put my feet up. Stick around.

Half an hour later I got up again and went out onto the balcony. Sometimes, when the smog is gone and the weather is clear, you can stand on the balcony and see all the way down Santa Monica Boulevard to the ocean. Now, the heat was up and the smog was in and I felt lucky to see across the street.

I went back in the office, dug around in the little refrigerator I have there, and found a bottle of Negra Modelo beer. Negra Modelo is a dark Mexican beer and may be the best dark beer brewed anywhere in the world. I sipped some and watched the Pinocchio clock. After a while I turned on the radio and tuned to KLSX. Bananarama singing it was a cruel summer. They're not George Thorogood, but they're not bad. I went back onto the balcony and looked out over Los Angeles and thought about what it would be like to marry and have children. I would have two or three daughters and we would watch *Sesame Street* and *Mr. Rogers* together and then roll around on the floor like puppies. When they grew up they would like Kenneth Tobey movies. Would they look like me, or their mother? I went back into the office, closed the glass doors, and sat in one of the director's chairs. You think the damnedest things when you're waiting for a call.

Maybe Lou Poitras had lost my phone number and was desperately searching the police computers in his attempts to contact me. Maybe he had obtained forbidden information concerning the two cops who'd fronted me and was now lying dead in a pool of blood behind the wheel of his Oldsmobile. Maybe I was bored stiff.

At five minutes after seven I was flat on my back on the floor, staring at the ceiling and wondering if aliens from space had ever visited the earth. At ten minutes after seven, the phone rang. I got up off the floor as if I had not been waiting most of the day, sauntered over, and casually picked up the receiver. "Laid-back Detectives, where your problems are no problem."

It wasn't Lou Poitras. It was Sheila Warren. She was crying. She said, "Mr. Cole? Are you there? Who is this?" The words spilled out around coughing sobs. It was tough to understand her. She still sounded drunk.

I said, "Is anyone hurt?"

"They said they would kill me. They said they would kill Bradley and me and that they would burn the house down."

"Who?"

"The people who stole the book. You've got to come over. Please. I'm terrified." She said something else but she was sobbing again and I couldn't make it out.

I hung up. One thing about this business, it doesn't stay boring for long.

6

When I got to the Warren home it was still standing. There was no fire, no hazy smoke blotting out a blood-red sun, no siege tower breaching the front wall. It was dark and cool and pleasant, the way it gets at twilight just as the sun settles beneath the horizon. Hatcher sat in the same light blue Titan Securities Thunderbird and watched me pull into the drive and park. He came over. He didn't look too worried.

I said, "Everything all right?"

"She phone you about the call?"

"Seemed pretty upset."

"Yeah. Well." He hacked up something thick and phlegmy and spit it at the bushes. Sinus.

I said, "You don't act like anything out of the ordinary has happened."

He patted his jacket below his left arm. "Anything out of the ordinary comes around here, I'll give it some of this."

"Wow," I said. "I'm surprised she bothered to call me with you out here."

Hatcher snorted and went back to the T-bird. "You'll see. You're around here enough, you'll see."

The voice of experience.

I walked over to the front door, rang the bell twice, and waited. In a little bit, Sheila Warren's voice came from behind the door. "Who's there?"

"Elvis Cole."

The locks were thrown and the door opened. She was wearing a silver satin nightgown that looked like it had been poured over her body and silver high-heeled sandals. Her eyes were pink and puffy and her mascara had run and been wiped away and not fixed. She was holding a handkerchief with dark blue smudges on it. The mascara. She said, "Thank God it's you. We've been terrified."

I shrugged toward the front gate. "Not much is going to get past Wyatt Earp."

"He could've been clubbed."

Some things you can't argue. I went in past her, watched her lock the door, then followed her back through the house. She walked with a slight lean to the right as if the floor wasn't quite level, and she cut too short through the doorways, brushing her inside shoulder. "Who's home?" I said.

"Just myself and Mimi. Mimi's in the back."

She led me to the den. The bar was in the den.

"Tell me about the call."

"I thought it was Tammy. Tammy's my girlfriend. We play tennis, we go to movies, like that. But it was a man." There was a capless bottle of Bombay gin and a short heavy glass with a couple of melting ice cubes in it sitting on the bar. She picked up the glass and finished what was left, and said, "Would you like something to drink?"

"You got a Falstaff?" I walked over to the big French doors that open out to the rear, and looked behind the drapes. Each door was locked and secure.

"What's that?" she said.

"This beer they brew in Tumwater, Washington."

"All we have are Japanese beers." Her voice took on an edge when she said it.

"That'll be fine."

She went behind the bar, put more ice in her glass, and glugged in some of the gin. That brought the Bombay down about to the halfway point. The bottle cap was sitting in an ashtray at the end of the bar. A strip of bright clean Bonded paper was lying beside it. The Bombay had been full when she'd started. She disappeared down behind the bar for a little bit, then stood up with a bottle of Asahi. There was a tight smile on her face and a smear of mascara on her left cheek like a bruise. "Did I tell you that I find you quite attractive?"

"It was the first thing you said to me."

"Well, I do."

"Everyone says I look like John Cassavetes."

"Do they?"

"I think I look like Joe Isuzu."

She cocked her hips and her head and rested her drink along her jawline, posing. She still hadn't given me the beer. "I think you look like Joe Theismann," she said. "Do you know who Joe Theismann is?"

"Sure. Used to quarterback for the Redskins."

She gave me a giggle. "No, you silly. Joe Theismann is married to Cathy Lee Crosby."

"Oh. That Joe Theismann."

She opened the Asahi, put a paper coaster that said New Asia Hotels on the bar, then set the Asahi on the coaster. She took an icy beer mug from somewhere beneath the bar and put it beside the bottle. I ignored the mug. "You were telling me about the call."

The smile went away. She looked down into her drink and swirled it and her eyes began to redden and puff. "He had an ugly voice. He said he had that goddamned book, and that he knew we had the police involved and that we had hired a private investigator. He said that was a mistake. He said if we didn't stop looking he was going to do things." Her voice got higher, probably the way it had been ten years ago. It was nice. "He said they were watching me and could strike at any time. He told me when I left the house this morning and what I was wearing and who I met and when I came back. He knew my perfume. He knew I use Maxipads. He knew Tammy came over at four and that we played tennis and that Tammy was wearing green shorts and a halter top and—" She closed her eyes and took more of the gin and said, "Damn."

"Did you call the police?"

She shook her head, keeping her eyes closed. "Bradley would shit."

"Calling the cops is the smart thing."

"We do things Bradley's way, mister, or we never hear the end of it." She shook her head again and had more gin. "God damn him."

I said, "Did you recognize the voice?"

She took a deep breath, let it out, then came

around to my side of the bar and stood next to me. Petulant. The first fright was past and the gin was working. She said, "I don't want to talk about this anymore. I needed someone here." I guess she hadn't recognized the voice.

"I know. I'll check the house and make sure it's tight. You'll be all right. A guy calls like this, it's only to scare you. If he was going to do anything, he'd have done it."

She gave her head a flick to get the hair out of her face. Her hair was lush and rich and if it was dyed it was a helluva good job. She reached out and touched my forearm with her finger. "I'll walk with you."

I moved my arm. "You look cold," I said. "Go put something on."

She looked down at herself. The silver gown made an upside-down V over each breast with a thin silver cord running from the apex of one V up her chest and around behind her neck and back down to the apex of the other V. Her shoulders were smooth and bare and tanned. She said, "I'm not cold. See?" She picked up my hand in both of hers and brought it to her chest.

I said, "Your daughter's in the house."

"I don't give a good goddamn who's in the house."

"I do. And even if she wasn't, your husband hired me, and he didn't hire me to lay his wife."

"Do you have to be hired for that?"

"Go put something on."

She pressed against me and kissed me. The silver gown felt warm and slick. I eased her back. "Go put something on."

"Fuck you." She slid past me and hurried out of

the room, bouncing a thigh off the near couch as she left. She hadn't seen her daughter standing in one of the doorways leading from the rear of the house, as motionless as a reed in still air. Neither had I.

I put the Asahi on the bar. "I'm sorry that happened," I said. "She's very scared and she's had too much to drink."

Mimi Warren said, "She's very good in bed. Everyone says so." Sixteen.

I didn't say anything to her and she didn't say anything to me, and then she turned and walked away. I watched little drops of condensation sprout on the Asahi until their weight pulled them down to the bar, then I took a rambling tour of the house, checking each window and door and making sure they were tight and locked and that the alarms were armed. I looked for the girl.

At the back of the house, a little hall branched away from the kitchen with a couple of doors on one side and glass looking out toward the pool on the other. If you looked out the glass you could see down across the lawn to the flat mirrored surface of the pool and the dark silhouette of palm trees behind it. I watched the quarter moon bounce on the pool's still surface, then tried the first door. It was open and the room was dark. I turned on the light.

Mimi was lying on her back across a single bed, legs straight up against the wall, head hanging down over the bedside, eyes wide and unfocused. I said, "You okay?"

She said nothing.

"You want to talk to your mom, we can do it together. That might be easier."

She did not move. The room was white on white, as stark and cold as the Wyeth landscapes she had been staring at earlier. There were no posters on the walls or record albums on the floor or clothes spilling out of a hamper or diet soda cans or anything at all that would mark the room as a sixteen-year-old girl's. On a glass-topped white desk at the foot of the bed there were three oversized art books by someone named Kira Asano and a paperback edition of Yukio Mishima's *The Sailor Who Fell from Grace with the Sea*. The Mishima looked as if it had been read a hundred times. There was a small Hitachi color TV on the desk, and a scent in the room that might have been marijuana, but if it was it was not recent.

I said, "You gotta be angry." Mr. Sensitive.

"To be angry is to waste life," she said, not moving. "One must have a cruel heart."

Great.

I finished my circuit of the house and found my way back to the den. Sheila was there, sitting on a bar stool, sipping from the short glass. She was wearing a man's denim work shirt buttoned over the gown and she'd done something about her makeup. She looked good. I wondered how anyone who drank so much could stay that lean. Maybe when she was on the court she played harder than I had thought.

I said, "The house is tight. All the windows are secure and the doors are locked. The alarm is armed and in order. With Hatcher out front, you're not going to have a problem."

"If you say so."

I said, "Your daughter saw you kiss me. You might want to talk to her."

"Are you scared Bradley's going to fire you?"

A pulse began behind my right eye. "No. You might want to talk to her because she saw her mother kiss a strange man and that had to be frightening."

"She won't tell. She never says anything. All she does is sit in her room and watch TV."

"Maybe she should tell. Maybe that's the point."

Sheila drained the glass. "Bradley's not going to fire you, if that's what you're worried about."

The pulse began to throb. "I'm not worried about it. I don't give a damn if Bradley fires me or not."

Sheila set the glass down hard. Red spots flared on her cheeks. "You must think I have it pretty good, don't you? Big house, big money. Here's this woman, plays tennis all day, what does she have to gripe about? Well, I've got shit is what I've got. What the hell's a big house if there's nothing in it?" She turned and stalked out the way she'd seen women do a hundred times on *Dallas* and *Falcon Crest*. Drama.

I stood by the bar and breathed hard and waited for something else to happen, but nothing did. Somewhere a door slammed. Somewhere else a TV played. Maybe this was a dream. Maybe I would wake up and find myself in a 7-Eleven parking lot and think, *Oh, Elvis, ha-ha, you really dreamed up some zingo clients this time!*

I let myself out and got in the Corvette and had to stop at the gate to let a yellow Pantera with two teenagers in it pass. Hatcher was in his T-bird, a smug grin on his face.

I leaned toward him. "If you say anything, Hatcher," I said, "I'll shoot you."

7

At nine-forty the next morning my phone rang and Jillian Becker said, "Did I wake you?"

"Impossible. I never sleep."

"We're back from Kyoto. Bradley wants to see you."

I had fallen asleep on the couch, watching a two A.M. rerun of *It Came from Beneath the Sea* with Ken Tobey and Faith Domergue. The cat had watched it with me and had fallen asleep on my chest. He was still there. I said, "I went by Bradley's house last night. Someone called and scared the hell out of Sheila."

"That's one of the reasons Bradley wants to see you. We're at the Century City office. May we expect you in thirty minutes?"

"Better gimme a little longer. I want to think up something real funny to see if I can make you laugh."

She hung up.

I lifted off the cat, went into the kitchen, filled a large glass with water, drank it, and filled it once more when the phone rang again. Lou Poitras. He said, "I made some calls. Those two guys who sixed you yesterday were Asian Task Force cops."

"Gee, you mean Nobu Ishida isn't a simple businessman?"

"If ATF people are in, Hound Dog, it's gotta be heavy."

Poitras hung up. Asian Task Force, huh? Maybe I had been right about old Nobu. Maybe he was the mastermind of an international stolen art cartel. Maybe I would crack The Big Case and be hailed as The World's Greatest Detective. Wow.

I fed myself and the cat, then showered, dressed, and was turning down Century Park East Boulevard forty minutes later. It was clear and sunny and cooler than yesterday, with a lot of women on the sidewalks, all of them wearing lightweight summer outfits with no backs and no sleeves. Century City was once the back lot of Twentieth Century-Fox Studios. Now it is an orchard of high-rise office buildings done in designer shades of bronze and black and metallic blue glass, each carefully spaced for that planned-community look and landscaped with small pods of green lawn and California poplar trees. The streets have names like Constellation Boulevard and Avenue of the Stars and Galaxy Way. We are nothing if not grandiose.

The Century Plaza Towers are a matching set of triangular buildings, thirty-five floors each of agents, lawyers, accountants, lawyers, business managers, lawyers, record executives, lawyers, and Porsche owners. Most of whom are lawyers. The Century Plaza Towers are the biggest buildings in Century City.

They have to be to squeeze in the egos. Warren Investments occupied half of the seventeenth floor of the
north tower. Rent alone had to exceed the Swedish
gross national product.

I stepped off the elevator into an enormous glass
and chrome waiting room filled with white leather
chairs that were occupied by important-looking men
and women holding important-looking briefcases.
They looked like they had been waiting a long time.
A sleek black woman sat in the center of a U-shaped
command post. She wore a wire-thin headphone set
that curved around to her mouth with a microphone
the size of a pencil lead. "Elvis Cole," I said. "For Mr.
Warren."

She touched buttons and murmured into the microphone and told me someone would be right out.
The important-looking men and women glared envi-
ously. Moments later, an older woman with gray hair
in a tight bun and a nice manner led me back along a
mile and a half of corridor, through a heavy glass
door, and into what could only have been an executive secretary's office. There was a double door wide
enough to drive a street cleaner through at the far
end. "Go right in," she said. I did.

Bradley Warren was sitting on the edge of a black
marble desk not quite as long as a bowling alley with
his arms crossed and a J. Jonah Jameson smile on his
face. He was smiling at five dour-faced Japanese men.
Three of the Japanese men were sitting on a white
silk couch and were old the way only Asians can be
old, with that sort of weathered papery skin and eter-
nal presence. The other two Japanese men stood at
either end of the couch, and were much younger and

much larger, maybe two inches shorter than me and twenty pounds heavier. They had broad flat faces and eyes that stared at you and didn't give a damn if you minded or not. The one on the right was wearing a custom-cut Lawrence Marx suit that made him look fat. If you knew what to look for, though, you knew he wasn't fat. He was all wedges and heavy muscle. The one on the left was in a brown herringbone, and had gone to the same tailor. Odd Job and his clone. Jillian Becker sat primly on the edge of a white silk chair, framed neatly in a full wall of glass that looked north. She looked nice. Yuppie, but nice.

"Where's Bush?" I said. "Couldn't he make it?"

Bradley Warren said, "You're late. We've had to wait." Mr. Personality.

"Why don't we cancel this meeting and schedule another to begin in ten minutes? Then I can be early."

Bradley Warren said, "I'm not paying you for jokes."

"I throw those in for free."

Today Jillian Becker was wearing a burgundy skirt and jacket with a white shirt and very sheer burgundy hose with tiny leaf designs and broken-leather burgundy pumps. With her legs crossed, her top knee gleamed. I gave her a beaming smile, but she didn't smile back. Maybe I'd go easy on the jokes for a while.

Bradley Warren slid off his desk and said something in Japanese to the men on the couch. His speech was fluid and natural, as if he had spoken the language as a child. The older man in the center said something back to him, also in Japanese, and everybody laughed. Especially Jillian Becker. Bradley said,

"These men are members of the Tashiro family, who own the Hagakure. They're here to make sure every best effort is made to recover the manuscript." The guy in the brown herringbone spoke softly in Japanese, translating.

"All right."

Bradley Warren said, "Have you found it yet?" I had expected him to ask about the threat against his wife first, but there you go.

"No." More mumbling from the guy in the brown herringbone.

"Are you close?"

"Hot on its trail."

The guy in the brown herringbone frowned, and translated, and the old guys on the couch frowned, too. Bradley saw all the frowning going on and joined in. So that was where he got it. He said, "I'm disappointed. I expected more."

"It's been two days, Bradley. In those two days I have begun identifying people who deal in or collect feudal Japanese artwork. I will do more of that. Eventually, one of the people I contact will know something about the Hagakure, or about someone who does. That's the way it's done. Stealing something like this is like stealing the *Mona Lisa*. There's only a half dozen people on earth who would do it or be involved in it, and once you know who they are it's only a matter of time. Collectors make no secret about what they want, and once they have it they like to brag."

Bradley gave the Japanese men a superior look and said, "*Harumph.*"

The Japanese man sitting in the center of the

couch nodded thoughtfully and said, "I think that he has made a reasonable beginning."

Bradley said, "Huh?"

The Japanese man said, "Has there been a ransom demand?" He was the oldest of the three seated men, but his eyes were clear and steady and stayed with you. His English was heavily accented.

I shook my head. "None that I'm aware of."

Bradley looked from the old man to me and back to the old man. "What's this about a ransom?"

The old man kept his eyes on me. "If a ransom is demanded, we will pay it."

"Okay."

"If you must pay for information, price is of no concern."

"Okay."

The old man looked at Bradley. "Is this clear?"

Bradley said, "Yes, sir."

The old man stood, and the large men quickly moved to his side in case he needed their help. He didn't. He stared at me for a very long time, and then he said, "You must understand this: The Hagakure is Japan. It is the heart and the spirit of the people. It defines how we act and what we believe and what is right and what is wrong and how we live and how we die. It is who we are. If you feel these things, you would know why this book must be found."

He meant it. He meant it all the way down deep where it is very important to mean what you say. "I'll do what I can."

The old man kept the steady eyes on me, then mumbled something in Japanese and the other two old men stood up. No one said *I'll be seeing you* or

Nice to have met you or *See you again some time*. Bradley walked the Tashiros to the door, but I don't think they looked at him. Then they were gone.

When Bradley came back, he said, "I didn't appreciate all the smart talk in front of the Tashiros. They're nervous as hell and breathing down my neck. You'd be a lot farther along without the wit."

"Yeah, but along to where?"

His jaw knotted but he didn't say anything. He strode over to the glass wall and looked out. Holmby Hills was due north. With a good pair of field glasses he could probably see his house. "Now," he said. "My wife is frightened because of this threat she received. Do you think there's any merit to it?"

"I don't know," I said. "It's not professional. You steal something, you're looking at ten years. You kill someone, you're looking at life. Besides that, the cops are already in and these guys know it. If they're hanging around, that means they want something else. What else do you have that they would want?"

"Nothing." Offended.

"Has there been any communication between you and them that I have not heard about?"

"Of course not." Pissed.

"Then I'd treat it seriously until we know more."

Bradley went back to his desk and began to flip through papers as if he couldn't wait to get back to work. Maybe he couldn't. "In that case, we should expand your services. I want you to oversee the security of my family."

"You've got Titan."

Jillian Becker said, "Sheila was not comfortable with Titan. They've been let go."

I spread my hands. "All right. I can put someone in your house."

Bradley Warren nodded. "Good. Just be sure that the Hagakure investigation continues to proceed." First things first.

"Of course."

"And the Man of the Month banquet is tomorrow," he said. "We can't forget that."

"Maybe you shouldn't go."

The frown came back and he shook his head. "Out of the question. The Tashiros will be there." He tamped some papers together and fingered their edges and looked thoughtful. "Mr. Tashiro liked you. That's good. That's very, very good." You could see the business wheels turning.

I said, "Bradley."

The frown.

"If someone is genuinely committed to killing you or your family, there isn't much we can do to stop them."

The skin beneath his left eye began to tic, just like it had in my office.

"You understand that, don't you?"

"Of course."

His phone buzzed and he picked it up. He listened for a few seconds, still staring at me, then broke into a Cheshire cat smile and asked someone on the other end of the line how the Graintech takeover had gone. He glanced at Jillian Becker and made a dismissal gesture with his free hand. Jillian stood up and showed me to the door. Bradley laughed very loud at something and put his feet up and said he'd like to get some of those profits into a new hotel he was building on Maui.

When we got to the door, Bradley cupped a hand over the receiver's mouthpiece, leaned out of his chair, and called, "Cole. Keep me posted, will you?"

I said sure.

Bradley Warren uncupped the receiver, laughed like he'd just heard the best joke he'd heard all year, then swiveled back toward the big glass wall.

I left.

With the security of his family now in my trusted hands, apparently it was safe to resume business.

8

Twenty minutes after Bradley and Jillian resumed business, I drove down to a flat, gray building on Venice Boulevard in Culver City, and parked beside a red Jeep Cherokee with a finish like polished glass. It's industrial down there, so all the buildings are flat and gray, but most of them don't have the Cherokee or an electronically locked steel door or a sign that says BARTON'S PISTOL RANGE. I had to ring a bell and someone inside had to buzz open the steel door before I could enter.

The lobby is big and bright, with high ceilings and Coke machines and posters of Clint Eastwood as Dirty Harry and Sylvester Stallone as Rambo. Someone had put up a poster of Huey, Dewey, and Louie, with a little sign on it that said WE ARE THE NRA. These gun nuts. There was a long counter filled with targets and gun cleaning supplies and pistols you could rent, and a couple of couches you could sit on while you were waiting for a shooting stall to open up. Three men in business suits and a woman in a jogging suit and another woman in a dress were waiting to shoot, but they weren't waiting on the couches. They were at the head of the counter and they didn't look happy. One of the men was tall and forty pounds too fat and had a red face. He was leaning over the counter at Rick Barton, saying, "I made an appointment, goddamnit. I don't see why I have to stand around and wait."

Rick Barton said, calmly, "I'm terribly sorry for the inconvenience, sir, but we've had to momentarily close the range. It will open again in about fifteen minutes."

"Closed my ass! I hear *somebody* shooting back there!"

Rick Barton nodded, calmly. "Yes, sir. Another fifteen minutes. Excuse me, please." Rick came down the long counter and nodded at me. He was short and slight and had put in twelve years in the Marine Corps. Eight of those years he had shot on the Marine Corps pistol team. He said, "Thank Christ you walked in. I hadda 'sir' that fat fuck one more time, I'da lubed his gear box for him."

"Ah, Rick. You always did have a gift for the public."

Rick said, "You want to pop some caps?"

I shook my head. "The gun shop said Joe was here."

Rick looked at his watch. "Go on back. Tell him he's got another ten, then I chuck his ass out."

He tossed me a set of ear covers, and I went back toward the range. Behind me, the fat guy said, "Hey, how come *he* gets to go back there?"

You go through the door, then down a long, dim

corridor with a lot of signs that say things like EAR AND EYE PROTECTION MUST BE WORN AT ALL TIMES and NO RAPID FIRING, and then you go through another sound-proofed door and you're on the firing range. There are twelve side-by-side stalls from which people can shoot at targets that they send down-range using little electric pulleys. Usually, the range is bright, and well lighted, but now the lights had been turned off so that only the targets were lit. A tape player had been hooked up, and Bob Seger was screaming *I like that old time rock 'n' roll* . . . so loud that you could hear him through the ear covers. Anyone else would find his partner on the golf course or the tennis courts.

Joe Pike was shooting at six targets that he had placed as far down-range as possible. He was firing a Colt Python .357 Magnum with a four-inch barrel, moving left-to-right, right-to-left, shooting at the targets in precise time with the music. *That kind of music just soothes the soul* . . . He was wearing faded Levi's and blue Nike running shoes and a gray sweatshirt with the sleeves cut off and a big steel Rolex and mirrored pilot's glasses. The gun and the glasses and the Rolex gleamed in the darkness as if they had been polished to a high luster. Pike moved without hesitation or doubt, as precise and controlled as a well-made machine. *Bang bang bang.* The Python would move, and flash, and a hole would burst near the center of a target. The dark glasses seemed not to adversely affect his vision. Maybe the sunglasses didn't matter because Pike had his eyes closed. Maybe somehow Pike and the target were one, and we could write a book titled *Zen and the Art of Small Arms Fire* and make a fortune. Wow.

He stopped to reload, still facing down-range, and said, "Want to shoot a few?" You see? Cosmic.

I went to the stall where he had set up Rick's tape player and clicked off the music. "How'd you know I was here?"

Shrug.

"We've got a job."

"Yeah?" Pike loves to talk.

We walked down-range, collected his targets, then examined them. Every shot had been within two inches of center. He was delighted. You could tell because the corner of his mouth twitched. Joe Pike does not smile. Joe Pike never smiles. After a while you get used to it. I said, "Eh. Not bad."

We gathered his things and walked back along the dim corridor, me telling him about Bradley and Sheila and the stolen Hagakure and the phone call from person or persons unknown that had scared the hell out of Sheila Warren.

He said, "Threat like that doesn't make any sense."

"Nope."

"Maybe there wasn't a threat. Maybe somebody's having a little fun."

"Maybe."

"Maybe the lady made it up."

"Maybe. But we don't know that. I figure you can stay with the woman and the kid while I look for the book."

"Uh-huh."

Pike was pulling off his sweatshirt when we walked

out into the lobby. The fat man said, "Well, it's about goddamned time," and then he saw Joe Pike and shut up. Pike is an inch taller than me, and more heavily muscled, and when he was in Vietnam he'd had a bright red arrow tattooed on the outside of each deltoid. The arrows pointed forward. There is an ugly pucker scar high on the left side of his chest from the time a Mexican in a zoot suit shot him with a gold Llama automatic, and two more scars low on his back above his right kidney. After the fat guy looked at the tattoos and the muscles, he looked at the scars and then he looked away. Rick Barton was grinning from ear to ear.

Pike said, "Use your shower, Rick?"

"No problem, bo."

While Pike was in the shower I used a pay phone to call Sheila Warren. "I'm on the way over," I said. "Bradley hired me to look out for you."

"Well," she said, "I should hope so."

"I'm bringing my partner, Joe Pike. He'll make sure the house and grounds are secure and be there in case there's a problem."

There was a pause. "Who's Joe Pike?"

Maybe I had lapsed into Urdu the first time. "My partner. He owns the agency with me."

"You won't be here?"

"Somebody has to look for the book."

"Maybe this Joe Pike should look for the book."

"I'm better at finding. He's better at guarding."

You could hear her breathing into the phone. The breaths were deep and irregular and I thought I could hear ice move in a glass but maybe that was the TV. I said, "You were pretty gone last night. How's your head?"

"You go to hell." She hung up.

Five minutes later Pike came back with a blue leather gym bag and we drove across town, me leading and Pike following in the Cherokee. When we got to the Warren house, Pike parked in the drive, then got out with the gym bag, walked back, and climbed into my car. Hatcher and his T-bird were gone. I told Pike about Berke Feldstein in the Sun Tree Gallery and Nobu Ishida and the two Asian Task Force cops.

"Asian Task Force are tough dudes," Pike said. "You think Ishida's got the book?"

"I think that a couple of hours after I saw him, someone threatened the Warrens. If Ishida doesn't have it, maybe he'll want to find out who does. Maybe he'll ask around."

Pike nodded. "And maybe you'll be there when he gets some answers."

"Uh-huh."

The twitch. "Nice."

The front door opened and Sheila Warren stepped out. She was in Jordache jeans over a red Danskin top that showed a fine torso. She put her palms on her hips, fingertips down the way women do, and stared at us.

Pike said, "The lady of the house?"

"Yep."

Pike opened the gym bag, took out a Walther 9mm automatic in a strap holster, hitched up his right pant, fastened the gun around his ankle, then pulled the pant down over it and got out of the car. Maybe he was saving the .357 for heavy work.

"Be careful," I said.

Pike nodded without saying anything, then took the gym bag and walked up to the house. He stopped in front of Sheila Warren and put out his hand and she took it. She glanced my way, then back up at Pike and gave him a big smile. Twenty kilowatts. She touched his gym bag and then his forearm and said something and laughed. She slid her hand up his arm to his shoulder and showed him into the house. I think she may have licked her lips. I eased the Corvette into gear and drove away. It's a good thing Pike's tough.

9

Little Tokyo was jammed with the lunch hour rush. Every restaurant on the block had a line of Caucasian secretaries and their bosses queued up out front, and the smell of hot peanut oil and vinegar sauces made my stomach rumble.

A small CLOSED sign was taped in the door at Nobu Ishida's place. It was one of those cruddy hand-lettered things and not at all what you would expect from a big-time importer and art connoisseur, but there you go. I turned into the alley behind Ishida's just to check, and, sure enough, it looked closed from back there, too. Probably out for lunch.

I turned back to Ki, then went up Broadway past the Hollywood Freeway into Chinatown. Chinatown is much bigger than Little Tokyo and not as clean, but the best honey-dipped duck and spring rolls in America can be had at a place called Yang Chow's on Broadway just past Ord. If bad guys can break for lunch, so can good guys.

I parked in front of a live poultry market and

walked back to Yang Chow's and bought half a duck, three spring rolls, fried rice, and two Tsingtao to go. They put extra spice in the spring rolls for me.

Ten minutes later I was back on Ki Street, pulling into a parking lot sandwiched between two restaurants. It was crowded but all of the lots this time of day were crowded. I was a block and a half down from Ishida's, and if anyone went into his shop through the front or came out through the front or turned over the CLOSED sign, I'd be able to see it. If they came or went through the back I was screwed. You learn to live with failure.

The parking attendant said, "You here to eat?"

"Yeah."

"Three-fifty."

I gave him three-fifty.

"Park anywhere. Give me the key."

I took a spot at the front of the lot, blocking in a white Volvo so that I had an easy eyes-forward view of Ishida's shop. I got out of the Corvette, pulled the top up to cut the sun, then climbed back in. I opened a Tsingtao, drank some, then went to work on the rice.

"I thought you here to eat." The parking attendant was standing by my door.

I showed him the rice.

"In there." He pointed at one of the restaurants.

I shook my head. "Out here."

"You no eat out here. In there for eating."

"I'm a health inspector. I go in there I'll close the place down."

"You got to give me key." Maybe he didn't believe me.

"No key. I keep the key."

He pointed at the Volvo. "What if owner come out? I got to move." He rapped knuckles on the Corvette's door.

"I'm here. I'll move it."

"You no insured here."

"Okay. I'll get out and let you move it."

"What if you leave."

"If I leave, I'll give you the key." People like this are put here to test us.

He was going to say more when two Asian women and a black man came out of the restaurant. The black man wore a navy suit and had a small mustache and looked successful. The attendant hustled over to them, got a claim check, then hustled to the back of the lot. One of the Asian women said something to the black man and they all laughed. The attendant drove up in a Mercedes 420 Turbo Diesel. Bronze. He closed the door after each woman, and the black man gave him a tip. Maybe the tip made him feel better about things. He went back to the little attendant's shack and looked at me but left me alone.

The honey-dipped duck was wonderful.

Four hours and twenty minutes later the Volvo was gone and the first of the early evening dinner crowd were starting to show up. The lot had emptied after lunch and another attendant had come on duty, an older man who looked at me once and didn't seem to care if I stayed or left or homesteaded. No one had gone into Ishida's shop or come out or touched the little CLOSED sign. Maybe nobody would, ever again.

At ten minutes after five the cop who had made me in the yakitori grill walked past carrying a large white paper bag and a six-pack of diet Coke. The Grateful Dead tee shirt was gone. Now it was ZZ Top. I got out of the car and watched him saunter down Ki Street and turn into a doorway next to the yakitori grill. I waited to see if he would come out and when he didn't I did a little sauntering myself and took a look. He and a cop I hadn't seen before were across from Ishida's in a State Farm Insurance office above the yakitori grill. Those sneaky devils. *Who watches the watchers?*

I walked back along Ki, crossed over at the little side street, and turned up the alley behind Ishida's shop. It looked the way it looked when I drove past six hours earlier. Empty. I went up to the loading dock doors and didn't like the lock and went over to the people door and took out the wires I keep in my wallet and opened it. If the cops had had the rear of the place staked out there would be trouble, but all the cops were on the street side eating cheeseburgers.

I let myself in, eased the door shut behind me, and waited for my eyes to adjust. I was in a dim, high-ceilinged freight room. Dirty light came through the little window beside the door and a skylight twenty feet up, but that was it. Boxes and crates were stacked ten feet up the wall. Some were wooden but most were cardboard, and most had Styrofoam packaging pellets or shredded Japanese newspapers spilling out. There was a metal stair against one wall that went up to a steel-grate catwalk and loft. There were more boxes and crates up there and a little office. If the Hagakure were here it should only take about six years to find it.

I went through a hall at the head of the freight

room and past shelves of bamboo steamers and into the showroom. The two desks were still there but the Hagakure hadn't been left sitting on them. No one had left a note suggesting a safe place to store the manuscript or a photograph of the new owner with his prize collectible. There were memo pads and paper clips and a little purple stapler and assorted pens and pencils and a Panasonic pencil sharpener and an old issue of *Batman* with the back cover gone. I was hoping for a clue but I would have settled for Ishida's home phone and address. *Nada*.

I went into the brighter light near the front of the shop, put my hands in my pockets, and wondered what to do. From the edge of the shadows you could see into the insurance office above the yakitori grill. The cop I didn't know was sitting a few feet back from the window with his feet up, drinking a diet Coke out of a can with a straw.

I went back into the freight room. Ishida had come from the back. Maybe the little office on the catwalk was where he worked. Maybe there would be a little desk with pictures of the kids and a note to bring home some sushi and a Rolodex or some personal correspondence that would tell me where he lived.

I climbed the steel stair and went along the narrow catwalk and opened the white door with the pebbled glass panel in it and smelled the blood and the cold meat and the death. It's the smell that comes only from a great quantity of blood and human waste. It can sting your nose and throat like a bad smog. It's a smell so strong and so alive that it has a taste and the taste is like when you were a kid and found a nickel in the winter and the metal was cold and you put it in your mouth to see what it would be like and your mother screamed that you would die from the germs and so you spit it out but the cold taste and the fear of the germs stayed.

The little office was heavy with shadow. I took out my handkerchief and found the light switch and snapped it on. The guy with the missing finger who'd been out front my first time around was curled atop a gray metal file cabinet. His head and his right arm were hanging over the edge. His neck was limp, the front and side of it purple as if he had been hit there very hard. Someone had cleared Nobu Ishida's desk of papers and ledgers and pencil can and phone. They had put all that on his swivel chair along with his clothes and then pushed the chair out of the way and tied Ishida spread-eagled on his desk, naked, arms and legs bound to the desk legs with brown electrical cord. They had used a knife on him. There were cuts on his arms and his legs and his torso and his face and his genitals. Some of the cuts were very deep. His bladder and his bowels had let go. The blood had crusted into delicate red-brown rivers along his arms and legs and had pooled on the desk and then dripped heavily onto the floor to mix with other things. The pool on the floor had spread almost to the door and looked slick and tacky. A gray stuffed Godzilla had been jammed in his mouth to smother the screams.

I stepped around the blood to the chair and looked through the things that had been on the desk. Ishida's wallet was still in his right back pants pocket. I took it out, opened it, copied down his home address, then put the wallet back the way I'd found it. I used my handkerchief to pick up the phone and called Lou Poitras. He said, "What now?"

"I'm at Ishida's place of business. He's dead."

There was a pause. "Did you kill him?"

"No." I watched the pool of blood.

"Don't leave the scene. Don't touch anything. Don't let anyone else in. I'm on my way. There'll be other cops but I'll get there first."

He hung up. I put the phone down and stepped around the blood back onto the catwalk and pulled the door closed. I worked up spit and swallowed and took several deep breaths. I expanded my lungs from the diaphragm and expelled the air in stages from the lower lobes to the mid-lobes to the upper lobes. I tried everything I could think of but I couldn't get rid of the taste or the smell. I never could. Like every encounter with death, it had become a part of me.

10

I went downstairs and sat at one of the two tables in the deepening darkness until Lou Poitras pulled up out front in a light green Dodge. A black-and-white pulled up behind him and the plain white van the crime scene guys use pulled up behind the van. Cops on parade.

I went to the front door and opened it. Across the street, the ATF cops were on their feet in the big window, ZZ Top screaming into the phone, the other one pulling on a jacket. I gave them a little wave.

Poitras said, "Knock off that shit and come in here."

If Lou Poitras wasn't a cop he could rent himself out as Mighty Joe Young. He spends about an hour and a half every morning six days a week pumping iron in a little weight room in his back yard in Northridge, trying to see how big he can get. He's good at it. I'd once seen him punch through a Cadillac's windshield and pull a big man out over the steering wheel.

He shouldered past me. "Where?"

"In the back. Up the stairs."

One of the uniforms was a black guy with a bullet head and a thick neck and hands four sizes too big for him. His name tag read LEONARD. His partner was a blond kid with a skimpy Larry Bird mustache and hard eyes. Leonard mumbled something and the blond kid took the crime scene guys into the back after Poitras.

"You don't want to see?" I said.

Leonard said, "I seen enough."

I went back to the two tables and sat. Leonard found the lights, turned them on, then went back up front. He leaned against a floor-to-ceiling case of toy robots with his arms crossed, and stared out into the street. You do this job long enough, you know what's going to be back there even without going back there.

The little door chime rang and the two ATF cops from the insurance office came in. They showed their badges to Leonard and then they went into the rear. When they passed me, the one in the ZZ Top tee shirt said, "You're in deep shit, asshole."

Lou Poitras came back around the bamboo steamers and said, "Jesus Christ." He looked pale.

I nodded.

The blond kid came out like it was nothing. He went back to Leonard and said, "You should see that, Lenny." His voice was loud.

In fifteen minutes the place was swarming with cops like flies on a nervous dog. Someone had found a Dunkin' Donuts and brought back two boxes of crullers and about twenty little Styrofoam cups of coffee. Crime scene specialists from the Hollenbeck Division were dusting everything and snapping pictures and asking me every two minutes if I had moved anything before they got there, and every time they asked I said no. Two guys came in from the L.A. County Medical Examiner's Office, but neither of them looked like Jack Klugman. One of them had a twitch. More than one cop came out of the back and sat down with his face in his hands, and everybody pretended not to notice when they did.

I was working on my second cup of coffee when the bell tinkled and the ATF cop with the bantamweight's face came in. He was wearing tan chinos and a pale lavender rugby shirt and a light khaki windbreaker and Topsiders with no socks. Like he'd been at home about to sit down to dinner with his family. Poitras went over and talked with him and then they went into the back. When they came back, ZZ Top was with them. Poitras and the bantamweight came over to me. ZZ Top pushed aside the cruller box, sat on the table, crossed his arms, and glared at me. Cops are tough when they've got you outnumbered.

Poitras said, "This is Terry Ito. He works out of the Asian Task Force, Japanese sub-unit."

I put out my hand. Ito didn't take it. He said, "What were you doing with Nobu Ishida?"

"Taking chopsticks lessons." The muscles in the tops of my shoulders and down through my midback were tight and aching.

Ito looked at Poitras. Poitras shrugged. "He's like that."

Ito looked back at me. "I think maybe you got shit for brains. You think that's possible?"

I looked from Ito to the cop at the cruller table and back to Ito. I could still smell what I'd smelled in Ishida's office. I said, "I think somebody dropped the ball. I think someone walked in here under ZZ Top's nose and did this and walked out again and nobody said dick."

The cop on the cruller table uncrossed his arms and stood up and said, "Fuck you, asshole."

"Good line," I said. "Schwarzenegger, right? *The Terminator*."

Poitras said, "Cut the bullshit."

Ito said, "Jimmy."

A tall black uniform came out of the back, took off his hat, and said, "Who'd do something like that?" Then he went outside. I was breathing hard and Jimmy was breathing hard but everybody else looked bored. Jimmy sat down again but didn't cross his arms.

Ito turned away from Jimmy and looked at me. "How long were you outside, hotshot?"

"Maybe six hours."

"You see anybody?"

I sipped some coffee.

Ito nodded. "Yeah, that's what I thought." He went over to the cruller table, picked up a cup of the coffee, peeled off its top, and took a long sip. Steam was rising off the cup but the heat didn't seem to bother him. He said, "Who's your client?"

"A guy named Bradley Warren. The Pacific Men's Club is naming him Man of the Month tomorrow."

"Man of the Month."

"Yeah. You should get in on that."

Jimmy said, "Shit."

I told them who Warren was and that he had hired me to find the Hagakure and that I had turned up

Nobu Ishida's name as a place to start. Terry Ito listened and sipped the hot coffee and stared at me without blinking. Detectives and crime scene guys and uniforms moved around us. The two guys from the ME's office went out to their van and came back with a gurney. Ito called to them.

"When did it happen?"

The shorter of the two said, "Maybe eight hours."

Ito looked at me and nodded. I shrugged. Ito looked at Jimmy, but Jimmy was staring at the floor and flexing his jaws.

I drank coffee and told them about my first visit to Ishida's shop and about the three guys sitting at the tables and about Ishida. I said, "The stiff upstairs with the missing finger was one of them. There was another guy with a bad left eye, and a big kid, young, named Eddie."

Ito looked at Jimmy again. Jimmy looked up and said, "Eddie have tattoos? Here?" He touched his arms just below the elbows.

"Yeah."

Jimmy looked at Ito and nodded. "Eddie Tang."

I said, "About three hours after I left Ishida's, the client's wife got a phone call saying they'd burn the house down if the Warrens didn't call off the cops. I wanted to work Ishida some more, maybe take a look around his house, that kind of thing, so I came back here today."

Jimmy said, "That's horseshit. You don't threaten somebody to make the cops back off."

I said, "Yeah. You cops are tough, all right."

Ito said, "You're some smart for a guy standing where you're standing."

"It's not hard in this company."

Jimmy didn't say anything.

I could feel the pulse in my temples and a sharp pain behind my right eye. It made me blink. Ito stared at me a long time, then gave a little nod. "Yeah, you're smart. Maybe if you're smart enough you can get what's in that room back there out of your head. Maybe if you're tough enough, what you saw back there won't bother you." His voice was softer than you would've expected.

I took a deep breath and let it out. I rolled my shoulders to try to work out some of the tension. Poitras was leaning against a shelf of tea trays and little lacquer cups with his arms crossed. Crossed like that, they looked swollen even more than normal. Ito was good, all right.

He said, "Thing is, what's back there ain't so special around here. This is Little Tokyo, Chinatown. You oughta see what the Mung have going down in Little Saigon."

Jimmy said, "How about those pricks in Koreatown?"

Ito nodded at him, then looked back at me. Thinking about those pricks in Koreatown made him smile. "This ain't America, white boy. This is Little Asia, and it's ten thousand years old. We've got stuff down here like nothing you've ever seen."

I said, "Yeah." Mr. Tough.

He said, "If Nobu Ishida wanted you out of the picture, he wouldn't do it by calling up some broad and making a threat." He swiveled around and looked at Jimmy. "Call Hollenbeck Robbery and see who has this book thing. Find out what they know."

"Sure, Terry." Jimmy didn't move.

I said, "What's the big deal with Nobu Ishida?"

Ito looked back at me and thought about it for a while. Like maybe he would tell me and maybe he wouldn't. "You know what the yakuza is?"

"Japanese mafia."

Jimmy smiled, wide and mindless, the way a pit bull smiles before he bites you. He said, "How about that, Terry. You think we got something as pussy as the mafia down here?"

Ito said, "Call Hollenbeck."

I said, "Ishida was in the yakuza?"

Jimmy smiled some more, then pushed off the cruller table and walked out. Ito turned back to me. "The yakuza is big in white slavery and dope and loan-sharking like the mafia, but that's where it stops. The stiff in back with the missing finger, he's what you would think of as a mafia soldier. But the mafia doesn't have any soldiers like him. These guys, they've got a little code they live by. Somewhere along the line this guy screwed up and the code required him to chop off his own finger to make up for it. I've seen guys with three, four fingers missing from one hand."

I drank more coffee.

Ito said, "The real headcases get their entire body tattooed from just below the elbows to just above the knees. Those guys are yakuza assassins." He touched his forehead. "Bug fuck."

"Eddie," I said.

Ito nodded. "Yeah. Eddie's a real up-and-comer. Local kid. Arrest record could fill a book. We got him made for half a dozen killings but we can't prove it. That's the bitch with the yakuza. You can't prove it.

People down here, something happens, they don't see it and they don't talk about it. So you've got to put a guy like Ishida's business under surveillance for eight months and pray some hotshot private license doesn't come along and tip him that he's being watched and blow the whole thing. You don't want that to happen because Ishida is overseeing a major operation to import brown heroin from China and Thailand for a guy named Yuki Torobuni who runs the yakuza here in L.A. and if you get Ishida maybe you get Torobuni and shut the whole fucking thing down." Behind us, the two guys from the coroner's office wheeled out the gurney. There was a dark gray body bag sitting on it. Whatever was in the bag looked rumpled.

I said, "If they're moving dope in, the guys down in Watts and East L.A. aren't going to like it. Maybe what happened in back is an effort to eliminate competition."

Ito looked at Poitras. "You were right, Poitras. This boy is bright."

"He has his days."

"Unless," I said, "it has something to do with the Hagakure."

Terry Ito smiled at me, then walked over to the cruller box and selected one with green icing. He said, "You're smart, all right, but not smart enough. This isn't your world, white boy. People disappear. Entire families vanish in the most outrageous manner. And there's never a witness, never a clue." Ito gave me a little more of the smile. "Have you read a translation of the Hagakure?"

"No."

The smile went nasty. "There's a little thing in

there called Bushido. Bushido says that the way of the warrior is death." Ito stopped smiling. "Whoever took your little book, pray it's not the yakuza." He stared at me for a little while longer, then he took his cruller and went into the back.

Poitras uncrossed the huge arms and shook his head. "Sometimes, Hound Dog, you are a real asshole."

"Et tu, Brute?"

He walked away.

They kept me around until a dick from Hollenbeck got there and took my statement. It was 3:14 in the morning when they finished with me, and Poitras had long since gone. I went out into the cool night air onto streets that were empty of round-eyed faces. I thought about the yakuza and people disappearing and I tried to imagine things like nothing I'd ever seen. I tried, but all I kept seeing was what someone had done to Nobu Ishida.

The walk to the car was long and through dark streets, but only once did I look behind me.

11

The next morning Jillian Becker called me at eight-fifteen and asked me if I had yet recovered the Hagakure. I told her no, that in the fourteen hours that had passed since we last spoke, I had not recovered it, but should I stumble upon it as I walked out to retrieve my morning paper, I would call her at once. She then reminded me that today was the Pacific Men's Club Man of the Month banquet. The banquet was to begin at one, we were expected to arrive at the hotel by noon, and would I please dress appropriate to the occasion? I told her that my formal black suede holster was being cleaned, but that I would do the best I could. She asked me why I always had something flip to say. I said that I didn't know, but having been blessed with the gift, I felt obliged to use it.

At ten minutes after ten I pulled into the Warrens' drive and parked behind a dark gray presidential stretch limousine. The driver was sitting across the front seat, head down, reading the *Times* sports section. There was a chocolate-brown 1988 Rolls-Royce Corniche by the four-car garage with a white BMW 633i beside it. I made the BMW for Jillian Becker. Pike's red Jeep was at the edge of the drive out by the gate. It was as far from the other vehicles as possible. Even Pike's transportation is anti-social.

When I rang the bell, Jillian Becker answered, her face tight. She said, "They've just gotten another call. This time the caller said they'd hurt Mimi."

She led me back along the entry and into the big den. Sheila Warren was sitting in one of the overstuffed chairs, feet pulled up beneath her, an empty glass on the little table beside the chair. She was wrapped in a white terry bathrobe. Joe Pike was leaning against the far wall, thumbs hooked in his Levi's, and Mimi Warren was on the big couch across from the bar. Her eyes were large and glassy, and she looked excited. Bradley Warren came in from his library at the back of the den, immaculate in a charcoal three-piece suit, and said, "Sheila. You're just sitting there. We don't want to be late."

I looked back at Jillian Becker. "Tell me about the call."

She said, "A half hour after you and I spoke the phone rang. Whoever it was started talking to Mimi, then must've realized she wasn't an adult and asked for her father."

"What'd they say, Bradley?"

Bradley looked annoyed. He adjusted each cuff and examined himself in the mirror behind the bar. Sheila Warren watched him, shook her head, and drained her glass. He said, "They told me that they knew we hadn't stopped searching for the Hagakure and that they were growing angry. They said they would be at the Man of the Month banquet and that if I knew what was good for me and my family, I'd call it off."

Sheila Warren said, "Bastards." Her *s*'s were a little slurred.

Bradley said, "They told me they knew our every move and we were at their mercy and if I didn't do what they said they'd kill Mimi."

I looked at Mimi. She was in a shapeless brown silk dress and flat shoes and her hair was pulled back. There still wasn't any makeup. I said, "Pretty scary."

She nodded.

I looked back at Bradley Warren. He was picking at something on his right lapel. "Is that the way they said it, using those words?"

"As near as I can remember. Why?" Not used to being questioned by an employee.

"Because it is so theatrical. 'If you know what's good for you.' 'Know your every move.' 'At their mercy.' Most of the crooks I know have better imaginations. Also, it's pretty clear now that we aren't just talking about robbery. The calls you're getting seem like harassment calls. Someone wants to hurt your business and embarrass you, and that's probably why the Hagakure was stolen."

I went over to the big couch and sat down next to Mimi. She was watching everything the way a goldfish watches the world from its bowl, all big eyes and vulnerability and with an assumption of invisibility. Maybe that was easy to assume when Bradley and

Sheila were your parents. I said, "What'd they say to you, babe?"

Mimi giggled.

Sheila said, "For Christ's sake, Mimi."

Mimi blinked. Serious. "He told me it wasn't ours. He told me it is the last legacy of Japan's lost heart and that it belongs to the spirit of Japan."

Sheila Warren said, "Spirit my ass." She got up from the chair and brought her glass over to the bar. She wasn't wearing anything under the robe. "Well, I guess it's time to get ready for the Man of the Month's divine moment." She said it loudly, then turned away from the bar and leered at Joe Pike. "Want to stand guard while I'm in the bath, rough guy?"

Jillian Becker coughed. Pike stood solemn and catlike, mirrored lenses filled with the empty life of a television after a station sign-off. Bradley Warren found a hair out of place and leaned toward the mirror to adjust it. Mimi's face grew dark and blotched. At the bar, Sheila shook her head at no one in particular, mumbled something about there being no takers, then left.

Bradley Warren stepped away from the mirror, temporarily satisfied with his appearance, and looked at his daughter. "Finish dressing, Mimi. We're going to leave soon."

"I hate to be the wet blanket," I said, "but maybe we should forgo the Man of the Month celebration."

Bradley frowned. "I told you before. That's impossible."

I said, "The banquet will be in a large ballroom at the hotel. There will be a couple of hundred people plus the hotel and kitchen employees. People will want to speak with you before the presentation and after, and with your wife, and your family will be spread all to hell and back. If we assume that there is merit to the threats you've received, you'll be vulnerable. So will your wife and daughter."

Mimi's left eye began to twitch in the same way that Bradley's had. What a trait to inherit. Her face was small and pinched and closed, but her eyes were watchful in spite of the tic, and made me think of a small animal hiding at the edge of a forest.

Bradley said, "Nothing's going to happen to my best girl." He went over to her with an Ozzie Nelson smile and put his hands on her shoulders.

Mimi jumped when he touched her as if an electrical current had arced between them. He didn't notice. He said, "My best girl knows I have to attend. She knows that if we're not at the banquet, the Tashiros will see me as weak."

His best girl nodded. Dutifully.

Bradley turned the Ozzie Nelson smile on me. "There. You see?"

"Okay," I said. "Go without your family. Pike will stay with them, here, and I'll go with you."

Ozzie Nelson grew impatient. "You don't seem to understand," he said. "What you're asking would be bad for business."

"Silly me," I said. "Of course."

Jillian Becker stared out the front window toward a grove of bamboo. Joe Pike moved to the bar and crossed his arms the way he does when he's disgusted. I took a deep breath and told myself to pretend Bradley Warren was a four-year-old. I spoke slowly and wished Mimi wasn't with us. I said, "A threat was made to your wife, and now a threat has been made to your daughter. A person who may or may not have been connected with the theft of the Hagakure was murdered. Whether the two are linked or not, I don't know, but the situation is worsening and it would be smart to take these threats seriously."

Jillian Becker turned from the window. "Bradley, maybe we should call the police. They could help with extra security."

Bradley made a face like she'd pissed on his leg. He said, "Absolutely not."

Mimi stood, then, and went over to her father. "I put on this dress especially for the banquet. Isn't it pretty?"

Bradley Warren looked at her and frowned. "Can't you do something about your hair?"

Mimi's left eye fluttered like a moth in a jar. She rubbed at the eye and opened her mouth and closed it, and then she left.

Joe Pike shook his head and he left, too.

Bradley Warren looked at himself in the mirror again. "Maybe I should change shoes," he said. Then he started out, too.

I said, "Bradley."

He stopped in the door.

"Your daughter is terrified."

"Of course she's frightened," he said. "Some maniac said he was going to kill her."

I nodded. Slowly. "The right thing for you to do is to call this off. Stay home. Take care of your family. They're scared now, and possibly in danger, and they need your help."

Bradley Warren gave me the famous Bradley Warren frown, then shook his head. "Don't you see?" he said. "A lot of cops would ruin the banquet."

I nodded. Of course. I looked at Jillian Becker, but she was busy with her briefcase.

12

"Who heads security at Bradley's hotel?"

Jillian Becker said, "A man named Jack Ellis."

"May I have his phone number?"

Jillian Becker held my gaze for a moment, then turned away and found Jack Ellis's number in her briefcase. I used the phone behind the bar, called Ellis at the hotel, told him what was going on and that I had been hired by Mr. Warren for Mr. Warren's personal security. Jillian Becker took the phone and confirmed it. Ellis had a thick, coarse voice that put him in his fifties. He said, "What do the cops think about all this?"

"The cops don't know. Mr. Warren thinks they'd be bad for business." When I said it Jillian Becker pursed her lips and went back to shuffling papers within the briefcase. Disapproving my tone of voice, no doubt.

Ellis said, "You like that?"

"I think it's lousy." More disapproval. The down-turned mouth. The posture. That kind of thing.

Ellis said, "I'll bring in my night people. That'll be enough to cover the Angeles Room, where they're gonna be, follow him in and out, watch the kitchen and the hallways." There was a pause. "He didn't tell the cops, huh?"

"Bad for business. Also, too many unsightly cops might ruin the banquet." Jillian Becker put the Cross pen down and looked at me with the cool eyes.

"Son of a bitch."

"That's right."

I hung up and looked at Jillian Becker looking at me. I smiled. "Want to hear my Mel Gibson imitation?"

She said, "If you knew more about Bradley, you wouldn't dislike him the way you do."

"I don't know. I sort of like disliking him."

"That's obvious. Either way, as long as you're in his employ, you might be more circumspect in sharing your feelings with fellow employees. It breeds discontent."

"Discontent. How Upper Management."

The nostrils tightened.

I said, "I think he's behaving like a self-absorbed ass, and so do you."

Her left eyebrow arched. "However he's behaving, he's still my employer. I will treat him accordingly. So should you." My country right or wrong.

Pretty soon Joe Pike came back, scrubbed and fresh and bright-eyed. It's never easy to tell if someone is bright-eyed when they're wearing sunglasses, but one makes certain assumptions.

He put his gym bag on the floor, then leaned with his back against the bar and his elbows up on the bar rail and stared out at infinity. "You really know how to pick'm," he said.

A little bit after that Bradley Warren came back resplendent in different shoes, and Sheila Warren came back smelling fresh and clean, and Mimi Warren came back looking and smelling pretty much the same, and we were all together. One big happy family. We trooped out to the limo, Bradley and Jillian and Sheila and me and Mimi and Pike, all single file. I broke into "Whistle While You Work," but no one got it. Pike might've got it, but he never tells. Bradley and Jillian took the forward-facing seat and Mimi and Sheila and I got the seat facing the rear, Sheila and Mimi on either side of me, Sheila sitting so that her leg was pressed against mine. Sheila said, "Don't they have a bar in these damn things?" Everyone ignored her. Pike said something to the limo driver, then went over to his Jeep. Sheila Warren said, "He's not coming with us?"

"Nope."

"Mother fuck."

Traffic was light. We went down Beverly Glen to Wilshire, then east. We stayed on Wilshire through Beverly Hills and past the La Brea tar pits with the full-sized models of the mammoths they have there and past MacArthur Park and into downtown L.A. until Wilshire ended at Grand. We went up to Seventh, then over on Broadway, and pulled up under the entrance of the New Nippon Hotel.

One thing you could say about Bradley Warren, he built a helluva hotel. The New Nippon was a thirty-two-story cylindrical column of metallic blue glass and snow-white concrete midway between Little

Tokyo, Chinatown, and downtown L.A. There were dozens of limos and taxis and MBs and Jaguars. Suitcases were going in and out and doormen in red uniforms were whistling for the next taxi in line and guys I took to be tourists who looked like they made a lot of money were with tall slender women who looked like they cost a lot of money to keep up. None of them looked like gunsels or thugs or art thief–maniacs, but you can never be sure.

"You got a McDonald's in there?" I said.

Bradley Warren smiled at me.

Sheila Warren murmured, "Piece of shit."

We pulled to a stop by a clump of men and women who smiled as they watched the limo drive up. Two doormen trotted over, one with a lot of braid who was probably the boss, and opened the doors. Pike pulled up behind us, gave his keys to a parking attendant, and moved to stand by the lobby entrance twenty feet away.

The group of smiling people gathered around Bradley and congratulated him and said it was long deserved and didn't Sheila look lovely and wasn't Mimi getting pretty. Somebody took a photo. Sheila gave everyone an arc-light smile and draped herself on her husband's arm and looked adoring and proud and was everything he could have wanted her to be. She didn't look like she hated it or hated him or hated the goddamned building. Nancy Reagan would've been proud.

A square-faced guy in gray slacks and a blue blazer and a gold and yellow rep tie moved up to Jillian's elbow, said something, then the two of them moved over to me. He put out his hand. "Jack Ellis. You Cole?"

"Yeah. Where'd you do your time?" Ellis wore *ex-cop* like a bad coat.

"You can tell, huh?"

"Sure."

"Detroit."

"Rough beat."

Ellis nodded, pleased. "Murder City, brother. Murder City." Murder City. These cops.

We moved into the lobby and up an escalator to the mezzanine floor. The lower three floors were boutiques and travel agencies and bookstores and art galleries surrounding a lobby interior big enough to park the Goodyear blimp. There was a sign at the top of the escalator that read PACIFIC MEN'S CLUB LUNCHEON with ANGELES ROOM beneath it and an arrow pointing down a short corridor. People who looked like guests milled around and two overweight guys dressed like Ellis stood off to the side, looking like security. Ellis said, "I've got eight people in for this. Two up here on the mezzanine, two more in the Angeles Room, two in the lobby, and two in the kitchen entrance behind the podium."

Bradley and his knot of admirers continued along the corridor, passing the Angeles Room. I thought about saying something, but after all, it was their hotel. They should know where we were going.

I said, "There any other halls or entrances off the Angeles Room besides the kitchen entrance?"

"The Blue Corridor. I got no people there because that's where we'll be. We wait in there and when they're ready for the show to start we can get into the Angeles Room from a side door."

I nodded and looked at Jillian Becker. "What's on the program?"

"It shouldn't take more than an hour and a half. First, lunch is served, then the president of the association makes a few introductory remarks, and then Bradley speaks for about fifteen minutes and we go home."

We went through an unmarked door and along a sterile tile corridor and through another unmarked door and then we were in the Blue Corridor and then the Blue Room. Both the corridor and the room were blue. Four successful-looking Asian-American men were there, along with a tall black man and an older white guy with glasses and the mayor of Los Angeles. Everybody smiled and kissed Sheila's cheek and shook Bradley's hand. There was back-slapping and more photographs and everybody ignored Mimi. She stood to the side with her head down as if she were looking for lint on her dress.

I leaned close to her and whispered, "How you doin'?"

She looked up at me the way you look at someone when they've said something that surprises you. I patted her shoulder and said softly, "Stay close, kid. I'll take care of you."

She gave me the serious goldfish face, then went back to staring at her dress.

"Hey, Mimi."

She looked at me again.

"I think the dress looks great."

Her mouth tightened and bent. A smile.

Jillian Becker came up behind me and tapped at her wrist. "Ten minutes."

"Maybe we should synchronize watches."

She frowned.

"I'm going to take a look outside. I'll be back in five." I told Ellis to stay with Bradley and told both Mimi and Sheila to stay put. Mimi made the crooked mouth again. Sheila told me she was horny, and asked wouldn't I like to do something about it. Nothing like cooperation.

I went along the Blue Corridor and out into what a little sign said was the Angeles Room and thought, nope, maybe the sign was wrong. Maybe this was really the UN. Maybe a king was about to be crowned. Maybe aliens had landed and this was where they were going to make their address. Then I saw Joe Pike. It was the Angeles Room, all right.

Eighty tables, eight people per table. Video cams set up on a little platform at the rear of a place that might be called a grand ballroom if you thought small. Press people. A dais with seating for twenty-four. Pacific Men's Club Man of the Month. Who would've thought it. About sixty percent of the faces were Asian. The rest were black and white and brown and nobody looked too concerned about making the next Mercedes payment. I recognized five city council members and a red-haired television newswoman I'd had a crush on for about three years and the Tashiros. Maybe the Pacific Men's Club was *the* hot ticket in town. Maybe Steven Spielberg had tried to get in and been turned away. Maybe I could get the newswoman's phone number.

Pike drifted up to me. "This sucks."

That Joe.

"I could off anybody in this place five times over."

"Could you off someone and get away with you here?"

Head shake. "I'm too good even for me."

I said, "It starts in ten minutes. Door I came from is off the Blue Corridor. They're in a room down the corridor. We come out that room, along the corridor, through the door, and up to the dais." I told him where Ellis had put his men. "You take the right side of the dais. I'll come out with them and take the left."

Pike nodded and drifted away, head slowly swiveling as he scanned the crowd from behind the sunglasses.

I went back to the Blue Room. Bradley Warren was seated on a nice leather couch, smiling with four or five new arrivals, probably people who would sit on the dais. The little room was getting crowded and smoky and I didn't like it. Jack Ellis looked nervous. Bradley laughed at something somebody said, then got up and went to a little table where someone had put out white wine and San Pellegrino water. I edged up to him and said, "Do you know all these people?"

"Of course."

"Any way to clear them out?"

"Don't be absurd, Cole. Does everything look all right?"

"You're asking my opinion, I say blow this off and go home."

"Don't be absurd." I guess he liked the sound of it. "All right."

"You're being paid to protect us. Do that."

If he kept it up, he was going to have to pay someone to protect him from me.

More people squeezed into the little room. Jack Ellis went out and then came back. There were maybe twenty-five people in the room now, more coming in and some going out, and then Jillian Becker went over to Bradley and said, "It's time," loud enough for me to hear. I looked around, figuring to get Sheila and Mimi and Bradley into a group. Sheila was nodding at a very heavy white guy who smiled a great deal. I said, "Where's Mimi?"

Sheila looked confused. "Mimi?"

I went out into the hall. There were more people coming along the corridor and others going into the Angeles Room but there was no Mimi. Jack Ellis came out and then Jillian Becker. Ellis said, "She asked one of the busboys for the bathroom."

"Where is it?"

"Just around the corner to the left. I got a man down there." We were trotting as he said it, picking up speed, Ellis breathing hard after twenty feet. We went around one corner then around another and into a dirty white hall with an exit sign at the far end. There was a men's room door and a women's room door halfway down its length. Jack Ellis's man was lying facedown in front of the women's room door with one leg crossed over the other and his right hand behind his back. Ellis said, "Christ, Davis," and puffed forward. Davis groaned and rolled over as he said it.

I pulled my gun and pushed first into the women's room and then into the men's. Empty. I ran down to the exit door and kicked through it and ran down two flights of stairs and through another door into the hotel's laundry. There were huge commercial washers and steam-circulating systems and dryers that could handle a hundred sheets at a crack. But there was no Mimi.

In Vietnam I had learned that the worst parts of life and death are not where you look for them. Like the sniper's bullet that takes off a buddy's head as you stand side by side at a latrine griping about foot sores, the worst parts hover softly in the shadows and happen when you are not looking. The worst of life stays hidden until death.

On a heavy gray security door that led onto a service drive beneath the hotel, someone had written WE WARNED YOU in red spray paint. Beneath it they had drawn a rising sun.

13

When the first wave of cops and FBI got there, they
sealed off the Blue Corridor and herded all the princi-
pals into the Blue Room and sealed that off, too. An
FBI agent named Reese put the arm on me and Ellis
and brought us outside and walked us past the restrooms and down the stairs. Reese was about fifty,
with very long arms and pool player's hands. He was
about the color of fine French roast coffee, and he
looked like he hadn't had a good night's sleep in
twenty years.

He said, "How long this guy Davis been working
for you, Ellis?"

"Two years. He's an ex-cop. All my guys are ex-
cops. So am I." He said it nervous.

Reese nodded. "Davis says he's standing down the
hall back up by the bathrooms grabbing a smoke
when the girl comes by, goes into the women's room.
Says the next thing he knows this gook dude is coming out the women's room and gives him one on the
head and that's it." Reese squinted at us. Maybe

doing his impression of a gook dude. "That sound good to you?"

Jack Ellis chewed the inside of his mouth and said, "Uh-huh."

In the laundry there were cops and feds taking pictures of the paint job and talking to Chicano guys in green coveralls with NEW NIPPON HOTEL on the back. Reese ignored them. "Didn't anybody tell the girl not to go off alone?" He squatted down to look at something on the floor as he said it. Maybe a clue.

Ellis looked at me. I said, "She was told."

Reese got up, maybe saw another clue, squatted again in a different place. "But she went anyway. And when she went, nobody went with her."

I said, "That's it."

He stood up again and looked at us. "Little girl gotta go potty. That's no big deal. Happens every day. Nothing to worry about, right?" A little smile hit at the corner of his mouth and went away. "Only when you got serious criminals out there, and they're saying things, maybe going potty, maybe that's something to think about. Maybe calling the police when the threats are made, maybe that's something to think about, too." He looked from Ellis to me and back to Ellis. "Maybe the cops are here, maybe the little girl does her diddle and comes back and this never happens."

Ellis didn't say anything.

Reese looked at me. "I talked to a dick named Poitras about you. He said you know the moves. What happened, this one get outta hand?"

Ellis said, "Look, Mr. Warren signs the checks,

right? He says jump, I say which side of my ass you want me to land on?"

Reese's eyes went back to Ellis and flagged to half-mast. I think it was his disdainful look. "How long were you a cop?"

Ellis chewed harder at his mouth.

I said, "You gonna bust our ass about this all day or we gonna try to get something done?"

Reese put the look on me.

I said, "We shoulda brought you guys in. We wanted to bring you guys in. But Ellis is right. It's Warren's ticket and he said no. That's half-assed, but there it is. So this is what we're left with. We can stand here and you can work out on us or we can move past it."

Reese's eyes went to half-mast again, then he turned to look at the door with the paint. He sucked at a tooth while he looked. "Poitras said you got Joe Pike for a partner. That true?"

"Yeah."

Reese shook his head. "Ain't that some shit." He finished sucking on the tooth and turned back to me. "Tell me what you got, from the beginning."

I gave it to him from the beginning. I had told it so many times to so many cops I thought about making mimeographed copies and handing them out. When I told the part about Nobu Ishida, Jack Ellis said, "Holy shit."

We went back up the stairs to the Blue Room. There were cops talking to Bradley Warren and Sheila Warren and the hotel manager and the people who organized the Pacific Men's Club luncheon. Reese stopped in the door and said, "Which one's Pike?"

Pike was standing in a corner, out of the way. "Him."

Reese nodded and sucked the tooth again. "Do tell," he said softly.

"You want to meet him?"

Reese gave me flat eyes, then went over and stood by two dicks who were talking to Bradley Warren. Sheila was sitting on the couch, leaning forward into the detective who was interviewing her, touching his thigh every once in a while for emphasis. Jillian Becker stood by the bar. Her eyes were puffy and her mascara had run.

When Bradley saw me, he glared, and said, "What happened to my daughter?" His face was flushed.

Jillian said, "Brad."

He snapped his eyes to her. "I asked him an appropriate question. Should I have you research his answer?"

Jillian went very red.

I said, "They knew you were going to be here. They had someone come up through the laundry. Maybe he waited in the restroom or maybe he walked around and was in here with us. We won't know that until we find him."

"I don't like these 'maybes.' Maybe is a weak word."

Reese said, "Maybe somebody shoulda brought the cops in."

Bradley ignored him. "I paid for security and I got nothing." He stabbed a finger at Jack Ellis. "You're fired."

Ellis really worked at the inside of his mouth. Bradley Warren looked at me. "And you? What did you do?" He looked at Jillian Becker again. "The one you insisted I hire. What did you say about him?"

I said, "Be careful, Bradley."

Warren pointed at me. "You're fired, too." He looked at Pike. "You, too. Get out. Get out. All of you."

Everyone in the small tight room was staring at us. Even the cops had stopped doing cop things. Jack Ellis swallowed hard, started to say something, but finally just nodded and walked out. I looked at Sheila Warren. There was something bright and anxious in her eyes. Her hand was on the arm of the big cop, frozen there. Jillian Becker stared at the floor.

Reese said, "Take it easy, Mr. Warren. I got a few questions."

Bradley Warren sucked in some air, let it out, then glanced at his watch. "I hope it won't take too long," he said. "Maybe they can still make the presentation."

Joe Pike said, "Fuck you."

We left.

14

Pike took me back to the Warren house, dropped me off, and drove away without saying anything. I got into the Corvette, went down Beverly Glen into Westwood, and stopped at a little Vietnamese place I know. Ten tables, most of them doubles, cleanly done in pale pinks and pastel blues and run by a Vietnamese man and his wife and their two daughters. The daughters are in their twenties and quite pretty. At the back of the restaurant, where they have the cash register, there's a little color snapshot of the man wearing a South Vietnamese Regular Army uniform. Major. He looked a lot younger then. I spent eleven months in Vietnam, but I've never told the man. I often eat in his restaurant.

The man smiled when he saw me. "The usual?"

I gave him one of my best smiles. "Sure. To go."

I sat at the little table for two they have in the window of the place and waited and watched the people moving past along Westwood Boulevard and felt hollow. There were college kids and general-issue pedestrians and two cops walking a beat, one of them smiling at a girl in a gauzy cotton halter and white and black tiger-striped aerobic tights. The tights started just above her navel and stopped just below her knees. Her calves were tanned. I wondered if the cop would be smiling as much if he had just gotten fired from a job because a kid he had been hired to protect had gotten snatched anyway. Probably not. I wondered if the girl in the white and black tights would smile back quite so brightly. Probably not.

The oldest daughter brought my food from the kitchen while her father rang up the bill. She put the bag on the table and said, "Squid with garlic and pepper, and a double order of vegetable rice." I wondered if she could see it on my forehead: *Elvis Cole, Failed Protector*. She gave me a warm smile and said, "I put a container of chili sauce in the bag, like always." Nope. Probably couldn't see it.

I went down to Santa Monica and east to my office. At any number of traffic lights and intersections I waited for people to look my way and point and say nasty things, but no one did. Word was still under wraps.

I put the Corvette in its spot in the parking garage and rode up in the elevator and went into my office and closed the door. There was a message on my answering machine from someone looking for Bob, but that was probably a wrong number. Or maybe it wasn't a wrong number. Maybe I was in the wrong office. Maybe I was in the wrong life.

I put the food on my desk and took off my jacket and put it on a wooden coat hanger and hung it on the back of the door. I took the Dan Wesson out of its holster and put it in my top right drawer, then slipped out of the rig and tossed it onto one of the director's chairs across from my desk, then went over to the little refrigerator and got out a bottle of Negra Modelo beer and opened it and went back to my desk and sat and listened to the quiet. It was peaceful in the office. I liked that. No worries. No sense of loss or unfulfilled obligations. No guilt. I thought about a song a little friend of mine sings: *I'm a big brown mouse, I go marching through the house, and I'm not afraid of anything!* I sang it softly to myself and sipped the Modelo. Modelo is ideal for soothing that hollow feeling. I think that's why they make it.

After a while I opened the bag and took out the container of squid and the larger container of rice and the little plastic cup of bright red chili paste and the napkins and the chopsticks. I had to move the little figures of Jiminy Cricket and Mickey Mouse to make room for the food. What was it Jiminy Cricket said? *Little man, you've had a busy night.* I put some of the chili paste on the squid and some on the rice and mixed it and ate and drank the beer. *I'm a big brown mouse, I go marching through the house, and I'm noooot afraid of anything!*

The sun was low above Catalina, pushing bright yellow rectangles up my eastern wall when the door opened and Joe Pike walked in. I tipped what was maybe the second or third Modelo bottle at him. "Life in the fast lane," I said. Maybe it was the fourth.

"Uh-huh."

He came over to the desk, looked in what was left of the carton of squid, then the carton of rice. "Any meat in this?"

I shook my head. Pike had turned vegetarian about four months ago.

He dumped what was left of the squid into the rice, took a set of chopsticks, sat in one of the director's chairs, and ate. Southeast Asians almost never use chopsticks. If you go to Vietnam or Thailand or Cambodia, you never see a chopstick. Even in the boonies. They use forks and large spoons but when they come here and open a little restaurant they put out chopsticks because that's what Americans expect. Ain't life a bitch?

I said, "There's chili paste."

Pike shook what was left of the chili paste into the rice, stirred it, continued to eat.

"There's another Modelo in the box."

He shook his head.

"How long since you've come to the office?"

Shrug.

"Must be four, five months." There was a door to an adjoining office that belonged to Pike. He never used it and didn't bother to glance at it now. He shoveled in rice and broccoli and peas, chewed, swallowed.

I sipped the last of the Modelo, then dropped the empty into the waste basket. "I was just kidding," I said. "That's really pork-fried rice."

Pike said, "I don't like losing the girl."

I took a deep breath and leaned back in the chair. The office was quiet and still. Only the eyes in the Pinocchio clock moved. "Maybe, whatever reason, Warren wanted the Hagakure stolen and wants people to know and also wants them to know that he's had a child kidnapped because of his efforts to recover it. Maybe he's looking for a certain image here, figuring he can make a big deal out of recovering the book and his daughter. That sound like Bradley to you?"

Pike got up, went to the little refrigerator, and took out a can of tomato juice. "Maybe," he said. "Maybe it's the other way. Maybe somebody wants Warren to look bad and they don't give a damn about the book just so they stir up as much publicity as they can. Maybe what they want is to make the big Japanese connections lose interest. Or maybe they just want to hurt him. Maybe he owes money."

"A lot of maybes," I said.

Pike nodded. "Maybe is a weak word."

I said, "Maybe it's the yakuza."

Pike shook the little can of tomato juice and peeled off the foil sealer tab and drank. A tiny drop ran down from the corner of his mouth. It looked like blood. He wiped it away with a napkin. "We could sit here maybe all night and the girl's still gone."

I got up and went to the glass doors and opened them. Traffic noise was loud but the evening air was beginning to cool. "I don't like losing her either. I don't like getting fired and told to forget it. I don't like it that she's out there and in trouble and we're not in it anymore."

Mirrored lenses caught the setting sun. The sun made the lenses glow.

"I think we should stay in," I said.

Pike tossed the little can on top of the empty Modelo bottles.

"We stay with the yakuza because they're what we

have," I said. "Forget the other stuff. We push until someone pushes back and then we see where we are."

"All we have to do is find the yakuza."

"Right. All we have to do is find the yakuza."

Pike's mouth twitched. "We can do that."

15

Nobu Ishida had lived in an older split-level house on a Leave-It-to-Beaver street in Cheviot Hills, a couple of miles south of the Twentieth Century-Fox lot. It was dark, just after nine when we rolled past his home, rounded the block, and parked at the curb fifty yards up the street. Somewhere nearby, a dog barked.

The house was brick and board and painted a light, bright color you couldn't make out at night. Ishida's Eldorado was in the drive, with a tiny, two-tone Merkur behind it. There was an enormous plate glass picture window to the left of the front door, ideal for revealing the house's brightly lit interior. A woman in her fifties passed by the window talking to a young man in his twenties. Both the woman and the man looked sad. Mrs. Ishida and a son. With Dad not yet cold in the grave, there was plenty to be sad about.

Pike said, "Me or you?"

"Me."

I got out of the car as if I were out for an evening stroll. A block and a half down, I turned, came back, slipped off the walk into the shadows, and went to the west side of the Ishida house. There were two frame windows off what looked like a bedroom. The bedroom was dark. Past the windows, there was a redwood gate with a neatly painted sign that said BEWARE OF DOG. I whistled softly through my teeth, then broke off a hedge branch and brushed it against the inside of the gate. No dog. I slipped back to the street, then followed a hedgerow to the east side of the house. The garage was on that side, locked tight and windowless, with a narrow chain link gate leading to the back yard. I eased open the gate and walked along the side of the house to a little window about midway down. A young woman in a print dress sat at the dining room table, holding a baby. She touched her nose to the baby's and smiled. The baby smiled back. Not exactly a yakuza stronghold.

I went back to the car. Pike said, "Just family, right?"

"Or clever impersonators."

Forty minutes later the front door opened and the young man and the woman with the baby came out. The young man had a pink carry-bag with teddy bears on the side, probably stuffed with Pampers and baby bottles and teething rattles and Bert and Ernie dolls. Mrs. Ishida kissed everyone good-bye and watched them walk out to the little Merkur and waved as they drove away. "You see that?" I said.

Pike nodded.

"Classic yakuza misdirection."

Pike said, "You're a pip on stakeout."

Just before midnight, an L.A.P.D. prowl car turned the corner and cruised the block, arcing its big spot over the houses to scare away burglars and peepers. At one-twenty, two men jogged down the middle of the street, one white, one black, breathing in unison, matching strides. By three, I was stiff and hungry. Pike had not moved. Maybe he was dead. "You awake?"

"If you're tired, go to sleep."

Some partner.

At twenty-five minutes after five, an Alta-Dena milk truck rolled down the street and made four stops. By six-oh-five, the sky in the east was starting to pinken, and lights were on in two houses down the block. At fourteen minutes after eight o'clock, after jobs had been gone to and children had been brought to school and lives had been put under way, Nobu Ishida's widow came out of her house carrying a Saks Fifth Avenue shopping bag and wearing a black suit. She locked the door, walked to the Eldorado, got in, and drove away.

I said, "Let's do it."

We climbed out of the Corvette, went through the little chain link gate next to the garage, then around to the back. There was a standard frame door off the kitchen, and French doors opening off the family room to a small, kidney-shaped swimming pool. We went in through the French doors.

Pike said, "I'll take the back of the house."

"Okay."

He disappeared down the hall without making a sound.

The family room was a nice-sized space with Early American furniture and pictures of the kids and a Zenith console color TV and absolutely nothing to indicate that Nobu Ishida had an interest in feudal

Japanese artifacts. *People* magazine sat on the hearth and a box of Ritz crackers was on the coffee table and someone was reading the latest Jackie Collins. Imagine that. Portrait of the criminal as a Middle-Class American.

There was a yellow dial phone on a little table beside a Barcalounger chair across from the Zenith. Beneath the phone was an address book with listings for things like paramedics, doctor, fire, police, Ed and Diane Waters, and Bobby's school. Probably code names for yakuza thugs. I put the address book down and went into the kitchen. There were messages held to the refrigerator by little plastic magnets that looked like Snoopy and Charlie Brown and baskets of flowers. A picture of Ishida's wife sat on the counter in a frame that said KISS THE COOK. She looked like a nice woman and a good mom. Did she know what her husband had done for a living? When they were young and courting, had he said, "Stick with me, babe, I'm gonna be the biggest thug in Little Tokyo," or had he simply found himself there while she found herself with children and PTA and a loving husband who kept business to himself and made a comfortable life? Maybe I should introduce her to Malcolm Denning's wife. Maybe they would have a lot to talk about.

Pike materialized in the doorway. "Back here," he said.

We went back through the family room and down a short hall to what had probably once been a child's bedroom. Now, it wasn't.

"Well, well, well," I said. "Welcome to Nippon."

We were in a small room with a lot of furniture and all the furniture was lacquered rosewood. There

was a low table in the center of the room with a pil-
low for a chair and one of those lacquered boxes with
a phone inside. A matching file cabinet stood in the
corner, and a low table ran along two walls. On the
table were four little stands, each stand holding a pair
of horizontal samurai swords, a longer one on the
bottom, a shorter one above it. The swords were in-
laid with pearls and gems and had silk ribbons wound
about the handles. Separating the stands were very
old samurai battle helmets shaped like the helmets
the Federation Storm Troopers had worn in *Star
Wars*. A beautiful silk robe was framed on the wall
above the helmets. It looked like a giant butterfly.
There were wood-block prints on the opposite walls
and a silk-screened watercolor under glass that
looked so delicate that a ripple of air might fray it,
and two tiny bonsai trees growing in glass globes. On
the outside wall, shoji screens softened and filtered
the early morning sunlight. It was a beautiful room.

Pike went to the low table and said, "Look."

Three books were stacked on the edge of the table.
The top book was an excerpted English translation
of the Hagakure. The second book was a different
translation. The third was titled *Bushido: The Warrior's Soul*. Pike thumbed through the top Hagakure
translation. "They've been read a lot."

"If Ishida had the real thing, maybe someone
found out and wanted it bad enough to try to make
him turn it over to them."

"Uh-huh." Pike found something he liked and
stopped to read.

"Perhaps we can find a clue as to whom."

Pike kept reading.

"As soon as we finish reading."

Joe read a moment longer, then put the book back on the table. "I'll go up front and keep watch."

When he was gone, I looked around. There was nothing on the low desk but the books and the phone, and nothing on the wall tables but the swords and the helmets. Not even dust. The file cabinet was absolutely clean, too, but at least there were the drawers to look into. The top drawer had neatly labeled files devoted to home and family: the kids' schools, medical payments, insurance policies. The bottom drawer held art catalogs, vacation brochures, and supply catalogs from Ishida's import business. There were no financial records from his business. Those were probably with his accountant. Filed under C for Crime.

In the third folder from the back of the drawer I found Ishida's personal credit card records. The charges were substantial.

Nobu Ishida had two Visa cards and two Master-Cards and American Express Platinum and Optima and Diners Club. Most of the charges were at restaurants or hotels or various boutiques and department stores. The Ishidas had gone out a lot, and spent a lot more than people living in this house in this neighborhood might spend. I was looking for patterns, but there didn't seem to be any. All the hotels were one-shots and so were most of the restaurants. Go someplace for a bite, maybe not go back for another couple of months, if you went back at all. There were a few repeats, but those mostly to places I recognized. Ma Maison is not a yakuza hangout.

I had gone through the old stuff and was working on the recent when I noticed that two or three times a week, every week for the past three months, Ishida had gone to a place called Mr. Moto's. There were mostly small charges, as if he had gone by himself to have a couple of drinks, but once every two weeks, usually on a Thursday, there was a single large charge of between four and five hundred dollars. Hmmmm.

I put the credit card receipts back in their file and the file back in its folder and left the cabinet as I had found it and went back to the low table. I used the phone and called information.

A woman's voice said, "What city?"

"Los Angeles. I need a number and address for a restaurant or bar named Mr. Moto's."

If all you want is a number, they put on the computer. If you want the address, a person has to tell you. The person gave me the number and the address and told me to have a good day. Something the computer never does. I hung up and wiped the beautiful lacquered box free of unsightly fingerprints, then went out to Joe Pike.

He nodded when he saw me. "Didn't take long."

"The best clues never do."

We let ourselves out, walked back along the side of the house, got into the Corvette, and drove to Mr. Moto's.

16

Mr. Moto's was a storefront dance club just off Sixth downtown. Hi-tech deco. Whitewashed front with porthole windows outlined in aqua and peach, and *Mr. Moto's* spelled out in neon triangles. Japanese and Chinese cuisine. Very *nouveau*. There would be buffalo mozzarella spring rolls and black pasta miso and waiters with new wave football player haircuts and more neon triangles on the inside. A sign on the door said CLOSED. Another sign said LUNCH—DINNER—COCKTAILS—OPEN 11:30 A.M. It was twenty minutes after ten.

We drove another three blocks and stopped at a Bob's Big Boy to clean up in their restroom. There was an older guy with a copy of the *Jewish Daily News* standing at one of the lavatories combing his hair when we walked in. Pike went to the lavatory next to him, pulled off his sweatshirt, then unhooked his hip holster and put his gun on top of the soap dispenser. The old man looked at the gun, then at Pike, then left. He forgot his newspaper.

When we were as clean as about a million paper towels and soap that smelled like Pledge could make us, we walked the three blocks down to Mr. Moto's. It was ten minutes before noon when we went in the front door and the slim Japanese maître d' said, "Two for lunch?" The hair on the right side of his head was shaved down to a quarter-inch buzz cut, the hair on the left was long and frizzed. New wave, all right.

I said, "We'll sit at the bar for a while."

It was a nice-looking place, even with the neon. The front was all aqua plastic tables and peach wrought iron chairs and a tile floor the color of steel. There was a sushi bar on the right, with maybe twenty stools and four sushi chefs wearing white and red headbands and yelling anytime somebody walked into the place. About halfway back, the room cut in half. Tables continued along the wall on the right all the way to the kitchen in the back. On the left, you could step up underlit tile steps to a full bar and a little drinking area they had there with more tables and plants and neon triangles. A modern steel rail ran around the edge of the drinking platform to keep drunks from falling into someone's California roll. There were three women together at one of the little tables up in the bar area, and four couples in the dining room. Business people on their lunch hour. Pike and I went back through the dining area and up the little steps to the bar, one of the three women staring at Pike's tattoos.

The bartender was a Japanese woman in her late twenties. Hard face and too much green eye shadow and a rich ocher tan. She was wearing black, sprayed-on pants and a blue and black *hapi* coat with red trim that had been tied off just below the breasts so her midriff was bare. A tattoo of a butterfly floated two inches to the right of her navel. She said, "What'll it be, guys?"

I said, "Not too busy."

"It picks up about twelve-thirty."

We ordered a couple of Sapporo in the short bottles, and Pike asked for the men's room. The bartender told him, and Pike went back through the kitchen. I said, "First time here. A friend of mine raves about the place, though. You might know him. A regular."

She reached under the bar and music started to play. A Joan Jett rip-off. "Who's that?"

"Nobu Ishida."

The bartender shrugged. "So many faces," she said.

A man and a woman took two stools at the end of the bar. The bartender went down to them. I leaned over the bar to watch her. Nice legs.

The three women at the table took their drinks and went down to the dining area. I brought my beer and Pike's and took their table. Pike came out of the back a couple of minutes later. He said, "Restroom in the back with a pay phone. L-shaped kitchen running the width of the building and a cold room. Door out the back. Office off the kitchen. Five men and four women working the place."

We sipped our beer. Mr. Moto's filled with lots of men in Giorgio Armani suits and women in black biking tights and female lawyers. You could tell the lawyers because they drank too much and looked nervous. There was a smattering of Asians in the place, but most everybody else was white or black. "You'll notice," Pike said, "that the only people in here who look like thugs are me and you."

"You, maybe. I look like Don Johnson. You look like Fred Flintstone."

Sixteen hours with nothing to eat and the Sapporo was working wonders. Pike flagged a waitress and we ordered sashimi, sushi, white rice, miso soup, and more Sapporo. Sapporo is great when your back is stiff from an all-night stakeout.

Several young women who looked like models came in. They were tall and thin and wore their hair in flashes and swirls and bobs that looked okay in a magazine but looked silly in real life. They spent a lot of time touching themselves.

Pike said, "Maybe we should interrogate them."

The food came. We'd ordered toro and yellowtail and octopus and freshwater eel and sea urchin. The urchin and eel and octopus were prepared as sushi, each slice draped over a molded bullet of rice and held there by a band of seaweed. Sashimi is sliced fish without the rice. The waitress brought two little trays of a dark brown dipping sauce with a sprinkling of chopped green onion in it for the sashimi. In an empty tray I mixed soy sauce and hot green mustard for the sushi. I dipped a piece of the octopus sushi in the sauce, let the rice absorb the sauce, then took a bite. Delicious. Pike was looking in his miso soup. "There's something in here."

"Black pasta," I said. "*Nouveau* cuisine."

Pike pushed the soup aside.

By one o'clock the place was packed. It was SRO up by the maître d' and the crowd noise was threatening to drown out the music. Just after one a second bartender came on duty. He was younger than the Butterfly Lady, with short spiky hair and very smooth skin and a little-boy face. Someone's grad student nephew, given a part-time job to make a few extra bucks during the summer. The Butterfly Lady said something and the new kid looked our way. Worried. I smiled at Pike. "Well, well. I think we're making progress."

I got up and went over to the new kid's end of the bar. "You guys have Falstaff?"

The grad student shook his head. The Butterfly Lady came over, gave me a look, said something in Japanese to the kid, then went back to her end of the bar. The grad student began building a margarita. I said, "How about Corona?"

"Just Japanese."

I nodded. "Sapporo in a short bottle. Two."

He poured the margarita mixture into three round glasses. The Butterfly Lady came back, got them, went away. I smiled at the kid. Mr. Friendly. "Get many thugs in here?"

He said, "What?"

I winked at him, and took the two Sapporos back to the table. Our dishes had been cleared. Pike said, "Look."

Across the room, at a little corner table by some leafy plants, three men were being seated. An older Japanese man, a much younger Japanese man with heavy shoulders, and a tall, thin black man. The black man looked like Lou Gossett except for the scar that started at the crown of his head and ran down across his temple and curved back to lop off the top of his left ear. The two Asian men were smiling broadly and laughing with a slight man in a dark suit whose long hair was pulled back in a punk version of the traditional Japanese topknot. Manager. "Something tells me we are no longer the only thugs in the place," I said.

"Know the black guy from when I was a cop," Pike said. "Richards Sangoise. Dope dealer from Crenshaw."

"You see," I said. "Gangsters."

"Could just be coincidence they're here."

"Could be."

"But maybe not."

"Maybe those two Asian gentlemen are yakuza executives in search of an expanding business opportunity."

Pike nodded.

I went back to the grad student and gave him the same Mr. Friendly. "Excuse me," I said. "Do you see the three gentlemen seated there?"

"Uh-huh." Uneasy.

"I have reason to believe that those men are criminals, and that they may be engaged in the criminal act of conspiracy, and I felt obligated to tell someone. You might want to call the police."

The kid gave me Ping-Pong ball eyes. I walked back and sat down with Pike. "Just a little push," I said.

We watched the bar. The grad student said something to the Butterfly Lady. She snagged a waiter, said something, and the waiter went down onto the main floor to the manager. The manager came back into the bar and went over to the Butterfly Lady. They looked our way, then the manager left the bar and went back toward the kitchen. A little while later he reappeared and came over to our table. "Excuse me, gentlemen." Mr. Cordiality. "We're terribly busy, as you can see. Since you've finished your meal, would it be too much of an imposition for me to ask that you make room for others?"

"Yes," Pike said, "it would."

I said, "My friend Nobu told me that if I came here I would be treated better than this."

The manager looked past me for a moment. "You're a friend of Mr. Ishida?"

I said, "Mr. Ishida is dead. Murdered. I want to know who he was with the last time he was in here."

The manager shook his head and gave me a smile that wobbled. "You should leave now."

"We like it here," Pike said. "We might stay forever."

The manager worked his mouth, then went back down to the dining room and into the kitchen. Pike said, "I think we're becoming a problem."

I nodded. "Fun, isn't it?"

Pike went down into the dining area and over to the table with the two Japanese men and the black man. He stood very close to the table, so that the men had to lean back to look up at him. He said something to Richards Sangoise. Sangoise's eyes widened. Pike leaned over, put a hand on Sangoise's shoulder, and said something else. Sangoise looked at me. I made a gun with my hand, pointed it at him, and pulled the trigger. Sangoise shoved his chair back and left. The younger Japanese man jumped to his feet. The older man looked from Pike to me and back to

Pike. Angry. They hurried out after Sangoise. The manager came running out of the back in time to see the end of it. He looked angry, too. The grad student looked even more worried and said something to the Butterfly Lady. She said something sharp and walked away from him. Pike came back to the table and sat down.

"Nice," I said.

Pike nodded.

When the grad student came out from behind the bar and went back toward the kitchen, I followed him.

The kitchen was all steel and white with a high industrial ceiling. It was hot, even with the kitchen's blowers going at top speed. There was a narrow hall at the right rear of the kitchen with a door that said OFFICE. On the left, there was another little hall with a pay phone and a sign that said RESTROOMS. I passed a woman carrying a tray of pot sticker dumplings and went into the men's room.

It was small and white, with one stall for the toilet and one urinal and one sink and one of those blowers that never get your hands dry and a smudged sign above the sink that said that employees MUST wash with soap. The grad student was standing at a urinal. He looked over and saw it was me and you would've thought I'd kicked him in the groin. I gave him the smile, then I threw the little bolt that locked the door. He said, "You'd better not touch me."

I said, "Is this place owned by the yakuza?"

Scared. Very scared. "Open the door. Come on."

"I'll open the door after we talk."

He zipped up and moved away from the urinal.

His mouth was working like maybe he'd cry, like he'd spent a lot of time thinking that something like this would happen one day and now it was. Malcolm Denning. I said, "The shit is about to hit the fan, boy. Do you know what the yakuza is?"

He shook his head.

I said, "Did you know a man named Nobu Ishida?"

He shook his head again and I slapped him in the center of the chest with an open right hand. It made a deep hollow thump and knocked him back and frightened him more than hurt him. I said, "Do not bullshit me. Nobu Ishida was in here three times a week for three months. He spent big and he tipped big and you know him."

Someone tried the door, then knocked. I opened my jacket to show the Dan Wesson to the kid and said, "Occupied. Out in a minute." The kids eyes were big, and his mouth opened and closed like a fish. Koi. He said, "I didn't know him. He was a customer."

"But you know the name."

"Yes, sir." Yes, sir.

I said, "Nobu Ishida was a member of the yakuza. Every two weeks he was here with other people and those people were probably in the yakuza, too. A girl named Mimi Warren has been kidnapped, maybe by the yakuza, and maybe by someone who knew Ishida. I want their names."

The kid looked up from the place under my jacket where the Dan Wesson lived. "Mimi was kidnapped?"

I looked at him. "You know Mimi Warren?"

He nodded. "She comes here sometimes."

"Here?"

"With her friends."

"Friends?" Witness interrogation had always been a strong point.

"A girl named Carol. Another girl named Kerri. I really didn't know them. They're around, you see them, you say hi. They'd come and dance and hang out. We get pretty good bands." He was looking past me at the door. Like maybe somebody was going to kick it in. "I don't know anything about a kidnapping. I swear I don't. They're going to miss me and come looking. I'll get in trouble."

"Tell me about Ishida."

The kid spread his hands. Helpless. "There were always three other men. The only one I know was Mr. Torobuni. He owns the place. *Please*." Terry Ito had said that Yuki Torobuni runs the L.A. yakuza.

I opened the door and let the kid out. A pink-faced guy in a nice Ross Hobbs suit gave me a helluva look when I walked out after the kid.

Mimi Warren? *Here?*

When I got back to the bar, three men were waiting at the table with Joe Pike. There was an older guy with a lot of loose skin and a cheap sharkskin coat over an orange shirt, and a very short guy with two fingers off his left hand and the sort of baleful stare you get when life's a mystery. There was also a tall kid with too many muscles in a three-quarter-sleeve pullover. Eddie Tang. He grinned at me. "What do ya know. It's Mickey Spillane."

Pike's mouth twitched. "You missed all the fun," he said. "While you were out, somebody phoned for reinforcements."

17

The older man in the cheap sharkskin looked at Eddie. "You know this one?" No accent.

Eddie nodded. "He came into Ishida s."

I said, "Wow, Eddie. Last week you're working for Nobu Ishida, then Ishida gets osterized, and now you're working for Yuki Torobuni. You're really on the rise."

Yuki Torobuni said, "How do you know who I am?"

"You're either Torobuni or Fu Manchu."

Torobuni dipped his chin at Eddie. "Let's go in the back."

Torobuni moved past me and went down the steps toward the kitchen. The midget swaggered after him the way midgets will. Pike and I went next, and Eddie trailed behind. The Butterfly Lady watched us go, lean hips moving to The Smiths, little butterfly dancing. Nice moves.

Eddie said, "You like that, huh?"

Some guys.

When we got into the kitchen, Yuki Torobuni leaned against a steel table and said, "Eddie." Everything was Eddie. Maybe the midget was a moron.

Eddie moved to pat Pike down. Pike pushed Eddie's hand away from his body. "No."

The midget took out a Browning .45 automatic about eighteen sizes too big for him. The smell of sesame oil and tahini and mint was strong and the kitchen help was careful not to look our way.

Eddie and Pike were just about the same height but Eddie was heavier and his shoulders sloped more because of the insanely developed trapezius muscles. Eddie sneered at Pike's red arrows. "Those are shit tattoos."

Torobuni made a little forget-it gesture with his left hand. "Let's not waste our time." He looked at me. "What do you want?"

"I want a sixteen-year-old girl named Mimi Warren."

Eddie Tang laughed. Torobuni smiled at Eddie, then shook his head and gave me bored. "So what?"

"Maybe you have her."

Torobuni said, "Boy, I never heard of this girl. What is she, a princess, some kind of movie star?" Eddie thought that was a riot.

I said, "Something called the Hagakure was stolen from her parents, and whoever got it kidnapped the girl to stop the search. It's a good bet that whoever wanted the Hagakure is also in the yakuza. Maybe that's you."

Torobuni's face darkened. He barked out a couple of words of Japanese and Eddie stopped laughing.

"Whoever stole the Hagakure kidnaps the girl to stop you looking for it?"

"That's the way it looks."

"Not too bright."

"Geniuses rarely go into crime."

Torobuni stared at me a moment, then walked over to a giant U.S. range where a woman was taking a fresh load of tempura shrimp from the deep fat. He mumbled something and she plucked out a shrimp on a little metal skewer and handed it to him. He took a small bite. He said, "Two years ago I had a man's face put in here." He gestured at the grease vat. "You ever see a fried face?"

"No. How'd it taste?"

Torobuni finished the shrimp and wiped his hands on a cloth that was lying on the steel table. He shook his head. "You're out of your mind to come here like this. You know my name, but do you have any idea who I am?"

"Who killed Nobu Ishida?"

He leaned against the table again and looked at me. Eddie shifted closer, his eyes on Pike. The midget with the .45 beamed. Torobuni folded the towel neatly and put it down. "Maybe you killed him."

"Sure."

Behind us cooking fat bubbled and cleavers bit into hardwood cutting boards and damp heat billowed out of steamers. Torobuni stared at me for another couple of centuries, then spoke again in Japanese. The midget put away the gun. Torobuni came very close to me, so close the cheap sharkskin brushed my chest. He looked first in my right eye, then in my left. He said, "Yakuza is a terrible monster to arouse. If you come down here again, yakuza will eat you." His voice was like late-night music.

"I'm going to find the girl."

Torobuni smiled a smile to match the voice. "Good luck."

He turned and went out the back of the kitchen, the midget swaggering behind him. Eddie Tang went with them, walking backward and keeping his eyes on Joe Pike. He stopped in the door, gave Pike a nasty grin, then peeled up his sleeves to show the tattoos. He worked his arms to make the tattoos dance, then snarled and flexed the huge traps so they grew out of his back like spiny wings. Then he left.

Pike said, "Wow."

We went out through the dining room and past the bar. The kid I'd talked to was gone. The Butterfly Lady was busy with customers. People ate. People drank. Life went on.

When we got back to the Big Boy lot, Pike said, "He knows something."

"You got that feeling, huh?"

Nod.

"Somebody else might know something, too. Mimi Warren used to come here."

The sunglasses moved. "Mimi?" He was doing it, too.

"She came with friends and she hung out and she probably met a wide variety of sleazy people. Maybe whoever grabbed her was someone she met here and bragged to about what her daddy had sitting in his home safe."

"And if we can find the friends, they might know who."

"That's it."

The sunglasses moved again. "Uh-huh."

Forty minutes later I pulled the Corvette into my carport, parked, went in through the kitchen, and phoned Julian Becker at her office. She said, "Yes?"

"It's Elvis Cole. I'd like to talk with you about Mimi and her father and all of this."

"You were fired."

"That may be, but I'm going to find her. Maybe you can help me do that."

There was a pause, and sounds in the background. "I can't talk now."

"Would you have dinner with me tonight at Musso and Frank?"

Another pause. Thinking about it. "All right." She didn't sound particularly enthusiastic. "What time?"

"Eight o'clock. You can meet me there, or I'll pick you up. Whichever you prefer."

"I'll meet you there." It was clear what she preferred.

After we hung up I pulled off my clothes, took a shower, then fell into a deep uneasy sleep.

18

I woke just after six feeling drained and stiff, as if sleeping had been hard work. I went downstairs and flipped on the TV news, and after a while there was something about Mimi's kidnapping.

A blond woman who looked like she played racquetball twice a day gave the update standing in front of the New Nippon Hotel, "site of the kidnapping." She said the police and the FBI still had no information as to Mimi's whereabouts or condition, but were working diligently to effect a positive resolution. The screen cut to a close-up of a photograph of Mimi with a phone number beneath her chin. After the blond woman asked anyone who might have information to call the number, the news anchor segued nicely into a story about a recruitment drive the L.A.P.D. was launching. There was a number to call for that, too.

Mimi Warren had been given seventeen seconds.

At seven o'clock I went into the kitchen, drank two glasses of water, then went upstairs to shave and shower. I ran the water hot and rubbed the soap in hard and after the shower I felt a little better. Maybe I was getting used to the pain. Or maybe it was just the thought of dinner with an MBA.

When I was dry and deodorized, I stood in the door to my closet and wondered what I should wear. Hmmm. I could wear my Groucho Marx nose, but Jillian already thought I joked around too much. My Metaluna Mutant mask? Nah. I pulled on a pair of brown outback pants and gray CJ Bass desert boots and a white Indian hiking shirt and a light blue waiter's jacket. I looked like an ad for Banana Republic. Maybe Banana Republic would give me a job. They could put my picture in their little catalog and under it they could say: *Elvis Cole, famous detective, outfitted for his latest adventure in rugged inner-city climes!* Did Banana Republic sell shoulder holsters?

I went downstairs, put out food for the cat, then locked up and drove down into deepest, darkest Hollywood. Yep. Thinking about dinner with Jillian was working wonders.

At two minutes before eight, I parked behind Musso and Frank's Grill on Hollywood Boulevard and went in. Jillian Becker walked in behind me. She was wearing a conservative eggshell pants suit over a light brown shirt and beige pumps. Her nails and her lip gloss were one of those colors between pink and flesh, and went well with the eggshell. Her fingers were slim and manicured and there was a single strand of white pearls around her neck. She looked tired and harassed, but I couldn't tell that until she was closer. She said, "I'm sorry I'm late." It was one minute after eight.

"Would you like a drink?"

"At the table."

A bald man led us into Musso's huge back room to a very nice booth. There's a long bar back there and leather booths and it looks very much the way it looked in 1918, when Musso's opened. A busboy came with sourdough bread and water, then a waiter appeared, giving us menus and asking if we cared for something to drink. I ordered a Dos Equis. Jillian Becker ordered a double Stoly on the rocks. Must have been some kind of day.

"This room," I said, "is where Dashiell Hammett first laid eyes on Lillian Hellman. It was a romance that lasted ages."

Jillian Becker glanced at her watch. "What did you want to talk about?" So much for romance.

"Have the cops come up with anything?"

"No."

"Have there been any demands from the kidnappers?"

"No. The police and the FBI talk to us a dozen times a day. They have a tap on Bradley's home phone. They have a tap on the office phone. But there's been nothing."

The waiter came back with the drinks. Usually it takes about a year to get your drinks, but sometimes they're fast. "Are you ready to order?" he said, pencil poised.

Jillian said, "I'll have the crab salad."

The waiter looked at me.

"Grilled chicken. Home fries. Broccoli."

He nodded twice and wrote it down and left. Jillian lifted her glass and took a long drink.

"Rough day?"

"Mr. Cole, I'd rather not discuss my day if it's all the same to you. You could have asked me what the police had over the phone."

"But then I wouldn't have been able to admire your beauty."

She tapped her glass with a manicured fingernail. Guess we'd proceed directly to business.

I said, "Have you ever heard the name Yuki Torobuni?"

"No."

"Yuki Torobuni owns a dance club downtown called Mr. Moto's. It's very new wave, very hip, cocaine in the bathrooms, that kind of place. Yuki Torobuni also heads the yakuza here in L.A. Do you know what the yakuza is?"

"Like the mafia."

"Yeah. How about a guy named Eddie Tang? Ever heard his name?"

"No." Impatient. "Why are you asking if I've heard of these people? Do you think Bradley's involved with them?"

"It crossed my mind."

She lifted her glass and took a careful sip, thinking about that. She thought about it for a very long time. When she put the glass down, she said, "All right. It's reasonable for you to consider every possible solution to a problem." Business school. "But Bradley is not involved with organized crime. I see where the money comes from, and I see where it goes. If there were something shady going on, I'd know it, or at least suspect it, and I don't."

"Maybe it's very well hidden."

She shook her head. "I'm too good for that."

I nodded. "Okay. Let's try this. I talked to a guy at Mr. Moto's who told me that Mimi came there often, and that she came with friends."

"Mimi?" Everybody does it.

"Uh-huh. A girl named Carol and another girl named Kerri."

Jillian took another sip of her drink. "She's never mentioned them to me. Not that she necessarily would."

"How about other friends?"

Jillian shook her head again. "I'm sorry. Mimi always seemed very withdrawn. Sheila complains endlessly that she never leaves the house." Jillian put her glass down and eyed it coolly. "Sheila is something else."

The waiter came with a little stand and all of our plates on a large oval tray. He put the stand down by the table, then the tray on the stand. He set out Jillian's crab salad, then my chicken and broccoli and home fries, and then he took the tray and the stand and left. The chicken smelled wonderful. It always did.

Jillian said, "Bradley's not going to pay you a dime, you know. He intends to sue you, if he has to, to recover the money he's already paid."

"He won't have to do that." Bradley Warren's blank check was still in my wallet. I took it out, tore it in quarters, and put it on the table by Jillian Becker's plate.

Jillian Becker looked at the check and then at me. She shook her head. "And you're still going to look for Mimi?"

"Yes."

"Why?"

"I told Mimi I would take care of her."

"And that's enough."

I shrugged. "It's an ugly job, but somebody has to do it."

Jillian frowned and ate some of the crab salad. I had some of the chicken, then a couple of the home fries. Excellent.

I said, "I need to find out who Mimi hangs out with. Bradley and Sheila might be able to tell me. If they won't talk to me, maybe you could talk to them for me."

Jillian frowned more deeply and put her fork in the crab but only played with it. "Bradley had to fly to Kyoto."

The Dos Equis was cold and bitter. I sipped it. I had a little more of the chicken. I had a little of the broccoli. Two guys at the edge of the bar crowd were looking our way. One of the guys was overweight and balding. The other guy was very tall with dark hair and thick glasses and a heavy jaw. He looked like Stephen King. The shorter guy was drinking what looked like scotch rocks. The taller, Campari and soda. They were staring at Jillian and the taller guy was smiling. "His daughter is gone," I said, "but business continues."

Jillian Becker's lips tightened and she put down her fork and I thought she was going to stand. She didn't. She said, "Bradley has been very fair to me. He's treated me just as he's treated everyone else in his organization. He's recognized and rewarded my abilities. It's a good job."

"And you've got the BMW to prove it."

"It's so easy for you, isn't it? Tearing up checks. Standing on your head in your office."

"How about Sheila? You think I could talk with her?"

Silence.

"Sheila went with him."

Slow nod.

I finished off the Dos Equis. "Parents of the Year, all right."

Jillian started to say something, then stopped. She looked angry and embarrassed.

I said, "You could get me into their house. We could look in Mimi's room."

"Bradley would fire me."

"Maybe."

Her jaw worked and she sipped some water and didn't say anything for a long time. When she did, she said, "I don't like you."

I nodded.

Her jaw flexed again, and she stood up. "God damn you," she said. "Let's go. I have a key."

19

We took two cars, Jillian pulling out in her white
BMW and me following her west along Sunset toward Beverly Hills, then up Beverly Glen to the Warrens'. Jillian parked by the front of the house and I
parked next to her. She had the front door open by
the time I got out of my car. She said, "Mimi's room
is in the rear. I'll walk back with you." She walked in
ahead without waiting.

The big house was as cold as a mausoleum, and
our footsteps echoed on the terrazzo entry. I hadn't
heard it when I'd been in the house before, but when
I was in the house before there'd been other people
and things going on. Now the house seemed aban-
doned and desolate. Life in an Andrew Wyeth landscape.

Mimi's room was big and white and empty the
way I remembered it. The single bed was made and
tight and the desk was neat and the walls bare and the
high shelf of *Britannica* and Laura Ingalls Wilder just
as it had been before. I had hoped that since the last

time I had seen the room, posters would have gone up on the walls and someone would have doodled on the desk and a pile of dirty clothes would've grown in the corner. Jillian said, "Sixteen years old." She was standing with her arms crossed and her hands cupping her upper arms, feeling the cold.

I nodded. "Uh-huh."

She looked at me. "As long as I'm here, I may as well help you."

"Take the desk."

"What are we looking for?"

"Address books, yearbooks, letters, a diary. Anything that might have names and phone numbers. Search one drawer at a time. Empty it item by item, then put it back together. Make yourself go slowly."

Jillian went over to the desk and opened the large bottom drawer. Hesitant. She said, "You do this a lot, don't you? Look through people's things."

"Yes. People keep secrets. You have to look into personal places to find them."

"It makes me uncomfortable."

"It makes me uncomfortable, too, but there's no other way."

She looked at me some more, then bent to the drawer and started taking out things. I went to the bed, stripped down the covers, threw them into the center of the room, and lifted the mattress off the box springs. No hidden diary. No secret compartments cut into the side of the mattress. I tilted the bed up on its edge. Nothing beneath the box springs. I put the bed back the way it had been, then I looked through the *Britannica* and the matched set of Laura Ingalls Wilder. A pink $50 Monopoly money bill fell out of volume E of the *Britannica*. The Laura Ingalls Wilder books had never been opened.

To the left of the desk there was a walk-in closet. A rail of clothes hung on the right side of the closet with a shoe board and shoes beneath the clothes, each pair neatly together and all the shoes forming a nice neat row. On the left side of the closet there were shelves with more books and game boxes. On the lowest shelf there was a blue hat that said *Disneyland* and a little stuffed monkey and what had once been an ant farm but was now just an empty plastic box. Next to the ant farm there was a very old set of a children's encyclopedia and a book about standard poodles that looked like it had been read a lot and four brochures on the work of a Japanese artist named Kira Asano. The brochures showed reproductions of bleak landscapes and described Asano as a dynamic, charismatic visionary whose gallery showings and lectures were not to be missed. One of the brochures had a picture of Asano made up like a samurai with a white and red headband, no shirt, and a samurai sword. Visionary, all right. Beneath the brochures were two slim volumes of what looked like Japanese poetry. There was something handwritten in Japanese in the front of each volume. I put the volumes of poetry aside and called Jillian.

"Can you read this?"

"Haiku by Bashō and Issa." She read the inscriptions and smiled. "They were a gift from someone named Edo. 'May there always be warm sun.'"

"Can Mimi read Japanese?"

"Maybe a little. I don't really know." Mimi Warren, the Invisible Child.

I put the poetry back on the shelf. "Did you finish going through the desk?"

"I didn't find anything."

I nodded. "Okay. I'll finish here in a minute."

"We could carry this stuff out and I could help."

"If we carried this stuff out, we wouldn't remember where it belongs."

She cocked her head at me. Curious.

"These aren't our things," I said. "We have to respect that."

She stared at me some more, then stepped back. "Of course. I'll wait in the front."

Halfway through the games, I found seven smudged envelopes in a Parcheesi box. They were postmarked Westwood and had been addressed to Ms. Mimi Warren at the Shintazi Hotel in Kyoto, Japan, and were return-addressed to Traci Louise Fishman, 816 Chandelle Road, Beverly Hills. Both the address and return had been neatly printed in bright, violet ink, with plenty of curlicues and swirls and hearts rather than dots over the *i*'s. I took out each letter and read it. Traci Louise Fishman was sixteen years old, and wondered why Mimi's father had to ruin every vacation by dragging her best friend off to Japan. In one letter, she had a crush on a boy named David who went to Birmingham High in Van Nuys, and desperately wanted him to "make her a woman." In another, David had become a stuck-up shit who wouldn't look at her, being a typical shallow Valley dude more interested in brainless bimbos with surfer-chick tans than women of intellect and sensitivity. Traci smoked too much, but was going to quit, having read a *Harvard Medical School Health Letter* which said that teenage girls who smoke would almost certainly have deformed children and breast cancer. She really really really liked Bruce Willis, but she'd just die if she could ever meet Judd Nelson, even though he had a funny-looking nose. Her dad had promised her a new car if she took two summer-session classes at the Glenlake School for Girls so maybe she could graduate one semester early. She was gonna do it 'cause what she wanted more than anything else in the world was a snow-white Volkswagen Rabbit convertible even though her old man was such a cheap shit it would probably never happen. She couldn't wait for Mimi to get home, she missed their talks soooooooo much! And—ohmyGod, fur shure!—she had spotted in a pair of white pants through a *Super* Tampax and was so embarrassed she thought she would die!!!! The letters went on. The stuff of life.

When I had read all seven letters, I returned them to the Parcheesi box, then went through the rest of the boxes, but found nothing else. When I left the closet, Jillian Becker was gone. I made sure the closet was as I had found it, fixed the bed, shut the light, then left and went back through the dark house to the front.

Jillian was leaning against a little table in the entry with her arms crossed when I got there. I thought she might have looked sad, but maybe not. She said, "Did you find anything?" Her voice was quiet.

"No mention of Carol or Kerri, but I found seven letters from someone named Traci Louise Fishman. Traci Louise Fishman told Mimi everything that was going on in her life. Maybe Mimi returned the favor."

Jillian uncrossed her arms. "Good. I'm glad this was helpful. Now let me lock up."

I went out and waited. It was cool in upper Holmby and the earth smelled damp from having been recently watered. When Jillian came out, I said, "Thanks for getting me in here."

She walked past without looking at me and went to her BMW. She opened her door, then she closed it and turned back to me. Her eyes were bright. She said, "I worked my butt off for a job like this."

"I know."

"You don't walk away from something you've worked so hard for."

"I know."

She opened her car door again, but still didn't get in. Out in the street some rich kid's Firebird with a Glaspak muffler blasted past, wrecking the calm. She said, "You go to school, you work hard, you play the game. When you're in school, they don't tell you how much it costs. They don't tell you what you've got to give up to get to where you want to be."

"They never do."

Jillian looked at me some more, then she said good night and got into her white BMW and drove away. I watched her. Then I drove away, too.

20

Glenlake School for Girls is on a manicured green campus at the border between Westwood and Bel Air, in the midst of some of the most expensive real estate in the world. It is a fine school for fine girls from fine families, the sort of place that would not take kindly to an unemployed private cop asking to be alone with one of its young ladies. Real cops would probably be called. As would the young lady's parents. When you got to that point, you could just about always count on the kid clamming up. So. Ixnay on the direct approach.

There were other options. I could go to Traci Louise's home, but that, too, would involve parents and an equal possibility of clamming. Or I could stake out the Glenlake campus and abduct Traci Louise Fishman as she arrived. This seemed the most likely option. There was only one problem. I had no idea what Traci Louise Fishman looked like.

The next morning I forwent my usual wardrobe and selected a conservative blue three-piece pinstripe suit and black Bally loafers. I hadn't worn the Ballys for over a year. There was dust on them. When the tie was tied and the vest buttoned and the jacket in place and riding squarely on my shoulders, the cat topped the stairs and looked at me.

"Pretty nice, huh?"

His ears went down and he ran under the bed. Some people are never happy.

At twenty minutes after nine I parked in the Glenlake visitors' lot, found my way to the office, went up to an overweight lady behind the counter, and said, "My name's Cole. I'm thinking about applying to Glenlake for my daughter. Would it be all right if I looked around?"

The woman said, "Let me get Mrs. Farley."

A thin woman in her early fifties came out of an office and over to the counter. She had blond hair going to gray and sharp blue eyes and a smile as toothy as a Pontiac's grill. I tried to look like I made two hundred thou a year. She said, "Hello, Mr. Cole, I'm Mrs. Farley. Mrs. Engle said you wished to see the school."

"That's right."

She looked me over. "Had you made an appointment?"

"I didn't think one was necessary. Should I have called?"

"I'm afraid so. I have an interview scheduled with another couple in ten minutes."

I nodded gravely, and tried to look like I would look if I was recalling an overbooked personal calendar, then shook my head. "Of course. Being a single parent and having just been made a partner in the firm, my schedule tends to get out of hand, but maybe I can get back in a couple of weeks." I let my eyes drift down the line of her body and linger.

She shifted behind the counter and glanced at her watch. "It seems a shame not to see the school after you've gone to such trouble," she said.

"True. But I understand if you can't make the time." I touched her arm.

The tip of her tongue peeked out and wet the left corner of her mouth. "Well," she said, "maybe if we hurry I can give you a short tour." She said it deviously.

Some guys can charm the stitches off a baseball.

Mrs. Farley came around the counter, put her hand on my back, and gave me the short tour. The short tour included a lot of laughing at unfunny things, a lot of her feeling my shoulder and arm, and a lot of her breathing in my face. Violets. We saw the new gymnasium and the new science labs and the newly expanded library and the new theater arts building and a lot of coeds with moussed hair and bright plastic hair clips and skin cancer tans. Five girls were standing in a little knot outside the cafeteria when Mrs. Farley and I walked past, Mrs. Farley's hand on my back. One of the girls said something and the others laughed. Maybe Mrs. Farley didn't require as much charming as I thought.

When we got back to the office, a man in a flowered shirt and a woman in sweat pants and a New Balance running shirt were waiting. Mrs. Farley's appointment. She smiled at them and told them she would only be another moment, then thanked me for my interest in Glenlake, holding my hand a very long time as she did, and apologized twice for not having more time. She offered to be available whenever I might have more questions. I asked her if it would be all right to take a short stroll around on my way out. She took my hand again and said of course. I smiled at the man in the flowered shirt and the woman in the sweat pants. They smiled back. To think that I dressed for this.

Two minutes later I was back in the library. There was a birch-and-Formica information table as you walked in, and a girl sitting behind the table chewing bubble gum and reading a Danielle Steel novel. The girl had the same moussed, sun-streaked hair and walnut tan that every other girl at Glenlake had, and the same large plastic hair clip. I said, "I thought Glenlake didn't require its students to wear uniforms."

She gave me blank eyes and blew a bubble.

"Where could I find last year's yearbook?"

The bubble popped. "In reference, over there on the shelf above California history. You see the David Bowie poster? To the left of that."

Traci Louise Fishman was on page 87 of last year's yearbook, sandwiched between Krystle Fisher and Tiffany Ann Fletcher. She had a heart-shaped face and a flat nose and pale frizzy hair and round, wire-framed glasses. Her lips were thin and tight, and her eyebrows looked like they would have a tendency to grow together. Like her friend Mimi, she wasn't what you would call pretty. From the look on her face, you could tell she knew it. I put the yearbook back on the shelf, left the library, went back to the Corvette, cranked it up, drove off the campus, and parked in the shade of a large elm just outside the school's front gate. Traci's letters to Mimi said she would be taking two morning classes to leave her afternoons free. It was 10:20.

At 11:45, Traci Fishman came around the rear of the administration building, walked into the student parking lot, and unlocked a white Volkswagen Rabbit convertible. Dad wasn't such a cheap shit after all. She was putting the top down when I walked up behind her. "Traci?"

"Yes?" She pronounced the word clearly.

"My name's Elvis Cole. I'm a private detective. Could I talk with you for a few minutes?" I showed her my license.

She stopped futzing with the top, looked at the little plastic card, then looked at me out of round, expressive eyes. No glasses. Maybe when you started thinking in terms of having some guy "make you a woman," you ditched the glasses and got contacts. "What do you want to talk with me about?"

I put my license away. "Mimi Warren."

"Mimi's been kidnapped."

"I know. I'm trying to find her. I'm hoping you can help me."

The big eyes blinked. The contacts didn't fit well, but in a world of plastic hair clips and chocolate fudge tans, she was going to wear them or die trying. Also, she was scared. She said, "I don't know. Are you working for her parents?"

"I was. Now I'm working for me."

"How come you're not working for Mimi's parents if you're trying to find Mimi?"

"They fired me. I was supposed to be taking care of her when she got snatched."

She nodded and glanced toward the front of the school. More girls were coming from behind the administration building and from other places and were going to their cars or heading through the gates to the street where parked cars waited. Traci chewed at her upper lip and stared at them through blinking alien eyes. Her frizzy hair was cut short and stuck out from her head. She was heavy and her posture was bad. Some of the girls looked our way. More than a couple traded looks and made faces. Traci said, "You want to sit in my car?"

"Sure." I held the door for her, then closed it and went around to the other side.

Three girls with moussed hair and plastic clips and mahogany tans and pearl-white lip gloss walked past the Rabbit to a catch-me red Porsche 944 Turbo. I watched Traci watch them. She tried to do it sneaky, out the corner of her eye so they couldn't tell. The girls at the Porsche leaned against its fenders and looked past each other so they could see the Rabbit and me and Traci, and there was lots of laughter. One of them stared openly. I said, "You think they share the same lip gloss tube?"

Traci giggled. She looked at me sort of the same way she looked at them, out from under her eyes, as if she really didn't want you to know she was looking, as if she thought that if you knew, you'd say something sharp or do something hurtful. "Don't you think they look like clones?" she said. "They have no individuality. They're scared of being unique, and therefore alone, so they mask their fear by sameness and denigrate those who do not share their fear." She just tossed that off, like saying, *Hey, buddy, how about a bag of nuts?* She said, "They're talking about us, you know. They're wondering who's that guy and why are you sitting with me."

"I know that."

"I knew they would. That's why I wanted us to get into the car."

"I know that, too."

She looked at me a long time, then looked away. "Do you think that's shallow? I hate to be shallow. I try not to be." Sixteen.

"Traci," I said, "I think maybe Mimi was mixed up with some people who might've had something to do with her kidnapping. People she might've thought were her friends and who she might've gone out with."

Traci pooched out her lips and chewed them and shrugged. "Friends?"

Even Traci Louise Fishman did it. I said, "Do you know a couple of Mimi's friends named Carol and Kerri?"

"Uh-uh."

"You sure?"

Traci chewed the lips some more and shrugged again. Nervous. "Why would I know them?"

"Because you guys were buddies."

Shrug.

I said, "Traci, I've seen seven letters that you wrote to Mimi last year when she was away. I've read them."

She looked shocked. "You read other people's mail?"

"Monstrous, isn't it?"

She chewed harder. "If you find her, what are you going to do?"

"Rescue her." Sir Elvis.

"You won't tell her that I'm the one who said?"

I said, "I know you want to protect your friend, babe, but you have to understand that right now she is in a world of trouble. We're not talking about her shoplifting a radio and you telling. Bad people have her and whatever you know might be able to help me find her."

She chewed harder and then she nodded. "You really think it was people she thought were her friends that did it?"

"Yes."

The irritated eyes grew pink and blinked faster. Maybe starting to cry. "It's just that Mimi liked to make things up, you know. She was always telling me about these stud guys and the parties they would have and how they would ride around in limousines and go to clubs and all these things that you just knew she'd made up."

"Bigger-than-life stuff."

"Uh-huh." She began to sniffle. "So when she told me about these new people, I didn't believe her at first. She said she had these new friends and that they weren't full of bullshit like everybody else in her life. She said she had a boyfriend and she said he was really buff and they partied every night and had real good cocaine and stuff and that they were the seeds of a revolution and all this crazy stuff, and after a while I said, 'Mimi, you're full of crap,' just like I always did, and she said it was true and she'd prove it."

Traci Louise Fishman dug through her purse and

took out a battered red leather wallet and dug through that and pulled out a bent color snapshot. "A couple of days later she gave me this. Kerri's the girl with the white hair. I don't know about Carol. I really don't."

The photograph had been taken on the street at night and was of half a dozen smiling young men and women. Mimi Warren was standing next to a girl with white hair, but Mimi Warren wasn't Mimi Warren as I had ever seen her. She had blue electroshock hair and heavy emerald eye shadow and she was giving the finger to the camera. She was also standing beside a big, good-looking kid with huge shoulders. The big guy was giving us the bird with his right hand and had his left hand on Mimi's breast. I took a deep breath, then let it out. Carol and Kerri didn't matter anymore. The big kid was Eddie Tang.

I touched his image in the photograph. "And this is Mimi's boyfriend?"

"Uh-huh. That's what she said."

21

One of the moussed girls by the 944 went around to the driver's side, got in, and leaned across to unlock the passenger door. The other girls climbed in, but the Porsche didn't start. One of the girls lit up. The one in the tiny back seat turned crosswise, and kept raking her fingers through her hair. Music blasted out of the Porsche's door-mounted speakers, rolling across the parking lot, and you could see them passing around an Evian bottle. They had gotten in the car, apparently, to better watch us from Black Forest comfort.

I looked at the photograph that Traci had given me and at the people in it. Eddie was the oldest, and the biggest. The other two guys were probably not out of their teens and were slight, one wearing narrow-legged jeans and a white shirt and a couple-of-sizes-too-big cloth jacket with a lot of buckles and studs, the other a uniform that looked like something a Red Chinese National would wear, all gray and plain with a single row of buttons down the front and a Nehru collar and a Red Army cap. The kid in the uniform was Asian. He didn't look like a yakuza thug, but maybe he was executive material. Kerri and the other woman were also Asian. The one Traci didn't know was dressed in Jordache jeans and a plaid shirt with the sleeves rolled up and a Swatch watch. Normal. Kerri was a Clorox blonde with a spike cut and a powdered face and neon-red lips and nails. There was a dog collar around her neck. Billy Idol. I said, "Traci, this is important. Did Mimi ever say what she talked about with these people?"

"Uh-huh."

"Was it about something called the Hagakure?"

"Uh-uh."

"What did she talk about?"

"Stuff I didn't understand. She said they were real. She said they loved her. She said they were the first people she'd ever met who truly had purpose." I looked out the window. Purpose. When you're sixteen, maybe all life is drama. I looked back at Traci. Her big eyes went from pink to red and she rubbed at them and said, "I gotta put in drops."

She took a little plastic bottle from her purse and put two drops of something into each eye and sat with her eyes closed for a couple of minutes. Trying not to cry.

"When was the last time you spoke to her?"

Nervous shrug. "About three weeks ago."

"Did she tell you what she would do when she was hanging out with these people?"

Traci stared at the photograph. I handed it back and watched her put it in her wallet like something precious that had to be handled carefully.

"She told me they went to all these clubs. She told me they did all these drugs and had sex and it sounded just like when she would make stuff up only this time I believed her. I said she ought not. I said she was gonna get in trouble or get fucked up or get arrested, and Mimi got real mad so I shut up. This one time she got so mad at me she didn't talk to me for a month. You have to be careful." Traci said it like she was telling me a secret that only she knew, like it was important and special and I had probably never heard anything like it ever before.

I said, "Mimi could sneak out, make herself up and change her clothes, and be with these people, then undo it all and go back home and be a different Mimi and her parents never knew."

Traci nodded, sniffling.

"Man." I stared out the front of the Rabbit at the Administration Building. It was large and clean and old with thick Spanish walls and a red tile roof. The hedges and the lawn and the trees were neat and well-groomed. Small knots of girls still moved along the walks, some carrying books, some not, but almost all were smiling. I shook my head.

Traci Louise Fishman picked at the steering wheel some more, then gave me the Special Secret look again. Like there was something else I'd never heard before, and something Traci had never been able to tell, and now she wanted to. "You want me to tell you something really weird?"

I looked at her.

"Last year, we were up in my room, smoking. My room is on the second floor and in the back, so I can open the window and no one knows."

"Uh-huh."

"We were smoking and talking and Mimi said, 'Watch this,' and she pulled up her shirt and put the hot part of the cigarette on her stomach and held it there." I sat in the Rabbit, listening to sixteen-year-old Traci Louise Fishman, and my back went cold. "It was so weird I couldn't even say anything. I just watched, and it seemed like she held it there forever, and I yelled, 'That's crazy, Mimi, you'll have a scar,' and she said she didn't care, and then she pushed down her pants and there were these two dark marks just above her hair down there and she said, 'Pain gives us meaning, Traci,' and then she took a real deep drag on the cigarette and got the tip glowing bright red and then she did it again." Traci Louise Fishman's eyes were round and bulging. She was scared, as if telling me these things she had been keeping secret for so long was in some way giving them reality for the first time, and the reality was a shameful, frightful thing.

I ran my tongue across the backs of my teeth and thought about Mimi Warren and couldn't shake the cold feeling. "Did she do things like that often?"

Traci Louise Fishman began to sob, great heaving sobs that shook her and made her gag. The secret had been held a long time, and it had been scary. Perhaps even incomprehensible. When the sobs died, she said, "You'll find her? You'll find her and bring her back?"

"Yes."

"I told her *I* was real. I told her *I* had purpose."

I nodded.

"She's my friend," she said. Her voice was hoarse and bubbly.

I nodded. "I know, babe."

The sobs erupted once more and took a long time to die. I gave her my handkerchief. With the pale skin and the out-from-under eyes and the heavy little-girl face, there was a quality of loneliness to her that comes when your only friend walks away and you don't know why and there's no one else and never will be. A left-behind look.

We sat like that for another few minutes, Traci rubbing at her flat nose and me breathing deeply and thinking about Mimi and Eddie Tang and what that might mean. Most of the cars had long since gone, but the red 944 still sat in its spot, music playing, girls within pretending not to stare toward Traci Louise Fishman's white Volkswagen Rabbit. After a while I said, "They're still watching us."

Traci nodded. The eyes weren't watering anymore and the nose was dry and she gave back my handkerchief. "They can't believe a good-looking guy like you is sitting here with me."

"Maybe," I said, "they can't believe a good-looking girl like you is letting me."

She smiled and looked down at her steering wheel again, and again picked at the plastic. She said, "Please bring her back."

I looked at the Porsche. The girl in the back seat was staring our way. I said, "Traci?"

She looked up at me.

I leaned across and kissed her on the lips. She didn't move, and when I pulled back she was a vivid red. I said, "Thanks for the help."

Her chin went down into her neck and she swallowed hard and looked mortified. She touched her lips and looked over at the girls in the Porsche. They were gaping at us. Traci Louise Fishman blinked at them, and looked back at me. Then she squared her shoulders, touched her lips again, and folded both hands very neatly in her lap.

I got out of the Rabbit, went back to the Corvette, and drove to my office.

22

I parked in the bottom of my building, went into the deli, bought a pastrami sandwich with Chinese hot mustard, then used the stairs to go up to the office. Walking the stairs made it easier not to think about Mimi Warren holding a lit cigarette to her skin. Maybe Traci Louise Fishman had made up that part. Maybe she'd made up all of it. Maybe if I didn't think about Mimi Warren or Traci Louise Fishman or Eddie Tang they would all disappear and living would be easy. Elvis Cole, Existential Detective. I liked that. Not thinking, properly done, creates a pleasant numbed sensation in the brain that I like a lot. There are women who will tell you that not thinking is one of my best things.

I let myself into the office, got a Falstaff out of the little fridge, put the sandwich on a paper plate, and called Lou Poitras.

Lou said, "Don't tell me. You've cracked the case."

I said, "The girl knew Eddie Tang."

He told me to hang on and then he put me on

hold. When he put me on hold, the phone started playing music. Michael Jackson singing about how bad he was. Our tax dollars at work.

Lou came back and said, "Go on."

"She used to sneak out of the house and go to clubs. She hung out and met people and one of the people she met was Tang. She might've mentioned the book to him. She told people that Eddie Tang was her boyfriend."

"She know Tang was yakuza?"

"I don't know."

"Eddie hears about the book, he maybe figures it's a good thing to steal."

"Uh-huh."

Lou Poitras didn't say anything for a while. He's got three kids. Two of them are daughters. "Thanks for the tip, Hound Dog. I'll look into it."

"Always happy to cooperate with the police."

"Right."

We hung up. I watched Pinocchio's eyes slide from side to side and ate the sandwich. Terry Ito had said Eddie Tang was on his way up. Maybe Eddie figured taking advantage of Mimi Warren and stealing the Hagakure were the keys to ascendancy. Hmmm. I finished the sandwich, then called the phone company. I asked if they had a street address for a guy named Eddie or Edward Tang. They did. Forty minutes later, I was there.

Eddie Tang lived in an apartment building in the flat part of L.A. just south of Century City off Pico Boulevard. It's older in there, and used to be middle class, but now there're lots of trendy restaurants and singles places and New Age health clubs. Eddie's complex had been redone about five years ago with mauve stucco and redwood inlays and black slate steps that twisted up from the walk in a slow curve to a glass security door. To the right of the entry a driveway angled down beneath the building and was blocked by a wrought iron gate. To either side of the garage, bougainvillea had been planted but not long enough ago to flourish. It was a good-looking building. Proof positive that crime pays.

I parked fifty yards down the block in the shade from a gum tree and waited. Maybe Eddie was home and maybe he had Mimi bound and gagged and hidden away in a closet, but maybe not. Boxes buried a couple of feet under the desert up in Sun Valley were more along the lines reserved for kidnap victims than upscale apartment houses in West Los Angeles.

At four-ten a brown unmarked copmobile pulled to a stop by the fire hydrant in front of Eddie's building. You know it's a copmobile because nobody in L.A. would buy anything as boring as a stripped-down four-door Dodge sedan except the cops. A bald-headed dick with freckles and a younger dick with a deep tan and heavy lines around his eyes climbed out and went up to the glass security door. The bald-headed guy was in a suit that looked like it hadn't been pressed in two months. The younger guy was in a dark blue Calvin Klein cord jacket and charcoal slacks with creases so sharp they could have been registered as deadly weapons. Poitras had made some phone calls and this was the follow-up.

They stood at the glass door and pretty soon a young woman in jeans and no shoes and a Sports Connection T-shirt came and opened the door. Manager. The younger cop showed her his badge and they all went inside and about fifteen minutes later they all came back out again. Eddie wasn't home, and Mimi hadn't been in a closet. The bald-headed cop went out to the car. The younger cop stood at the security door and talked to the woman for a while, both of them smiling a lot. When the woman went back inside, the younger cop watched her closely. Probably alert for suspicious moves. The cops left.

Just before five, Eddie Tang came down the street in a dark green Alfa Romeo Spider. There might've been blood stains on Eddie's shirt, but if there were, I couldn't see them. The garage gate lifted and Eddie Tang disappeared beneath his building and the gate closed and I waited.

At a quarter after six, the garage gate lifted again and Eddie and the Alfa turned north past me, heading toward Olympic. I followed him. We turned west on Olympic, then south to Washington, and stayed on Washington until we came to a clapboard warehouse in Culver City three blocks from MGM. Eddie pulled into the warehouse, then almost lost me when he pulled out again while I was looking for a place to park. We went west into Marina del Rey. Eddie drove slowly, as if he wasn't sure where he was going, and that made it tough. I had to keep cars between us and I had to drop further and further back to do it. In the Marina, we turned off Washington onto Via Dolce Drive and passed tall, cubist houses on little tiny lots that sold for over a million bucks each. Eddie parked at the curb of a brick and wood monstrosity with a sea horse in the window and got out of the Alfa carrying a red nylon gym bag. A slender man with a beard and thick glasses opened the door, took the gym bag without a word, then closed the door. Criminals rarely observe the social graces. We went back out to Washington and drove east. After a while Eddie stopped at a Texaco station and used the pay phone, then drove south to pick up the 1-10 freeway. In Hollywood, a heavily muscled black guy in a tank top climbed into Eddie's car and the two of them talked, the black guy getting agitated and waving his arms. Eddie threw a snapping backfist, and after that the arm-waving stopped. The black guy put a handkerchief to his mouth for the bleeding. There was more driving and more stops and more phone calls and not once did I see anyone dressed like a ninja or carrying a sword.

At eight-twenty that evening, Eddie Tang turned west onto Sunset from Fairfax, drove two blocks, and pulled to the curb at a new wave dance place called the Pago Pago Club. We were right in the heart of the Sunset Strip. There were two men and three women waiting for him. One of the women was Mimi Warren.

Kidnapped, all right.

23

Mimi Warren wasn't tied up and no one was holding a gun on her. She was wearing tight white pants and a green sequined halter top and spike-heeled silver sandals. Her hair stuck out at odd angles and her nails were bright blue and she wore too much makeup the way teenage girls do when they think it's sexy. She still wasn't very pretty. Eddie pulled to the curb and gave her a big smile.

I drove past the club, turned around at Tower Records, and crept back. The Strip was bright with flashing neon signs and the sidewalks were jammed with overage hipsters trying to look like Phil Collins or Sheena Easton. There were two baby-blue spotlights on the back of a flatbed trailer parked in front of a shoe store. The lights arced in counter-rotating circles, the light shafts crisscrossing again and again like matched sabers.

When I got back, Mimi and the white-haired girl Traci Louise Fishman had identified as Kerri were climbing into the Alfa. Eddie gave Mimi a kiss. There was a lot of laughing and a lot of waving and then they drove away, heading west on Sunset across Beverly Hills. I thought about shooting out the tires, but that would have been showing off.

Eddie turned north, following Rexford as it turned into Coldwater Canyon, and climbed into the Santa Monica mountains. He wasn't bringing her home and he wasn't bringing her back to his place. Maybe he was bringing her to a party. There's always a party in Hollywood.

At the top of the mountain, Eddie turned west on Mulholland Drive. Mulholland runs along the top of the mountains like some great black python. There were no streetlights and no other cars. The only light came from the waxing moon high overhead and from the San Fernando Valley, spreading out on the right like gold and yellow and red glitter. I turned off my headlamps and dropped back and hoped nothing was lying in the road.

Just before Benedict Canyon, the Alfa's brake lights flared and it pulled into a drive cut into the hillside. The drive was private and well lit and there was a modern metal gate growing out of the rock and one of those little voice boxes so you can announce yourself. The gate rolled out of the way and the Alfa went in. Then the gate closed.

I stopped about a hundred yards short of where the Alfa disappeared, backed into another drive, and killed the engine. The air was chill and clean and there was a breeze coming up the canyons. If you listened hard, you could hear the faraway hiss of the Ventura Freeway riding the breeze. I sat for twenty minutes and then the gate opened again and the Alfa came out. Eddie was still driving, but if Mimi and Kerri were with him, they were in the trunk.

Hmmm.

I got out of the Corvette, walked up to the gate, and took a look. The drive followed the curve of the hillside for about sixty yards to where the mountain had been cut away for a large neat lawn and a large, well-lit Bauhaus house. There were garages on the right of the property with what looked like a tennis court peeking out from behind, and a guy and a girl standing just outside the entry to the house. They were both wearing pale gray pants and pale gray Nehru jackets with black leather belts. That good old Red Army look. Mimi and Kerri were framed in a large picture window to the left of the entry, talking with another boy and girl. The boy was Asian, but the girl wasn't. The girl wore the same pale gray uniform. The boy wore baggy white pants and a too-big tee shirt. The four of them stood in the window for a while, then walked out of my line of sight. There came no cries for help, no sharp crack of gunfire, no blood-curdling screams.

I went back to the Corvette, got in, and stared at the gate. Mimi was in the house, and it appeared that she planned to stay there. It also appeared that she was safe. The smart thing would be to find a phone and call the cops. It was also the obvious thing. I sat there and stared, and after a while I started up and drove west.

Just off Beverly Glen at Mulholland I found a Stop & Go convenience store and used their pay phone. I called the phone company again, gave them my name and the number off my license, then told them the

Mulholland address, and asked who lived there. The phone company voice said that there were four numbers installed at that address, all unlisted, two being billed to something called Gray Shield Enterprises and two being billed to a Mr. Kira Asano, all billings being sent care of an accountancy firm with a Wilshire address. I said, "Kira Asano, the artist?"

The voice said, "Pardon me, sir?"

I hung up.

I went into the Stop & Go, got more change, then called the *Herald Examiner* and asked if Eddie Ditko was on the night desk. He was.

Eddie came on with a phlegmy cough and said, "Elvis Cole, shit. I heard you got shot to death down in San Diego. What in hell you want?" Eddie loves me like a son.

"Know anything about a guy named Eddie Tang?"

"What, I'm supposed to know about some guy just because we got the same goddamn first name?" You see? Always the kind word.

"Try out Yuki Torobuni."

Eddie made a gargling sound, then spit.

"How about a guy named Kira Asano?"

"Asano's the gook artist, right?"

"That's what I like about you, Eddie. Sensitive."

"Shit. You want Asano or you want sensitive?"

"Asano."

"Okay. Made *Time* back in the sixties. Back then, he was some kinda hot shit artist from Japan, mostly because of a lot of minimalist landscape work showing empty beaches and crap. He stopped painting and came here, saying America was gonna be the new

Japan, and he was gonna instill the samurai spirit in American youth. Some shit, huh?"

"The Hagakure," I said.

"Huh?"

"What else?"

Eddie made the gargling sound again, then said, "Jesus. You wouldn't believe what I got coming out of me." That Eddie. "Asano founded something called the Gray Army and got a couple hundred kids to join. That was a long time ago, though. Old news. I ain't heard about him in years."

I said, "Is he dangerous?"

"Hell, *I'm* dangerous. Asano's just crazy."

I hung up and got back in the Corvette but didn't start it. Sonofagun. Maybe Kira Asano was behind the theft of the Hagakure. Mimi would have gotten involved with his organization because she didn't have anything else in her life, and Asano would've pointed out what a grand fine place the Hagakure would have in the movement. Only now Eddie knew about the Hagakure, and wanted it, and was playing on Mimi to get to it. *You and me, babe.* My, my.

A fat man in baggy shorts came out of the Stop & Go with a brown paper bag. Inside, the Persian clerk stared at a miniature TV. The fat man looked at me, nodded, then got into a black Jaguar and drove away. When the Jaguar was gone, the little parking lot was quiet except for the insectile buzz of the street lamps. Here in the mountains, the Stop & Go was an island of light.

I had come to rescue Mimi, and that would be easy enough. I could call the cops, and let them do it, or I could return to Asano's, crash through the gate, and drag Mimi back to the safe tranquility of Holmby Hills and her mother and father. Only she probably wouldn't stay. Something had driven her away. Something had turned her into a kid who burned herself with cigarettes and adopted a different personality for everyone in her life and had made her want to get away from home so badly and hurt her parents so much that she had gone to incredible lengths to do it. Something wasn't right.

I sat and I stared into the warm light of the Stop & Go and I thought about all the different Mimis. The Mimi that I'd met and the Mimi that Bradley and Sheila knew and Traci Louise Fishman's Mimi and the Mimi who thought the kids in the gray uniforms had "purpose." *I'm with people who love me now.* Maybe there would even be a different Mimi tomorrow. Maybe I needed to know which Mimi was the real Mimi before I'd know what to do.

At eighteen minutes after ten I started my car, pulled out onto Mulholland Drive, and went home.

24

At nine-forty the next morning I drove back along Mulholland, pulled up at Asano's gate, and pressed a blue metal button on the call box. A female voice said, "May I help you?"

I said, "Yes, you may. My name is Elvis Cole, and I'd like to speak with Mimi Warren."

Nothing happened.

I pressed the call button again and said, "Knock, knock, knock! Chicken Delight!"

The female voice said, "There is no Mimi Warren here."

"How about I come in and talk with Kira Asano."

"Do you have an appointment, sir?"

"Yes. Under the name George Bush."

A male voice came on. "Sir, if you'd like to make an appointment with Mr. Asano, we should be able to fit you in sometime toward the end of next week. If you do not wish an appointment, please clear the driveway."

"Nope."

There was a long pause. "If you don't clear the drive, sir, we'll phone the police."

"Okay."

I turned off the Corvette, got out, crossed my arms, and leaned against the fender. After about fifteen minutes the front door opened and two Asian guys came out and started down along the drive. They wore the same cute little gray jumpsuit some of the kids wore. Gray Army. Only these guys weren't kids and they weren't cute. They were close to my age and had flat faces and eyes that didn't think much was funny. The guy on the left walked with his hands floating out from his legs like he was a gunfighter. The guy on the right bounced a nightstick off his thigh in rhythm with their stride and looked pleased with himself. When they got to the gate I said, "Hey, Kira didn't have to send a welcome wagon. I'm touched."

The guy with the priest said, "You're going to be more than touched if you don't move that shit pile outta here."

I said, "Shit pile?"

The gunfighter said, "You got no business here. You're also trespassing. Beat it."

I took out my license and held it up. "Mimi Warren is being sought by the police and the FBI as the victim of a kidnapping. I know Mimi Warren is in there because I saw her. If I have to leave here without speaking with her, I'll call the cops and the FBI and you can play tough with them."

The guy with the priest said, "Open the gate, Frank. Lemme kick his ass." The license impressed the hell out of 'm.

Frank ignored him. "You're mistaken. There's nobody here named Mimi Warren or anything like that." Frank looked as if he didn't like the thought of the Feds coming around. Probably had a couple of outstanding traffic warrants.

I said, "There is, and I'm going to stay here until I see her."

Nightstick gave me you've-done-it-now eyes and slapped his open palm with the priest. "Open the gate, Frank. How 'bout it?" Neither Frank nor I looked at him.

Frank said, "You gotta go."

I said, "You won't be able to move me without the cops."

Nightstick said, "Oh, man." He was smiling.

Frank said, "Maybe not." He was looking at me the way you look at someone when you're remembering things you learned the hard way. He'd probably learned some things the guy with the nightstick would never know. He raised his right arm, and the gate lurched inward.

Nightstick stepped back out of the way, then came around. He was smiling like a loon, gripping the stick tightly with his right hand. "Last time, asshole. Move it or lose it."

I hit him on the side of the head with a reverse spin kick just about the time he said *lose it*. The priest spun off against the gatepost and clanged against the gate and he was down on the drive. He didn't try to get up. Frank hadn't moved. He said, "What style?"

"Tae kwon do. Know a little kung fu. Know a little wing chun, too."

He nodded. "Yeah. Saw the kung fu there in the leg move."

"Where are we?" I said.

Frank shrugged. "Guess I'll go in and tell'm you're serious about staying. The man says move you anyway, guess I'll come out and give it a try. I'm better than Bobby."

"Yeah. I guess there's that chance."

Frank hefted Bobby over a shoulder in a fireman's carry, then went back up the drive. The gate closed. I went back to leaning against the Corvette. I waited.

Twenty minutes later I was still waiting. Frank hadn't come back, and it didn't look like the cops had been called. Maybe they thought I bored easily and would soon grow tired and lax in my vigil. Maybe they were planning to wait me to death. Maybe they were all out back at the pool, grilling hamburgers and drinking cold beer while I stood around out front trying to look tough.

I left the Corvette blocking the gate, walked back along Mulholland and around Asano's ridge to a fire trail, and followed it away from the road. The fire trail angled down into a little erosion gully, then slowly wrapped around the ridge toward Asano's estate. It flattened out across the ridge crest and came out behind a little concrete retaining wall. I scrambled up the slope and the concrete wall and found myself standing by a pool. The pool decking was stained and cracked and needed repair. The pool itself was a fifty-foot oval with a discolored bottom. A slim young man in black racing goggles and a black Speedo suit was swimming laps. He wouldn't notice the Circus Vargas troupe rumbling past.

At the far left edge of the pool was a tennis court. The court looked old and was flaking surface paint. Beyond it, the ground had been terraced in ascending levels up to the house. I walked along the length of the pool and up three stone steps and passed two young women coming around the tennis court. One wore red pants and a white blouse, the other a sleek lapis lazuli one-piece swimsuit. The one in the suit was quite pretty. Neither of them was Mimi Warren. I nodded and smiled and kept walking as if I had just had a nice conversation with the young man swimming laps.

I walked along beside the tennis court until they were out of sight, then turned up a walk past several dwarf orange and lemon and kara tangerine trees. Fruit had dropped to the ground, and no one had bothered to pick it up. At the main house, a boy in the nifty Gray Army uniform was coming out of a set of French doors. I said, "They told me Mimi would be out by the pool, but I just went there and she wasn't. Any idea where I could find her?"

"Try the community room on the second floor."

I gave him a big smile and went in. The house was as large and open as it looked from the outside, with high ceilings and blond wood floors and plenty of glass to let in the view. It might have been nice except that the walls needed painting and the floors were due wax and there were cobwebs in the high corners. Maybe when you're founding a revolution, basic maintenance just sort of gets away from you.

Every room and every wall contained large wash paintings of beaches and dunes and flat placid lakes and other lonely places, all in pale, cold colors. There were quite a few tall and spindly steel sculptures. Some of the work was impressive. All of it was signed by Kira Asano.

I was halfway up a wide curving staircase when Mimi Warren and her friend Kerri came around the corner and started down. Mimi's nose was red and her hair looked like she hadn't brushed it. When she saw me she took a half step back up toward the landing, then stopped. "How did you find me?"

I spread my hands. "You're supposed to be kidnapped. You go to clubs on Sunset Boulevard, you gotta expect to be found."

Kerri said, "Who is this?"

I said, "Peter Parker."

Kerri looked confused.

"Most people know me as The Amazing Spider-Man."

Kerri turned and ran back up the stairs.

"Mimi," I said, "you and I have to talk." Somewhere deep in the house, doors opened and closed and footsteps sounded on hardwood floors.

She said, "I won't go back."

"I won't make you go back."

She said, "You won't?"

Frank, Bobby, and another man came out of a door on the ground floor and looked up at me.

Bobby's cheek was swollen and beginning to color but he still managed a grin. Probably because he had a Ruger .380 automatic in his left hand instead of a nightstick. He aimed it at me and said, "Here's where I put the fuck on you, asshole."

That Bobby. What a way with words.

25

Frank shook his head like Bobby was backward, and pushed the Ruger down. "Don't be stupid." He looked at the third man. "This is the guy from out front. Elvis Cole."

The third man was in his early sixties and good-looking in a solid, muscular way. He was deeply tanned and had crew cut hair and the sort of nose you get when you spend a little time in the ring. Kira Asano. He said, "What's the meaning of this?"

"Gosh," I said, "I never heard anyone say that in real life."

Asano stepped forward and put his fists on his hips.

I looked at Mimi. "Are you all right?"

She blinked big eyes and scratched herself.

"Answer me."

She nodded.

I looked back at Asano. "You're in a world of shit, old man."

Half a dozen kids had gathered below us in the big

room, watching. Asano glanced over them, let his fists drop from his hips, and turned away. "Bring Mr. Cole along, would you, Frank?"

Frank took the gun away from Bobby and held it down along his leg. Frank looked at me. He wasn't Bobby, all right. "Come on."

We followed Asano across a large sunny room with a pool table and into a smaller room that looked out over the tennis court and pool and most of the San Fernando Valley. I didn't see any more of the Gray Army. Maybe there weren't any more. Eddie Ditko had said that once there had been a couple hundred members, but that was a long time ago. Maybe, like the house, the Gray Army's time had passed and its smell had grown musty and it had fallen into disrepair. Old news.

There was a glass desk in the room and some modern chairs and about a million photographs on the walls. On the largest wall there were several mounted samurai swords and a Japanese flag and a portrait of Asano in a Japanese military uniform. He looked young and strong and proud. The portrait had probably been done very close to the end of World War II. Asano went behind the glass desk, crossed his hands behind his back, and stared at me. When Asano walked, he had a tendency to strut, and when he stood, he had a tendency to posture, but there didn't seem to be a lot of confidence to it, more like the strutting and posturing were habits he had developed a long time ago. He said, "You have no right to be here, Mr. Cole. This place is a private home which you have entered against my wishes. You are not welcome."

"I rarely am, but that's beside the point," I said. "Mimi Warren is a minor whom the police and FBI believe is the victim of a kidnapping. They're looking for her and they'll find her. I'm interested in her well-being."

Asano smiled reasonably. "Why would anyone think Mimi has been kidnapped? Does she look kidnapped to you?"

"She staged a phony kidnapping when she ran away from home."

"Ah."

"Mimi seems to have a lot of anger toward her parents. I think she saw it as a way to hurt them."

"Ah."

"I think you had something to do with it."

Asano sat down. He put his hands on the desk in front of him and laced his fingers. "Don't be absurd. I am the leader of a movement, Mr. Cole, a locus for the lifeblood of a system as old as any on earth!" He made a fist and gestured with it.

I said, "Jesus Christ, Asano, I'm not fourteen years old. Save all the Divine Wind crap for someone else."

Bobby said, "Hey." Bobby had been recruited a long time ago and nothing better had come along. He probably wasn't bright enough to know, one way or another. Frank had been around a while, too, but he was smarter. He put a hand on Bobby's arm. Waiting to see what I had.

Asano made the reasonable smile again. He said, "If Mimi has done something as foolish as involving the police in a false crime, I certainly know nothing about it. Mimi is free to come and go as she pleases. Everyone here has that freedom. Gray Shield Enterprises and the Gray Army are duly licensed nonprofit political organizations of the state of California."

"Really aboveboard and oh-so-legal, huh?"

Asano nodded.

I said, "Is Eddie Tang a member?"

Asano's eyes flickered.

I said, "Here's what I think. Maybe you didn't participate in the runaway or the fake kidnap, but I'll bet you knew about it and that makes you eligible for a contributing charge. And I'll bet you've got the Hagakure. That puts you on deck for grand theft, receiving stolen goods, and accessory before and after the fact."

When I said it about the Hagakure his hands started to shake and all the hard edges softened and he looked like an old man caught on the toilet. It hadn't been Eddie, all right.

Bobby said, "Jesus, Frank, shoot the motherfucker." Frank shifted behind me.

"The Hagakure has to go back," I said.

Asano said, "What are you talking about?" His voice sort of croaked and he looked at Frank. It made me wonder who ran the place. It made me wonder a lot of things.

"She's a screwed-up kid with garbage for parents and she came to you looking for something, and you screwed her, too. You had her steal the Hagakure for you."

"No."

"The kids you've got out there are here because they've got no place else to go. Not because of any ideal. The Gray Army movement is dead, and having the Hagakure isn't going to bring it back to life."

Asano stood up. He started to say something, but nothing came out. He looked confused. Frank took a step toward him, then stopped. The Ruger was up now and pointing at me but Frank didn't seem interested in using it. He said, "If that's the way it is, why aren't you here with the cops?"

"Because the cops are going to want a piece of Mimi for setting all this up and wasting their time. If the cops were here they'd drag her home or maybe to juvie detention." I looked at Bobby. "You remember juvie detention, don't you, Bobby?"

Bobby said, "Fuck you."

I said, "Maybe there's a better way to do this than bringing in the cops right now."

Frank looked at me a little more and the gun lowered. "What do you want?"

"The kid doesn't want to go home and I won't know what I should do about that until I talk with her. Maybe there's a way to get her back home that will make things right for her."

Frank said, "Okay."

I looked at Asano. "Either way, the book has to go back. Maybe if the book goes back, nobody has to take a fall. Maybe, if things work out and certain people keep their mouths shut, the cops can be smoothed out."

Frank said, "That sounds good."

Asano went to the wall with all the photographs. There were pictures of Asano speaking to crowds and Asano with his Gray Army recruits and Asano riding in an open convertible in a parade. They weren't recent pictures.

Frank said, "If no one takes a fall, the Gray Army stays in business."

"Yeah."

"Everything stays like it is."

"Maybe so."

Asano blinked the way Traci Louise Fishman had blinked, but he wasn't wearing contacts. He said, "Mimi has indeed been very distraught. Almost certainly due to the state of her home life."

"Uh-huh."

"If there were some way to ease those tensions. If there were some way we could bring the child and parents together."

"My thinking exactly," I said.

Kira Asano let his eyelids flag closed, and then he raised a finger. "Get Mimi, would you, Frank? If Mr. Cole can help the child in any way, we should encourage it."

Frank nodded and left. Asano watched him go, then drew himself up and turned to stare at his photographs, his only army an army of memories.

His shoulders were wide and his arms were muscular and his legs powerful. His neck was taut and corded. Long ago, when his dreams were alive, he had probably been something to see.

26

When Frank came back with Mimi, I took her out the back and down along the terraced walks and past the rows of little potted fruit trees with their fruit rotting on the ground. Frank and Bobby walked behind us, the Ruger still dangling down alongside Frank's leg.

At the tennis court, I opened the gate and said, "Let's go out here."

Mimi and I went to a table and some chairs they had near the outer edge of the court. Bobby started out on the court after us, but Frank pulled him back to wait at the gate.

The court had been cantilevered out over the slope, which fell away sharply and bowled down into a deep ravine. On the fall-away side, the chain link fence hadn't been woven with green fabric so you could enjoy the view while you played. Standing there was like being at the edge of a cliff.

I said, "You want to sit?"

Mimi went to the table and sat.

I said, "You don't have to sit if you don't want to."

Mimi stood.

"You staying here full time?"

"Uh-huh."

"Anyone forcing you to do something you don't want to do?"

"Uh-uh."

"Could you leave now?"

"I don't want to."

"If you wanted to."

"Uh-huh." Mimi was staring down at the court. Little scout ants were searching along the white court lines as if they were great white bug highways. Maybe she was watching the ants.

I leaned against the fence and crossed my arms and stared at her. After a while she looked over and said, "Why are you staring at me?"

"Because I am the Lord High Keeper of the Knowledge of Right and Wrong, and I am trying to figure out what to do."

She blinked at me.

"Jiminy Cricket," I said. "He was also Counselor in Moments of Temptation, and Guide Along the Straight and Narrow Path. You need that."

Mimi shook her head. "You can't make me go back."

So much for Jiminy Cricket.

"Yeah, I could. I could shoot Frank and Bobby and throw you over my shoulder and bring you home." The skin around her eyes looked soft and nervous. "But I couldn't make you stay. You don't want to be there and you'd leave again as soon as you could. Besides that, I don't think your going home is necessarily the best thing."

She looked at me with Traci Louise Fishman out-from-under eyes. Suspicious. She said, "You don't bring me home, my dad is gonna fire you."

"He already did."

"He fired you?"

"Yeah."

"Why?"

"Because I was supposed to provide security for his family and it didn't stop his daughter from being kidnapped."

Mimi giggled that sort of nervous, red-nosed giggle, like maybe she was giggling at something else, not what you thought she was giggling at. She took a crumpled pack of Salem Lights out of her pocket and lit one with a blue Bic lighter. She took a quick, nervous puff. I said, "Was Asano part of that?"

She shook her head.

"You get Eddie to help you?"

She cocked her head. "How do you know about Eddie?"

"The Blue Fairy told me."

"You're strange."

"You know what the yakuza is?"

Shrug. "I don't care."

"Eddie's in the yakuza. He's a professional thug. You like him and you think he likes you, but all Eddie wants is the Hagakure."

She took a nervous drag on the Salem, then pushed it out through the fence and let it drop down the slope. Mid-summer with the brush dry, the whole ridge could burn off.

I said, "I'm trying to figure out what to do, kid, and you're not helping me. You have supposedly been kidnapped, and the cops and the FBI are involved. They are looking for you and they are looking for the book. They are going to find you, and when they do they are going to take you home. They won't stand around and wonder what's best."

She crossed her arms and chewed at her upper lip. The lip was chapped and split and had been chewed a lot. "I won't go back."

I said, "Your parents are assholes, and that's rough, but it's not the end of the world. You can survive them, and you don't need guys like Eddie Tang or Kira Asano to do it. You can work past them to be the person you want to be. A lot of kids do."

For just a moment the nervousness seemed to pass and Mimi grew still. She looked at me as if I were a silly, offensive man and then she rubbed at her face with her hands. She said, "You don't know anything."

"Maybe not. If you don't want to go home, there are other places."

"I like it here."

"Here sucks. You're going to have to talk to the cops and let them know what's going on and deal with them. They don't like it when people steal valuable things and pretend to be kidnapped and cost the taxpayers a lot of time and money."

She recrossed her arms so that her right hand was beneath her left arm. The right fingers began to pinch her left side. Hard, nervous pinches. "You don't understand," she said slowly. "I will kill myself first."

Great. High drama in Teen Town. "You've been found. Sooner or later you are going to have to talk to your parents."

"No."

"Now, without the cops involved, is better. There are people that work with kids and their parents who can be there to help. They've been known to help bring a family close together again."

Mimi Warren made the little smile, then looked directly at me. "My father is close enough."

I took slow deep breaths and felt myself grow cold. She pinched at her side and chewed at her lip, then stared down into the valley at things that were too far away to see. Her eyes took on the jumpy vacant look I'd seen on street kids down on Hollywood Boulevard, kids who'd had it so hard back home in Indianapolis or Kankakee or Bogalusa that they weren't right any more and never would be. When she said she would kill herself, she had meant it. "Mimi, does your father have sex with you?"

The red eyes leaked and she began to rock. She said, "I hope they changed their minds and didn't give him that fucking award." She didn't say it to me. She just sort of whispered it.

I said, "Does your father sexually molest you?"

The right fingers moved faster, digging into the soft flesh of her side and squeezing. She probably didn't even know she was doing it. I wanted to reach out and stop her.

"Does your mother know?"

Shrug. The tears dropped down her cheeks and into her mouth. She dug out another cigarette and lit it. Her fingers were wet from wiping away tears and left gray marks on the paper. She made the giggle and it was confused and crazy. She said, "Eddie and I are going to get married. He said we're going to live in a penthouse apartment on Wilshire Boulevard in Westwood and I'm going to have babies and we'll go to the beach a lot." She said it in the to-herself voice.

"You want to stay at my place?"

She shook her head.

"There's a woman I know named Carol Hillegas. She works with kids who have problems like this. What if I take you there?"

She shook her head again. *I'm with people who love me.*

I took a deep breath, let it out. "Okay. I'm going to let you stay here. I'm not going to call the cops, and I'm not going to tell your parents. You won't have to go home and you won't have to see your father if you don't want to." I took out one of my cards and I put it in her hand and she looked at it but probably didn't see much. "That gets me at home or my office, and if I'm not there a machine picks up. I want you to stay here. I don't want you to go nightclubbing and I don't want you to go out with Eddie Tang."

The giggle.

"Eddie Tang is a bad man, babe."

The giggle again, and then she made a wet sound. Her slight body shook and heaved and she put her face in her hands and she cried. I put my arms around her and I held her and I glared at Frank. I said, "I can't tell you things are going to be wonderful. I can't tell you that things will ever be right. All I know is that things have happened to you that shouldn't have and you're going to need help straightening it all out and I will make sure you get that help. Okay?"

She nodded. She was still rocking. She said, "I'm so messed up. I don't know what to do. I don't know. I don't know."

I held her until she ran out of tears. I said, "I'll talk to Carol Hillegas and then I'll give you a call. We can fix this."

She nodded again.

When I left, Mimi Warren was standing at the edge of the tennis court, staring out at the valley, rocking. Bobby stood in the gate, blocking my way and acting tough. He said, "Have a good time?"

I went very close to him and said, "If anything happens to her, I will kill you."

Bobby stopped smiling. Frank took a step in, then pulled Bobby back. Bobby licked his lips and didn't move. Frank looked at me. "Forget him," he said.

I stared at Bobby hard enough to stop his heart, and then I left.

27

I walked out the long drive toward Mulholland. The gate swung open when I got there, and I went through, and then the gate closed. I got into the Corvette and closed the door and took a deep breath and rubbed very hard at my eyes. I pressed my fingers into my cheeks and under the line of my jaw and behind my neck and over my temples. The muscles in my neck and at the base of my skull and the tops of my shoulders were as tight as spinnaker lines and I couldn't make them loosen.

I drove back along Mulholland to the Stop & Go, and called Carol Hillegas. In the past, when I've had to find runaways who'd taken to the streets, Carol has always proven a help. She knows kids, and counsels them at her halfway house in Hollywood. I gave her the short version and said I needed her help and asked if I could stop by. She told me she'd make some time around eleven. I hung up, then called Jillian Becker. I said, "I need you to meet me in Hollywood in half an hour."

She said, "I'm really very busy."

"It's about Mimi."

"Have you found her?" She said it slowly. Scared, maybe.

"Will you meet me?"

She didn't answer.

I said, "This isn't a time to worry about business. I know where she is and I've spoken with her and now there are some things that have to be discussed. Is Bradley back from Kyoto?"

"Yes."

"I don't want to involve Bradley or Sheila until after we've talked."

"Why not?"

I didn't say anything.

After a very long while, she said, "All right. Where should I go?"

When I got to the halfway house, Jillian Becker was out front, leaning against her BMW. She was wearing a cream-colored pants suit with a white silk blouse and black Sanford Hutton sunglasses with electric-blue mirrorshade lenses. The halfway house was in what used to be a two-story pre-war apartment building on a ratty street called Carlton Way, one block south of Hollywood Boulevard, off Gower. There was a liquor store on the corner where guys with no place to go sat on the curb, and old Taco Bell cups littered the street, and a stack of empty Texaco oil cans on a plot of dead grass, and a tiny bungalow house with a hand-painted sign hanging from the porch that said PALMISTRY. The halfway house had a neat lawn and a fresh coat of paint and was the best-kept property on the street. I think Jillian Becker was hiding behind the sunglasses.

I said, "One thing about me, I really know how to show a girl a good time."

She said, "Is Mimi in there?"

"No."

"Why do you want me here and not Bradley and Sheila? If this has to do with Mimi, Bradley and Sheila should be here."

"No," I said, "if Bradley were here I would shoot him."

Jillian Becker stared at me through her mirror-shades, then looked over at the unshaven men sitting on the curb, then looked back at me. She said, "You really mean that, don't you?"

"Let's go inside."

We went through the little gate and up the walk and into the house. There was a tiny entry with a hardwood floor and an old-fashioned coat rack and a sign that said LEAVE THE BULLSHIT AT THE DOOR. To our left there was a stair that went up to the second floor, and to our right there was a little reception area with a yellow Formica counter and a telephone and a blackboard for group announcements. A blond boy with long straight hair and a little blue cross tattooed on the back of his left hand was sitting behind the counter. He was reading a worn-out, spine-rolled copy of Robert Heinlein's *Stranger in a Strange Land*. He looked up when we walked in. "Hi," I said. "We're here to see Carol."

The blond kid closed the Heinlein on a finger, said he'd tell Carol, and came around the counter to take the stairs up two at a time.

Jillian Becker took off the mirrorshades and stood stiffly by the Formica counter. "What kind of place is this?"

"Halfway house for kids. Most of the kids here are runaways from middle-class homes and middle-class mommas and daddies. Things got a little out of hand back in Ohio. Sometimes things got a lot out of hand. So they end up here in the Land of Dreams hooking or peddling dope or scamming and they get grabbed by the cops. If they are very lucky, the cops give them over to Carol."

The blond kid came back down the stairs, said Carol was making coffee, and that we could go on up. We did. There was a narrow landing on the second floor and a long hall that went past four dormitory rooms, two for boys and two for girls. A girl who couldn't have been more than twelve was on her hands and knees scrubbing the baseboard. She had a bright pink scar running along the length of her left tricep. Knife. Jillian Becker stared at the scar.

Carol Hillegas's office was at the end of the hall. She appeared in the door, took my hand, gave me a kiss, then introduced herself to Jillian Becker and showed us in. Carol Hillegas was tall and thin and wearing her hair shorter than the last time I'd seen her. There were new streaks of gray in it. She had a long face and thin lips and was wearing a pair of faded Levi's and a green Hawaiian shirt with flowers and birds on it and open-toed Mexican sandals. She wore the shirt tucked into her pants. The office had a new coat of paint, but the secondhand desk was the same and so were the wooden chairs and the text-books and file cabinets and diplomas on the wall.

There was an aluminum-frame sliding window in the north wall. If you looked out, you could see the big red X of the Pussycat Theatre up on Hollywood Boulevard. "Very nice, Carol," I said. "Upgrading."

"It's all this government subsidy. I'm thinking about putting in a Jacuzzi."

When we were seated and had coffee, Carol looked at Jillian and smiled. "What's your position in this case, Ms. Becker?"

"I work for the girl's father. I'm not related to her."

I said, "Jillian's here because I'm going to need help with the parents. The more she knows, the more help she'll be."

"So far," Jillian said coolly, "I don't know anything. He hasn't told me what's going on."

Carol gave Jillian a warm smile. "He's like that. Secrets give him a sense of power."

"Bitch," I said.

Carol laughed, then leaned back in her chair and said, "Tell me about this little girl."

I told Carol Hillegas all of it. When I got to the part about the cigarettes, Jillian Becker sat forward and brought one hand to her mouth and stayed like that. I told them about Eddie Tang and following him to the Pago Pago Club and finding Mimi, and then following her to Kira Asano's. When I mentioned Asano, Jillian moved her hand from her mouth and said, "Bradley opened a hotel in Laguna Beach last summer. Asano had a showing in the hotel gallery."

I said, "Would Mimi have gone to the opening?"

"Yes. She probably went down with Sheila."

I told them about my talk with Mimi, and about her refusal to return home. Then I told them why.

"She said she couldn't go home because her father sexually molests her."

Jillian Becker drew in a breath as sharp as a rifle's crack. She said, "My God." Then she stood up and went to the window.

Carol said, "You left her at Asano's?"

"Yes."

Jillian Becker shook her head and said, "This can't be. I've known these people for years." She shook her head twice.

Carol Hillegas got up and poured herself another cup of coffee. I'd once seen Carol Hillegas drink fourteen large cups of 7-Eleven coffee in a single Saturday morning. She said, "Leaving her at Asano's was probably all right. Mimi's there because she feels secure, and that's probably the most important thing right now. In an environment where there is an incestuous relationship, the child loses all sense of security because there is never a safe, nurturing time. The person whom the child should be able to trust most is the source of fear and anxiety."

Jillian Becker turned away from the window, came back, and sat on the edge of her seat. "I can't believe Sheila could even suspect this and keep quiet." She looked at me. "You've seen how she is."

Carol drank more coffee and leaned back in her chair. She looked at Jillian and her face took on a more female quality, as if what she were about to say was somehow more female than male. "The mother might not know. She might only suspect, and there is a high likelihood that she would reject that suspicion out of hand. Somewhere along the line whatever the mother had with the father stopped, and he turned to their daughter. A way to look at it is that the daughter has usurped the mother's power and position in the household. The daughter has proven herself more desirable and more satisfying to the male. More womanly. That's not an easy thing to accept."

"Sheila has a tough household position," I said. "Wow."

Carol looked at me and the female thing in her face was cool. "Understand that incest is a family problem with a tremendously complex dynamic. It is also one of the most socially shameful things a person can confront. No one wants to admit it, everyone feels guilty about it, and everyone is afraid of it."

I said, "Great."

"Something like this cannot be handled privately. By law, any licensed therapist or counselor has to report a suspected or admitted case of incest to the Department of Public Social Services Child Abuse Unit. The Department dispatches a field investigator who works with the private therapist, if there is one, or the district attorney's office and police, if those two agencies are required. Incest is a violation of the criminal code and charges can be filed, but they usually aren't if the offending parent and family agree to participate in therapy."

Jillian said, "What if the parent refuses?"

"As I said, charges could be filed, but if the child won't testify, and most of them won't, there's really nothing that can be done. The child would have to go into single therapy, but unless the parent and child work together, it is very difficult to get past the scars this kind of thing leaves."

I said, "What about Mimi?"

"There's no way I can make a diagnosis based on hearsay. You have to work with the client, and it can take many, many hours over many, many weeks. But clearly this girl is demonstrating severe aberrational behavior. She repeatedly inflicts pain upon herself, and she went to bizarre lengths to escape her environment. Most kids want to run, they just run. They don't need to stage a phony kidnapping. The anger this child must be feeling is enormous, and most of it is directed at herself. That's why the masochistic behavior. Another reason is that, subjectively, Mimi is looking for someone who will love her. When a person hurts herself the way Mimi has, they're doing it because they want someone to make them stop."

Jillian was nodding. "And the person who makes them stop is the person who loves them."

Carol Hillegas said, "Essentially, yes. Sexual abuse isn't love. It's abuse." She looked at me. "Mimi is like everyone else. She just wants to feel loved."

"Should I call the cops?"

Carol shrugged. "The cops won't kill her. They'll take her in and when this comes out they'll refer it to the DA and to Social Services and they'll get her a counselor. Your instinct was to avoid the trauma of the arrest and the questioning, and in an ideal world that would be the best way to go. Mimi's had enough trauma."

I said, "If I can get Mimi and her parents to agree to come in, will you help?"

"Yes."

"What's the most trauma-free way to do it?"

"The girl should be in a stabilized environment, and should have established some trust with the therapist. If that's me, I'd like to spend some time with her and some time with the parents before we try to bring them together. After we're used to each other, we can begin the group work on neutral ground and see where it leads us."

Jillian Becker said softly, "Bradley will never agree."

I looked at her and leaned forward in my chair. "Yes, he will."

She looked at me.

"I'm going to talk to Bradley and Sheila and I'm going to get them to agree to this, but I don't want to do it at Bradley's office. I want you to get them together at home. Can you do that?"

Carol Hillegas said, "How are you going to convince them?"

I ignored her. "Can you do that, Jillian?"

"Yes."

"Will you?"

"Yes."

I stood up. "Then let's do it."

28

I went to my office and Jillian went to hers, and fifty minutes later she called and told me to be at the Warrens' home at three that afternoon.

When I got there, Jillian's white BMW was parked behind Bradley's chocolate-brown Rolls convertible. The Rolls's top was down and it looked very sporty. Sort of like a tank with the turret blown off. A sky-blue Mercedes 560SL was parked in one of the garages just past the motor court. That would be Sheila.

At three in the afternoon, it was clear and bright and warm in Holmby Hills. Quiet. Mockingbirds chirped and bees floated around the snapdragons and poppies that lined the drive, and high overhead a single light plane buzzed east. Out on the street, somebody's Salvadoran housekeeper walked toward Sunset Boulevard and her bus stop. She didn't look at me and she didn't look up at the plane.

I went to the front door, knocked, and Sheila Warren let me in. She was wearing a white and pink Love tennis outfit and had a short glass containing ice and

a dark liquid in her hand. Always after five somewhere in the world. She looked defiant and sullen, a
woman who'd had to make too many sacrifices to get
where she was. "I certainly hope I was called off the
court for a good reason."

Sacrifices.

She closed the door and we went into the den.
Bradley Warren was half sitting on one of the bar
stools, thumbs hooked in his vest's watch pockets,
looking sour. The stern affluent businessman as pic-
tured by *GQ*. Jillian Becker was standing by the other
end of the bar, not looking at him and not looking at
Sheila. Bradley said, "Let's get something straight,
Cole, and get it straight now. You are not in my employ, nor have you been since you were terminated, so
I don't intend to pay you a dime. If this is just a ploy
to maneuver yourself back onto my payroll, you can
forget it."

Sheila said, "I didn't leave the court to listen to
you. If he knows something about Mimi, for God's
sake, let's hear him."

Jillian said, "I'll wait outside."

Bradley said, "You stay here. I want a witness in
case this fraud claims I agreed to pay him for addi-
tional services."

Jillian's face was pale. She looked like she had
been hoping no one would notice her. "I can't do
that, Bradley." She started for the door.

Bradley said, "What do you mean, you can't do
that? I want you to stay."

She kept going. "Not this time."

Bradley said, "What do you mean, not this time?

You made me come here. You'd better remember who you work for."

Jillian stopped at the door. She looked at me, then Bradley. She looked at him for a very long time. "Bradley," she said. "Go fuck yourself." Then she left.

Sheila Warren laughed. Bradley said, "Jillian," but he said it to a closed door. He looked back at me. "Jesus Christ. I don't have time for this. Tell me about Mimi. Is Mimi all right?"

"No," I said. "Mimi is not all right."

Sheila stopped smiling and put her drink on the bar.

"Mimi has not been in an accident and has not suffered a physical injury and isn't in a hospital somewhere, but she is not all right."

Bradley said, "What the hell does that mean?"

Looking at them, I could feel the muscles in my neck and shoulders tighten the way they had tightened when I was with Mimi. I said, "Mimi wasn't kidnapped. She ran away. I found her and talked with her."

Sheila said, "Good Lord, why didn't you bring her home?"

"She didn't want to come home."

Sheila opened her mouth, then closed it. "Well, what kind of answer is that? Where is she?"

"I won't tell you that."

The famous Bradley Warren frown. "What do you mean? You have to."

"No. I don't."

Bradley looked at me the way you look at someone when you're thinking maybe they're up to something. Then he started around the bar for the phone. "I'm going to call the police."

I said, "We're going to talk about some very personal things now. You're not going to want the cops here."

Bradley stopped, his hand on the phone. Sheila's eyes wobbled from me to Bradley and back to me. She said, "What's going on here? What's this about?"

I was looking at Bradley. "Mimi has the Hagakure, Bradley. She stole it to hurt you and she pretended to be kidnapped for the same reason."

Bradley moved slightly as if a strong wind had pushed him. "Mimi has the Hagakure."

"Yes."

"And you didn't bring it back."

"No."

"She stole it to hurt me, and now she is pretending to be kidnapped."

Sheila said, "That's silly." She made a little gesture of dismissal with her left hand, picked up the drink with her right, and had some.

"Your daughter is in trouble. She's got serious problems and she's had them for years and she will probably need professional help for a long time if she's ever going to have a chance to be right. You're going to have to be a part of that."

Sheila said, "I don't know what all this is about. Teenage girls get confused. It's hormonal."

"It has to start now, Bradley. The problems have to come out in the open now and the healing process has to begin." It was just me and Bradley. Sheila might just as well have been on Mars. "Mimi will have to go into a halfway house for a while or you will have to leave home."

Bradley's left eye started to spasm and veins bulged in his forehead and on the sides of his neck. He said, "I don't know what you're talking about."

"Tell Sheila, Bradley."

The spasm got worse. He shook his finger at me. Angry. "You'd better tell me where the Hagakure is, goddamnit. That book is priceless. It's irreplaceable."

"Tell Sheila about Mimi."

Sheila put the glass down again. The defiance and the sullenness were gone. Bad dreams coming true. "Tell me what?"

"I don't know what he's talking about. What did Mimi say? What's this all about?" You could see his hands tremble.

I said, "Bradley, your daughter is never going to have a chance to heal until you admit that you've been molesting her."

Sheila's face faded and went pale and became something ghostlike. She didn't move and Bradley didn't move and then Bradley shook his head and smiled. It was the sort of smile you give to someone you don't know well when you're correcting them. He said, "That's not true."

Sheila made a small sound, very much like her daughter's giggle.

Bradley said, "Mimi made it up. You said she wanted to hurt me."

Sheila threw what was left of her drink in his face. Her eyes filled and her nose grew red and she said, "You bastard. You no good shit bastard." She hit him. She flailed wildly, slapping and punching and calling him a bastard, her face blotchy, spit flying. He didn't move.

The hitting went on until I went over and caught her wrists and pulled her in close to my chest. She said, "You bastard," over and over.

Bradley spread his hands the way they do in a comic strip. His you-must-be-mistaken smile didn't waver. "Why would Mimi say such a thing? It's not true. It's outrageous." The eye fluttered madly.

I brought Sheila over to one of the couches and sat her down. "Sheila. There's a woman named Carol Hillegas who is a counselor who's worked with people who've had to go through this. You can talk to Carol, and she will talk to Mimi, and then she will talk to all of you together. Will you do that? Will you talk to Carol?"

Sheila held herself as if there were something hard and painful in her chest. She nodded.

Bradley said, "I'm going to sue you if you spread rumors about this. There's no proof."

I left Sheila and went around behind the bar to where Bradley was standing and took out the Dan Wesson.

Bradley backed up until he hit glass shelves lined with liquor bottles and then he couldn't back up anymore. He said, "Hey."

I pulled back the hammer until it locked and I pointed the muzzle at the center of his forehead. "Bradley, your child needs you and you are going to do right by her." My voice was even and calm. "Do you understand?"

He did not move. "Yes."

"She needs you to be honest about this. She needs

you to admit that this should never have happened and that this is not something she precipitated and that she is not at fault. Do you understand that?"

"Yes."

"The Department of Social Services is going to be notified, and one of their people is going to work with you and a counselor and Sheila and Mimi. It is very, very important for Mimi that you accept the therapeutic process and participate in it. Do you understand that?"

"Yes."

I stared at Bradley Warren past the Dan Wesson, and then I moved a half step closer. I said, "I'm told that what has happened here is complex and that you are not what we less sophisticated types call a bad man. That may be. I don't give a rat's ass if you are helped in this process or not. I don't care if you have to fake every moment of therapy for the next ten years. You will see to it that everything that can be done to help your daughter will be done. If you do not, I will kill you, Bradley. Do you understand that?"

He nodded.

"Say it."

"Yes."

"Say it all the way."

"You will kill me."

"Do you believe that?"

"Yes."

"Stay here. Don't go back to your office. Carol Hillegas will call you. If you don't come through with this, Bradley, I will be back."

We stood like that for another few seconds, then I lowered the gun and left.

Jillian Becker was sitting inside her BMW. Even with the mirrorshades you could see that she'd been crying. I went around to her side of the car and squatted down by the window. "You learned a very hard thing today," I said. "Time passes, you'll steady down. You'll see if you can live with it or if you'll have to make some changes."

She took a deep breath, then sighed it out. "Do you have to do that much? Make changes?"

"Sometimes. Sometimes you can change what's there, sometimes what's there changes you."

She nodded and looked toward the house. Big changes coming. She said, "I was thinking of what Carol said about people who hurt themselves, about how what they're really doing is looking for someone who loves them enough to make the pain stop."

I didn't say anything.

Jillian Becker started the BMW and put it in gear and looked at me.

After a while she drove away.

29

When I got home I called Carol Hillegas and told her that I had spoken with Bradley and Sheila and that they were expecting her call. After Carol hung up, I called Kira Asano's place and asked for Mimi. Bobby came on and said, "Who's this?"

"The Shell Answer Man."

"Eat shit."

Frank came on and said, "Are the cops on the way here?"

"No."

"She's in the back. Wait."

In a little while Mimi said, "Uh-huh?" She sounded like she maybe expected that her parents were really on the other end of the line and about to start yelling at her.

I said, "It's Elvis."

"Uh-huh."

"I spoke with your parents. They're not going to make you go home. You're going to have to leave Asa-no's, but you can stay at a halfway house Carol Hillegas owns. If that doesn't work out, you can go home and your father will move out, whichever you prefer."

She didn't say anything.

"Mimi?"

"I don't want to go home." Dull. I wondered if she was loaded on something.

"I'll come get you tomorrow morning. If you want we can have breakfast and then I'll take you to Carol's place, and I'll stay with you there for as long as you need me to, okay?"

"Okay."

"Put Frank on."

There were noises and voices and then Frank came on. "What's up?"

"I'm going to come get her tomorrow. I'm going to get the book, too."

"Are you going to be able to keep Mr. Asano out of it?"

"I don't know. I'm not going to bring him into it, but I don't know what Mimi is going to tell the cops when they talk with her. You live up to your end and help me with the kid and I'll see that the parents don't try to press you if the cops come in. I'll tell them that you guys cooperated with me and wanted the best for the girl."

"That oughta cut a lot of ice."

"It's what I can do."

"Yeah." Frank hung up.

I put down the phone and went into the kitchen and poured myself a glass of apple juice and drank it. I went back into the living room and turned on the evening news. I put my hands in my pockets and shook my head and thought, sonofagun, this thing is coming together. I went back to the phone and called Joe Pike but he wasn't home. I dug through my wallet and found Jillian Becker's home number and gave her a call. Nope. She was out, too. The cat door clacked in the kitchen and hard food crunched. I went back into the kitchen and looked at him eating and said, "Well, I guess it's just you and me."

He didn't bother to look up.

I got us a couple of Falstaff out of the refrigerator and put on some music and after a while I went to bed.

At five minutes after eight the next morning my phone rang. I picked it up and said, "Elvis Cole Detective Agency. Let us get on your case!"

Jillian Becker said, "What's going on?"

I said, "What do you mean, what's going on?" This sort of thing is covered in Advanced Interrogation at the Private Eye Academy.

"Mimi called Bradley fifteen minutes ago. She told him she wanted to give the Hagakure back and asked him to meet her. I thought you were supposed to pick up Mimi and bring her to Carol Hillegas."

"Did Bradley go?"

"Two minutes ago. I told him he shouldn't. I told him he should wait."

"Are you in your office?"

"Yes."

I told her I'd call her back, then I hung up and dialed Kira Asano's. I dialed the four numbers I had and each of the four rang but no one answered. I didn't like that. I called Jillian. "I couldn't get anyone at Asano's. Did Bradley say where he was going to meet Mimi?"

"She wanted to see him at a construction site on Mulholland just east of Coldwater. He said he told her that was silly, that she should come to the office or that he would go to where she was staying but she said she would feel safe there and that's where she wanted to do it. Why would Mimi want to give back the book like this? Why would she want to be alone with him?"

There were a couple of reasons but I didn't like them much. I said, "I'm on my way now. Call the North Hollywood PD and ask for Poitras or Griggs or Baishe. Tell them you're calling because I told you to and have them send a car. Tell them to hurry."

Mulholland was five minutes away down Woodrow Wilson, then a single broken-backed sprint west toward Coldwater. Just past Laurel, Mulholland is woodsy and the houses have been there forever, but farther west more and more ridges were being cut and scraped and developed for homesites. A mile short of Coldwater, Mulholland flattened out and signs said HEAVY EQUIPMENT AHEAD. I slowed down. A large ridge grew away to the north, rising off the road toward the San Fernando Valley. The ridge was big and white and had been graded clean. A fresh tarmac road had been cut up to the ridge top and clean white sidewalks paralleling the road had been poured and cement drains set. When all this was finished there would probably be guards and ornate street lamps and no trees and no coyotes and no deer. Just what the locals had in mind when they bought up here ten years ago.

There was a chain link fence running the perimeter of the site. A sign on the wire and pipe gate that should have blocked the road said S&S CONSTRUCTION—KEEP OUT. The gate was open. I turned through the gate, and followed the road up.

The top of the ridge had been sliced off to make a broad flat plateau with a jetliner's view of the valley. On the plateau, the road made a wide circle so that view homes that sold for eight hundred thousand dollars could be built along the rim of the circle. Luxury living. There was a sixty-yard dumpster and two Cat bulldozers and a Ryan backhoe parked on the far side of the circle. Bradley Warren's brown Corniche convertible and a beat-up green Pontiac Firebird were by the dumpster, and Mimi and Bradley were standing by the Firebird. Mimi saw me first. She was wearing a loose red and white cotton shirt over blue jeans and black, high-top shoes. There was a pink leather purse slung over her shoulder and her face looked pale and wild and blotchy from crying. She reached into the purse and took out a small black revolver and pointed it toward her father and I yelled and she shot him. There was one sharp POP. Bradley looked down at himself, then looked back at his daughter, then went forward onto his hands and knees.

Mimi dropped the gun and climbed into the Firebird and screeched away. I jumped the curve and revved the Corvette across the island's rough ground. Bradley stayed on his hands and knees for the time it took me to cross the ridge top and get out of the car, then he keeled sideways onto his side and began to make flapping movements with his arms, trying to get up. "She shot me," he said. "My God, she shot me."

"Stop trying to get up. Let me see it."

"It hurts!"

I put him on his back and looked at him. There was pink froth at the corner of his mouth and when he spoke his voice was wet the way it gets when you've a bad cold and the mucus fills your throat and sputters when you try to breathe. There was a red spot about as big around as a medium-sized orange just to the right of the center of his chest. It was growing.

I took out my handkerchief and put it on the spot and pressed hard. "I have to get you to a hospital," I said.

Bradley nodded, then blew a large red bubble and threw up blood. His eyes rolled back in his head and he shuddered violently and then his heart stopped.

"God damn you, Bradley!" I was yelling.

I pulled off my shirt and his belt. I bundled my shirt, put it over the red spot, then wrapped the belt around his chest to maintain some pressure. When there is arterial bleeding you are not supposed to use CPR, but when there is no pulse, there's not much choice. I cleared his throat and breathed into his mouth and then pressed hard on his chest twice. I repeated the sequence five times and then I checked for a pulse but there was none.

A single hawk floated high above, looking for mice or other small living things. Out on Mulholland cars passed. None of them saw, and none stopped to help. Somewhere a motorcycle with no muffler made sounds that echoed through the canyons.

I breathed and pressed and breathed and pressed and breathed and pressed, and that's what I did until the cops that Lou Poitras sent found us and pulled me off. All the breathing and pressing hadn't done any good. Bradley Warren was dead.

30

Six copmobiles came and two wagons from the Crime Scene Unit and a van from the coroner's office and a couple of Staties and a woman from the district attorney's office. The Crime Scene people outlined the body and the gun and measured a lot of tire tracks. The coroner's people took pictures and examined the body and pronounced Bradley Warren officially dead. Bradley was probably glad to hear that. Being unofficially dead must be a drag.

The woman from the DA's office and a tall blond detective I didn't know talked to the Crime Scene guys and then came over and talked to me. The detective had sculptured, air-blown hair that was out of style ten years ago. The woman was short with a big nose and big eyes. I was looking good with blood on my pants and my hands and my shirt and my face. The blond said, "What happened?"

I told it for the millionth time. I told them where Bradley Warren had stood and where Mimi had stood and where Mimi's car had been parked and how she had taken the gun from her purse and fired one shot point-blank and killed her father.

The blond dick said, "She drops the gun after she pulls the trigger?"

"Yeah."

"A sixteen-year-old kid with no gun and you couldn't stop her."

"I was busy trying to keep her father alive." Asshole.

A dark cop with a cookie-duster mustache came over with the gun in a plastic bag. He showed it to the woman. "Gun's a Ruger Blackhawk. Twenty-two caliber revolver. Loaded with twenty-two long rifle ammo. One shot fired."

The woman looked at the gun, gave it back, and said, "Okay." The dark cop left and took the blond cop with him. The woman said, "What kind of car was she driving?"

"Dark green Pontiac Firebird. Couple of years old. I didn't get the plate."

"Anyone else in the car?"

"No."

The woman took out her handkerchief and gave it to me. "Wipe your face," she said. "You look like hell."

Just before ten, Poitras and Griggs and Terry Ito pulled up in a blue sedan. Griggs was in the back seat. They talked to the woman from the DA's office and then the Crime Scene people and then they got to me. Nobody looked happy. Lou Poitras said, "Half the cops and Feds in L.A. looking for this kid, Hound Dog, how'd you happen to be up here with her and her old man?"

I told him. As I said it, Ito's face darkened and you could tell he wasn't liking it. Hard to blame him. I wasn't liking it, either. Midway through the telling Jillian Becker's white BMW nosed up to the ridge top and stopped by one of the coroner's vans. Jillian Becker and a short man in a tweed sport coat got out. One of the dicks and the woman from the district attorney's office went over to them. Jillian Becker looked at me. Her face was drawn. Terry Ito said, "You found the girl, and followed her to Kira Asano's and you decided not to tell anyone."

"Yeah."

"Even though you knew the police and the Feds were searching for her."

I said, "She looked safe at Asano's so I let her sit until I knew what was going on and then I talked with her. She was a mess, Ito. She had run away and couldn't go home because her father was sexually molesting her."

Poitras said, "Jesus Christ."

Ito took a breath, let it out, and shook his head. He looked out off the ridge toward the valley. The hawk was gone.

I said, "I wanted to get the kid some help before she'd have to deal with you people."

Across the ridge top, the woman from the district attorney's office opened the coroner's van and showed Jillian Becker and the short man what was inside. Jillian stood stiff and nodded, then turned and quickly walked back to her BMW. The short man went with her. VP from the company, no doubt.

Poitras said, "Why'd she kill him?"

"I don't know."

Griggs was staring at his hands. "Maybe she just had to," he said, quietly.

Ito looked at Griggs, then took off his sunglasses and stared at them as if there was a bad smudge on the lenses. He put the sunglasses back on. Poitras said, "As far as you know, she still staying at Asano's?"

"Yes."

"Let's go get her."

We got into the blue sedan, Poitras driving, me and Griggs riding in back. I told Poitras to go west on Mulholland toward Beverly Glen. He did. The cop sedan with its heavy-duty suspension rolled easily along Mulholland's curves. Poitras had the windows up and the air conditioning on and no one said anything. All you could hear in the car was the hiss and chatter of the radio. I couldn't understand what the radio voices said, but Poitras and Griggs and Ito could. Cops get special ears for that.

When we got to Kira Asano's, Griggs said, "Man, this guy must be loaded."

The gate was open. We went up the drive without announcing ourselves and stopped about halfway to the house. We had to stop because Frank was lying facedown in the drive. His legs were bent and his right arm was under his body and the left half of his head was missing. Poitras and Griggs both leaned to the side to free their guns and Ito called in a request for backup. I said, "There were about a dozen kids here. Some of them were wearing gray uniforms. There was another guy like the one on the drive named Bobby, and Asano, and Bobby probably has a gun."

Poitras steered the car out onto the lawn around

Frank's body and stopped by the front door. The front door was open.

Poitras and Griggs went around the side past the garage, and Ito and I went in through the front. No one tried to shoot us. There wasn't anyone around to try.

Cabinets had been emptied and furniture upended and Asano's paintings torn from the walls in every room. Poitras and Griggs came in from the back and said they'd found a guy who was probably Bobby with two bullets in his chest out by the little fruit trees. They'd seen no sign of the girl or anyone else.

We found Asano in his office. He was lying on the floor in front of his desk, clutching the grip of a samurai sword. He had been shot once in the chest and once in the side of the neck. The sword was bloodied. There was a short, muscular man sitting on Asano's couch. The man and the couch were sprayed with blood, and the man's eyes were slightly crossed and sightless. There was a slash along the top of his left shoulder and two puncture marks in his abdomen and a black automatic pistol in his right hand as if Asano had attacked him with the sword and he had killed Asano and then staggered to the couch to finish dying. The little finger was missing from his left hand. Somebody said, "Sonofabitch." I think it was Griggs.

Ito looked at the left hand and then at me. "You say Asano had the book."

"Yeah."

Ito looked at the left hand again. "Yakuza."

We looked through the rest of the house. In an upstairs bedroom we found two girls holding each other under some rags in a closet. They screamed when we opened the door and begged us not to kill them and it was quite a while before they believed that we would not. One of them was Kerri.

We went through every room and every closet. There was no sign of either the Hagakure or Mimi Warren. When we had made the complete circuit and were back at the front of the house again, Ito shook his head. "So," he said. "You left her here because she was safe, huh?"

I didn't bother to look at him.

31

We brought Kerri and the other girl down to the big open room with the French doors and put them on a couch beneath an enormous watercolor of an old woman sharpening a sword. The old woman was sitting in the snow, and was barefoot, but did not look cold.

The girls were scared and the smaller one had red puffy eyes from crying. We offered them blankets even though it was eighty degrees outside. Kerri kept sneaking glances at me, probably because she had seen me before. She said, "Are you a policeman?"

"Private eye," I said. I gave her a little eyebrow wiggle. Elvis Cole, Master of Instant Rapport.

"You're the guy who came here looking for Mimi."

"Yeah. You know where she is?"

"They took her."

Poitras said, "Who's they?"

The other girl pulled her knees up to her chin and locked her arms around her shins. She squeezed her eyes shut. Kerri said, "These four men came. They just came in and started yelling and shooting and tearing up the house. I saw them shoot Bobby, and then I ran."

Terry Ito said, "All Japanese men?"

Kerri nodded.

Poitras asked her when.

Kerri looked at the other girl but the other girl's chin was between her knees and her eyes were still clamped shut. Kerri said, "I dunno. Maybe seven. I had just got up. I dunno. I ran into the bedroom with Joan and we hid." Joan was the quiet one.

Poitras looked at me. "That was before she called Bradley?"

"Yeah." I said, "Kerri, was Eddie Tang one of the men?"

"Uh-uh." She shook her head.

"You sure?"

"Uh-huh."

Ito said, "You know what they were after?"

"They wanted this book."

Ito gave me a look, then he and Griggs went out to the car. Pretty soon the same uniforms who had been at Bradley's murder site came, along with a couple of dicks from Beverly Hills and three more guys from Asian Task Force. The uniforms got the girls' names and parents' phone numbers and made some calls to try to get them picked up. The ATF guys brought in big photo albums with known yakuza members and had each of the girls look through them. One of the uniforms and I made instant coffee in the kitchen. I put three cups of coffee on a plate and brought it out and sat by the girls while they turned the pages. I said,

"Kerri, did Mimi say anything to you about leaving here?"

"No."

"I was supposed to come get her this morning. She and I had talked about it and she said okay."

Kerri turned each page slowly, lifting the next page and scanning the pictures at the same time. "I think she changed her mind."

"Why?"

"Eddie came over last night." Eddie. Great.

"What happened?"

"They had this big fight. She said he didn't really love her. She said all he wanted was the book and that he didn't care about her and that no one cared about her. Then he left." Joan finished one album and started another. She hadn't said a word in hours.

"But he didn't come back?"

"Uh-uh."

In a little bit a couple of the ATF cops came over and Kerri and Joan identified three of the four men who had raided the house. One of the three was the stiff in Asano's office.

A short ATF cop with a puckered scar running along his right jawline said, "You think this is connected with the torture-murder down in Little Tokyo?" He got a kick out of saying torture-murder.

Ito said, "Yeah. I think our boy Eddie was making a power grab. He figured Ishida had the book, so he did Ishida to get it. Only Ishida didn't have it. Asano did. So he went after the girl. When she wouldn't come across, he sent in some goons this morning." He looked at me. "Sound good to you?"

I gave it a shrug. "Some of it. Some of it has holes you could put a Cadillac through."

The short cop with the scar smirked.

Ito put his hands in his pockets. "I'm listening."

I said, "Eddie was working the girl a long time before Ishida was done. He'd know Asano had the book."

"Okay. What about this morning?"

"If the yakuza grabbed her, how'd she get away to kill her old man?"

Ito said, "I hear a lot of questions. You got the answers?"

"I don't know. I just know something isn't adding up."

Ito thought about that, and me, then finally shook his head and walked away. "Well, you had her for a little while."

Poitras and Griggs and I stood there and watched Ito and the guy with the scar walk away and nobody said anything. After a while, Poitras told me I looked like I'd been through a Cuisinart and asked me if I was okay. I said sure. He wondered if I needed to see a doctor. I said no. He put a hand the size of a manhole cover on my shoulder, gave me a squeeze, and said if I wanted to call him at home later that it would be fine. I said thanks. Charlie Griggs drove me back to my car. Bradley's body was gone. There were just a couple of newsmen poking around, along with a motorcycle cop who was making out like he'd just busted the Hillside Strangler. We sat there a while, in Griggs's car, and he asked if I wanted to have a couple of drinks. I told him maybe later. When I got home I went in through the garage and took off the blood-stained shirt and pants and washed my hands and face in the kitchen sink. I put the shirt and pants in the sink and rubbed the bloodstains with Clorox Prewash and let them sit while I went up and took a shower. I used a cloth and lots of soap and hot water and scrubbed myself pink. I used a small brush to get Bradley Warren's blood from around and beneath my fingernails. When I was finished I threw the brush away. *Well, you had her for a little while.*

I put on a loose pair of dojo pants, then went downstairs and put the clothes into the washer. Cold water. I opened a Falstaff, drank most of it, and called Jillian Becker at her office. Her secretary was subdued and distracted and told me Ms. Becker wasn't in. Probably with Sheila. I hung up and drank the rest of the Falstaff. It was so good I opened another. I stood with it in the center of my quiet house and thought about Mimi Warren out there wherever she was and whom she might be with and what she might be doing and I drank more beer. I opened the big glass doors to let in the air, then turned on my stereo and put on an old Rolling Stones album. *Satisfaction.* Great bass. I made a sandwich out of some sliced turkey breast and egg bread and tomato and had another beer. *Got family problems? Hire Elvis Cole, The Family Detective. Guaranteed to make things worse or your money back!*

I called Joe Pike.

"Gun shop."

"It's me. I found the girl."

He grunted.

"I lost her again."

He said, "You been drinking?"

"No." I sounded fine to me.

He said, "You at home?"

"Uh-huh."

He hung up.

Half an hour later Pike was in the living room. I hadn't heard him knock or use a key. Maybe it was teleportation. He was dressed exactly as always: sweatshirt with no sleeves, faded Levi's, blue Nike running shoes, mirrored sunglasses. I said, "Are those new socks?"

There was a pretty good-sized pyramid of Falstaff cans on the coffee table. He looked at it, then went into the kitchen and rattled around. After a while he said, "Come to the table."

He had put out a ranch omelet with cheese and tomatoes, and whole wheat toast with butter and strawberry jam. There was coffee and a small glass of milk and a little bottle of Tabasco sauce and two glasses of water. The water was all he was having. I sat down and ate without saying anything. The omelet was fluffy and moist and perfectly cooked. The cat door made its noise and the cat walked through the kitchen and hopped up onto the table. The cat watched me eating, his nose working at the odors, then he walked over and sat down in front of Pike and purred. Pike's the only person besides me that the cat will let touch him.

When I finished, I closed my eyes and held my head and Pike said, "Can you tell it now?"

"Yes." I drank more coffee and then I told him what had happened to Bradley Warren and I told him why. I told him everything I knew about Mimi Warren, and how she was, and why she was that way. I told him about finding Mimi at Asano's and arranging to bring her to Carol Hillegas's and Eddie Tang and the Hagakure. I told him that there were things that didn't add up and that I didn't have answers for and that maybe I didn't give a damn anymore. Pike listened without moving. Sometimes, Pike might not move for as long as you watch him. There are times I suspect that he does not move for days. When I finished he nodded to himself and said, "Yes."

"And you're thinking you had something to do with her killing her father."

I nodded.

Pike took a bit of egg off my plate and held it up for the cat. "You were doing your best for her, something that no one in her life has ever done."

"Sure." Mr. Convinced.

"Ever since the Nam, you've worked to hang on to the childhood part of yourself. Only here's a kid who never had a childhood and you wanted to get some for her before it was too late." Joe Pike moved his head and you could see the cat reflected in his glasses. The cat finished the bit of egg.

I said, "I want to find her, Joe. I want to bring her back."

He didn't move.

"I want to finish it."

Pike's mouth twitched. I cleared my place and washed the dishes. I went back upstairs, took another shower, then dressed and put the Dan Wesson under my arm.

When I went downstairs again, Joe Pike was waiting.

32

It was midafternoon when we got to Mr. Moto's. The lunch crowd was gone and so were most of the employees, except for a couple of busboys mopping the floor and setting up for happy hour. The manager with the hi-tone topknot was sitting at a table with the Butterfly Lady, going through receipts. He stood up when he saw us and started to say something about us not being welcome when I grabbed his throat and walked him halfway across the dining room, bent him back over a table, and put the Dan Wesson in his mouth. "Yuki Torobuni," I said.

The Butterfly Lady stood up. Pike pushed her back down. He pointed at the busboys, then pointed at the floor. They went down fast.

I said, "Yuki Torobuni."

Mumbles.

"I can't hear you."

More mumbles.

I took the Dan Wesson out of his mouth. He

coughed and licked at his lips and shook his head. "He's not here."

I let the gun rest against his jaw. "Where is he?"

"I don't know."

I dug my fingers into his throat and squeezed. I said, "Remember Mimi Warren? I am going to find her and I won't think twice if I have to kill you to do it."

His eyes opened wider and his face got purple and after a while he gave us Yuki Torobuni's address.

Torobuni lived in a treesy section of Brentwood, just east of Santa Monica, in a large sprawling ranch house more appropriate to a western star than a yakuza chieftain. There were wagon wheels lining the drive and a genuine old west buckboard converted into a flower planter and a gate featuring a rack of longhorn horns. Ben and Little Joe were probably out back. Joe Pike stared at it all and said, "Shit."

Ben and Little Joe weren't around, and neither was anyone else. No Torobuni. No guys with tattoos and missing fingers and stupid eyes. After a lot of knocking and looking in windows we turned up a Nicaraguan housekeeper who said that Mr. Torobuni wasn't home. We asked her when he had left. She said he wasn't home. We asked her when he might be back. She said he wasn't home. We asked her where he had gone. She said he wasn't home.

Pike said, "I guess he's not home."

"Maybe he's with Eddie Tang," I said, "Maybe they're reading the Hagakure and celebrating Eddie's promotion."

Pike liked that. "Maybe we should go see."

When we got to Eddie Tang's there was a black-

and-white parked at the fire hydrant out front with the same nondescript cop sedan I'd seen before double-parked beside it. Pike said, "I'll wait in the Jeep. One of them might know me."

I nodded and got out. The glass security door was propped open by a large potted plant so the cops could come and go as they wanted. I trotted up the little curved steps and through the open door like I owned the place. There was a landing and a couple of indoor trees and a circular step-down lobby with a brace of nice semicircular couches for waiting and chatting. There was a small elevator to the right and a very attractive suspended staircase to the left that curved up to the second floor. A chandelier that looked like a spaceship hung from the high ceiling and a door under the staircase probably went down to the garage and the laundry facility.

Two kids maybe eleven or twelve were standing by the elevator. One of the kids had a skateboard with a picture of a werewolf on it and the other had thick glasses. The kid with the glasses looked at me. I said, "What's going on with the cops?"

The kid with the glasses said, "I dunno. They went upstairs looking for some guy."

"Yeah? They find him?"

"Nah." Well, well.

The other kid said, "We thought they were gonna bust down the door or something but the manager let'm in."

I said, "What room is that?"

"212."

"The cops still up there?"

"Yeah. They're talking with the manager. She wants to screw one of them."

The kid with the skateboard smacked the kid with the glasses on the arm. The kid with the glasses said, "Hey, she screws everybody."

I said, "Well, you guys take it easy." I walked across the little lobby and out through the rear door and down one flight of bare cement steps to the garage. There was a little hall with a laundry room across from the stairs. The other end of the hall opened out to the garage. I went out to the garage and walked around. Nope. No dark green Alfa Romeo. Eddie was out, all right.

I went back to the laundry room and lifted myself atop an avocado-colored Kenmore dryer and waited. After about ten minutes I heard the door at the top of the stairs open, so I hopped off the dryer, fed in a couple of quarters, and turned it on. A uniformed cop in his early forties with tight sunburned skin came down the stairs and looked in. I frowned at him and shook my head. "Damn towels take forever," I said.

He nodded, continued on out into the garage, then went back up the stairs. I gave it another hour, then I went up to the lobby and looked out front. The cops were gone, and Pike had parked the Jeep across the street. I opened the door for him. We took the stairs to the second floor, went down the hall to 212, and let ourselves in.

Eddie had a narrow entry with mirrors on the walls and ceiling, and some kind of imitation black marble floor. There was a little guest bath on the left. To the right a short hall went to a bedroom that had been refitted as an exercise room, then on to what looked like another larger bedroom. The entry stepped down into a long living room which opened onto a balcony. The living room elled left for a dining area and the kitchen. The living room walls were crowded with trophies for excellence in the martial arts. Hundreds of them. Gleaming first-place cups and championship belts from exhibitions and tournaments all over the United States. Best All-Around. In Recognition of Excellence. Black Belt Master. Over-All Champion. "Don't worry about this stuff," I said. "The guy probably bought'm."

Pike said, "Uh-huh."

Joe went into the kitchen and I went into the bedroom. Eddie had a king-sized walnut platform bed with matching nightstands and a long low dresser and a mirror on the ceiling above his bed. I looked twice at the mirror. It had been years since I had seen a mirror above a bed. On the wall opposite the bed there were about a million framed photographs of Eddie Tang breaking bricks and flying through the air and accepting trophies and competing in martial arts tournaments and raising his hands, sometimes bloodied, in victory. In the earlier pictures he couldn't have been more than eight. Maybe he hadn't bought the trophies after all.

The master bath was as tastefully decorated as the rest of the apartment. Lots of mirrors and imitation black marble and flocked wallpaper. There were dirty underwear and socks in a plastic hamper and stains around the lavatory and in the tub. I looked in the medicine cabinet and the cabinet beneath the sink. There was no toothbrush and no toothpaste and no razor and no deodorant. Either Eddie was lax about personal hygiene, or those things were missing.

I went back into the bedroom. I looked through the chest and the dresser and the nightstand. A stack of well-thumbed *Penthouse* magazines sat on the nightstand along with a couple of old Sharper Image catalogs and one of those globe lamps that makes electrical patterns when you touch it. In the night-stand drawer there were five lavender-scented notes from someone named Jennifer professing her love for him and half a dozen snapshots of Eddie with different women in different places and two postcards from a United Airlines flight attendant named Kiki saying she wanted to see him when she got back to town. There was nothing of Mimi. No snapshots, no notes, no proof of her presence in his life, nothing to indicate a Westwood apartment house or babies or any sort of shared dreams, *I'm with people who love me.* Sure, kid.

There were also no clues to indicate where Eddie Tang might be or if Mimi Warren was with him or, if she wasn't, what had been done with her.

I put everything back the way I had found it and went out into the living room. Pike was waiting by the door. He said, "There used to be a suitcase in this closet. It's gone."

I told him what I hadn't found in the bathroom. "If Eddie went, he'll be back. We can wait."

Pike stared at the trophies. They were clean and bright and had been dusted regularly. He said, "Why not."

Outside, we parked the Jeep down the block in front of a condominium that was being built. We decided to split shifts, six on, six off. I said I'd take the first shift. Pike said that was fine. He walked away without another word.

I sat in the Jeep and waited. Two hours later the same unmarked cop sedan eased down the street and stopped by the fire hydrant. A cop in a brown suit got out, looked into the garage, then got back in his car and drove away. People went in and out of Eddie's building and cars moved up and down the street and a woman walked a little black dog and slowly the sky grew deeper until it was night. There was a nice summer chill in the air and a breeze coming in from the water, and the breeze made the palm fronds move and whisper and remind me of old songs I did not know. If I could just wait long enough, Eddie would come. When Eddie came, I could find Mimi. Waiting doesn't look like much, but it is something very important. Waiting is passive hunting.

At ten minutes after twelve that night, Joe Pike slipped into the Jeep with a brown paper bag. He said, "I've got it. Take a break."

I shook my head. "Think I'll just sit."

He nodded and took out two sandwiches. He handed one to me and kept one for himself. I didn't open it. I wasn't hungry.

Pike pulled a translation of the Hagakure from the bag. Imagine that. He sat, and read in the dark, and neither of us spoke.

Sometime very late that night I fell into a sort of half-sleep and dreamed I was having dinner with Mimi Warren. We were at a center table in the big back room at Musso & Frank's Grill, the only diners there. Pristine white tablecloths and shining cutlery and the two of us eating and drinking and talking. I could not hear what we said. I had the same dream every time I dozed over the next three days as Pike and I waited for Eddie Tang. The dream was always the same, and I could never hear what we said. Maybe the saying wasn't important. That we were together, maybe that was what mattered.

On the fourth day, Eddie Tang came home.

33

It was twenty of ten in the morning. The metal garage gate lifted and Eddie's Alfa cruised past and swung down into his garage. The Alfa was spotted and dust-streaked and there were mud splashes behind the wheel wells. Eddie had driven a long way.

Pike said, "Now or later?"

"Let's see what unfolds."

We sat. We waited.

One hour and ten minutes later a long white stretch limo came slowly up from Olympic and stopped in front of Eddie's building. The driver was the midget with the stupid eyes who'd been with Torobuni at Mr. Moto's. "Better," I said.

The midget got out of the limo, strutted over to the glass door, and buzzed Eddie's apartment. He got up on his toes for the intercom, then swaggered back to the limo and leaned against the door. He didn't even make it up to the top of the car.

Eddie came out three minutes later in light blue slacks and a navy jacket and a yellow shirt with a white button-down collar and a pink tie. Sweet. Maybe Eddie had been away taking yuppie lessons. The midget climbed in behind the wheel and Eddie got in back, and a few minutes later we followed them down to Olympic, then west to the San Diego Freeway, then south. The limo stayed in the right lane and took it slow. Just before lunchtime, traffic was light, and it was easy to stay back and not worry about being seen. We went south past the Mormon Temple and the Santa Monica Freeway, then took the Century Boulevard exit toward LAX.

I said, "If he gets on a plane, we've got trouble."

"No," Pike said. "We just shoot it down."

I looked at him. You never know.

We stayed two cars back and followed the limo onto Century Boulevard and past the airport hotels and into the LAX complex. Los Angeles International Airport is designed in two levels, the lower level for arriving flights, the upper level for departing flights. Eddie's limo didn't mount the ramp for the departure level. Pike looked disappointed. There went the ground-to-air.

The limo followed the huge U-shaped design of the airport around to the Tom Bradley Terminal, where international flights are based, then pulled to the pickup curb and parked. Eddie got out and went inside. After a while, he reappeared with three Japanese men and a redcap with a load of baggage. Two of the men were in their late fifties and dignified, with dark hair shot through by gray, powerful faces, and stern mouths. The third man was in his early thirties and taller than the other two, almost as tall as Eddie, with a hard bony face and broad shoulders. His hair was short except for a lock growing directly out the back of his head. The lock was long and braided and fell down his back. Well, well, well. "How much you want to bet," I said, "that those gentlemen run the yakuza in Japan?"

"A visit from the home office?"

"Yep."

"The Hagakure," Pike said.

I nodded. "Eddie gives it to Torobuni, Torobuni gives it to them. Everybody moves up."

Eddie and the three men got into the limo while the redcap and the midget loaded the trunk. When all the bags were stowed, Eddie leaned out of the car, gave the redcap a tip, and then the limo pulled away.

We looped back around to the San Diego Freeway again, headed north to the 1-10, then went east across the center of Los Angeles. We cut just south of the downtown area, then up past Monterey Park, and pretty soon downtown and its skyscrapers fell away to an almost endless plain of small stucco and clapboard houses. Past El Monte and West Covina, the traffic thinned and the houses gave way to undeveloped land and railroad spur lines and industrial parks. The limo settled into the number two lane and stayed there for a very long time, and for a very long time there was nothing to see. We rolled past Pomona and Ontario and by early afternoon we approached San Bernardino. Service roads appeared, lined with Motel 6's and Denny's Coffee Shops and middle-of-nowhere shopping malls featuring BEDROOM SPECIALISTS and INDIAN DINING and UNFINISHED FURNITURE. At the southern edge of San Bernardino, we turned north on the San Bernardino Freeway toward Barstow.

I said, "How we doing for gas?"

Pike didn't answer.

The San Bernardino forked to the right under a sign that said MOUNTAIN RESORTS, and that's the way we went. A little bit later it forked again, and this time when we followed we began a long slow climb into the San Bernardino Mountains toward Lake Arrowhead. The limo stayed in the slow lane and Pike dropped very far back. Maybe these guys were on their vacation. Maybe they were going to do a little fishing and water-skiing on the lake and grill some wienies down on the dock. That would be fun.

The mountains were vertical giants, rocky and bare except for their shoulders and ridges, which were laced with a stegosaurus-like spine of ponderosa pine trees. Every couple of miles there were signs that said DEER CROSSING or SLOWER TRAFFIC USE TURNOUTS or BEWARE FALLING ROCKS.

It took a half hour to reach a sign that said 5000 FEET ELEVATION, then the highway stopped climbing and leveled out in a heavy forest of ponderosas so improbably tall that we might have been in Oz. Two miles later the road forked again and another sign said BLUE JAY. An arrow pointed toward the left fork. That's where the limo went. That's where we went.

The road was narrow and winding and little clapboard cabins and weekender houses began to pop up amidst the pines. Most had small boats out front or muddy motorcycles leaning against native-stone garage walls. More and more houses sprouted, and pretty soon there was a Pioneer Chicken and a couple of banks and a shopping center and two coffee shops and a Jensen's Market and a U.S. Post Office and crowds of people and we were in Blue Jay. Up so high, Lake Arrowhead was a good twenty degrees cooler than San Bernardino below, and every summer the hordes ascended, desperate to escape the sweltering weather down in the flatland.

The limo didn't stop. It rolled slowly through the three-block stretch that was urban Blue Jay, and then the road forked once more. The town ended and houses reappeared but now the houses were larger and more expensive, big two- and three-story structures with lots of decking and stairs and high slanted roofs to shed the snow. We climbed, then leveled off, and we could see the lake, big and wide and gleaming in the summer sun. There were dozens of boats and skiers on the water, the powerboats and jet skis buzzing like angry mutant wasps.

On the north shore, the limo turned off the main road and eased down a gravel and tarmac lane for a mile and a half past large older homes. Big money was on the north shore. These were old vacation mansions built back in the thirties and forties for Hollywood celebrities and movie moguls who hoped to get away for a little hunting and fishing. Clark Gable and Humphrey Bogart and those guys. Wonder what Bogie would think if he knew a scumbag like Yuki Torobuni was living in his house?

Pike pulled off the road and parked. "We follow down there," he said, "they'll spot us."

We got out and trotted after them on foot.

A quarter of a mile ahead, the limo stopped at a private gate. The rear window on the driver's side

went down and Eddie Tang said something to an
Asian man who was leaning against a cranberry-
colored Chevrolet Caprice. The guard opened the
gate and the limo went in. Pike and I moved off the
lane into the woods and made our way past another
couple of houses until we got to Torobuni's place.
There was a native-stone wall running from the road
back into the woods. We followed it until we were
hidden from the road, then I went up for a look and
Pike continued on toward the lake.

The grounds were ten acres easy, with a looping
gravel drive and a huge stone mansion with a man-
sard roof and a smaller carriage house to the side.
Ponderosas and Douglas firs grew naturally about the
grounds, and in back there were gardens and flower
beds and stone pathways and swings for lazy summer
afternoons. The property ran a good four hundred
feet in a gentle slope down to the lake. At the lake
there was a stone entertaining pier and boat house
and four boat slips. The three men Eddie Tang had
brought were smiling and shaking hands with Yuki
Torobuni at the limo while a lot of guys who were
probably just hired muscle watched. Torobuni made
a big deal out of pumping each man's hand and bow-
ing and there was a lot of back slapping. Home office,
all right.

After they'd had their fill, Torobuni and the Big
Shots went inside, and Eddie went over to a thin guy
with nothing for a mustache and said something to
him. The thin guy went into the main house and
Eddie strolled around to the carriage house. After a
while the thin guy came out of the big house with
Mimi Warren and walked her over to the carriage

house. He knocked once, the door opened, Mimi went in, and then the door closed. The thin guy took a walk down to the water.

I stayed at the top of the wall between the branches of a Douglas fir and I did not move until something touched my leg. Joe Pike was on the ground below me.

"Not now," he said. "It's too light, and they're too many. Later. Later, we can get her."

34

Riding back toward Blue Jay, Joe Pike said, "We can wait for dusk, then come in from the water. If we come in behind the boat house, the guards won't be able to see us, then we can move up along the wall to the carriage house."

I nodded.

"Or we could call the cops."

I looked at him.

Pike's mouth twitched. "Just kidding."

At Blue Jay, we turned east along the southern edge of the lake and drove to Arrowhead Village. The village is a two-tiered shopping and hotel complex on the southeast rim of the lake. On the upper tier there's a Hilton hotel and a Stater Brothers market and a video rental place and a narrow road that brings you down to the lake. On the lakeside level there's a McDonald's and an ice cream shop and an arcade and a couple of million gift shops and clothing stores and real estate offices. There is also a place that will rent you a boat.

Joe parked in a spot by the ice cream shop, and took a canvas Marine Corps duffel bag from the Jeep's cargo space and slung it over his shoulder. Probably packed a big lunch. We walked down past the McDonald's to the lake, stopped by a wharf they have there, and looked out. This close, the lake was huge, all dark flat planes and black deep water. There was a little girl with very curly hair on the wharf, throwing white bread to the ducks. She was maybe eight and pretty and gave me a happy smile when she saw me. I smiled back.

Then I looked across the lake again and the smile faded. There was about an hour of light left. Plenty of time to call the cops. I said, "If we call the cops, they might blow it. The guys across the lake are pros. They're there to protect Torobuni and those other guys, and they won't hesitate to pull the trigger. I want the girl and I want her safe and if it's me over there I won't be worrying about something else when I should be worrying about her."

He looked at me through the mirrored lenses with no expression. "You mean us over there."

"Yeah."

The little girl tossed her last piece of bread, then ran back up the wharf into the arms of a tall man with glasses. The tall man scooped her up and heaved her toward the sky. Both of them laughed.

Pike said, "You're riding the edge on this one."

I nodded.

"Be careful."

I nodded again. "No one has ever been there for her, Joe."

The little girl and the tall man walked back toward the parking lot. Holding hands.

Pike and I went along the shore past boat slips and a tour boat dock and several small shops to a wooden wharf with a flotilla of little aluminum boats around it. There were kids on the wharf, and moms and dads wondering whether or not it would be safe to rent one of the boats so late in the day. At the end of the wharf there was a wooden shed with a rail-thin old man in it. He needed a shave. We went out on the wharf past the moms and dads and kids and up to the shed. I said, "We'd like to rent a boat, please."

"I got'm with six- or nine-pony 'Rudes. Which you want?"

"Nine."

He turned a clipboard with a rental form toward me. "Fill that out and gimme a deposit and you're all set."

He came around with a red plastic gas can and got into one of the boats and filled its tank. "Watch out for those rat bastard ski boats," he said. "Damn rich kids come out here and run wild all over the goddamn lake. Swamp you sure as I shit peanuts." He was a charming old guy.

"Thanks for the tip," I said.

He looked at Pike's duffel bag. "You plannin' on doin' some fishin'?"

Pike nodded.

The old guy shook his head and hawked up something phlegmy and spit it in the water. "Rich little bastards in their ski boats ruined that. You ain't gonna catch shit."

"You'd be surprised at what I catch," Pike said.

The old man squinted at Pike. "Yeah. I guess I would."

It took twenty minutes to cross the lake. There was mild chop and wakes from the ski boats but the little Evinrude motor gave us a steady dependable push. Halfway across we could make out the houses that dotted the north shore, and a little past that I turned to a westerly heading, looking for Torobuni's.

Pike took the Colt Python out of the duffel and clipped it over his right hip. He snapped a little leather ammo pouch beside it. The pouch held two six-round cylinder reloads. He went back into the duffel and came out with a sawed-off Remington automatic shotgun and a bandolier of Hi-Power shotgun shells. It was a 12-gauge skeet gun with a cut-down barrel and an extended magazine and a pistol grip for a stock. It looked like an over/under, but the bottom tube was the magazine and had been modified to hold eight rounds. Pike had done the modifications himself. He put the bandolier around his waist, then took out eight shells and fed them into the shotgun. Buckshot.

Torobuni's elaborate dock with its boat house and slips and bright yellow sun awning wasn't hard to spot. The stonework was intricate and beautiful and gave a sense of enduring wealth. It was easy to imagine long-ago times when life resembled an Erté painting and men and women wearing white stood on the dock sipping champagne. I said, "You see it?"

Pike nodded.

From the water you could see up past the dock and the boat house and along the walks that wound through the trees up to Torobuni's mansion. The carriage house was to the right of the main house and about sixty yards up from the lake. On both sides of the property big walls started at the water. There were two guys sitting under the awning and another guy walking up toward the carriage house. One of the guys under the awning went into the boat house, then came back with a third guy. A man and a woman on jet skis buzzed around the point, looped into the cove, then out again. The woman was maybe twenty-five and had a lean body and the world's smallest bikini. One of the guys under the awning pointed at her and the other two laughed. Nothing like America.

Pike said, "Property to the right is what I was talking about. We put the boat in there and come around the wall, the guys under the awning won't be able to see us."

The home next to Torobuni's was a sprawling Cape Cod with a sloping back lawn and a new wooden dock. The trees had mostly been cleared from the east side of its property, but Torobuni's side was still wooded and trees kneed out into the water. A sleek fiberglass ski boat was in one of the house's two slips, tied down and tarped, and the house was shuttered tight. Whoever owned the Cape Cod probably wouldn't be up until the weekend.

We stayed well out in the cove until we were past Torobuni's, then turned in and crept back along the shoreline. The sun was painting the western rim of the mountains and the sky was green and murky and cool. End of the day, and you could smell burning charcoal as people fired their barbeques. We tied up by the ski boat, then crept along the shore to the clump of pines at the end of Torobuni's wall. We stepped into the lake and went around the wall and into the trees, Pike keeping the Remington high and out of the water. There were voices from the far side of the boat house and music from the main house and somewhere someone smoked a cigarette, and men laughed. We waited. The sun sank further and the sound of ski boats was replaced by crickets and pretty soon there were fireflies.

We moved up along the wall to the carriage house and waited some more and pretty soon a short guy with thick shoulders and no hair drifted out of the main house carrying a couple of Coors. He came over to the carriage house, kicked at the door, and said something in Japanese. The door opened and the guy with the cheap mustache stepped out. The mustache took one of the Coors, and the two of them headed down to the lake. Pike and I looked in a side window. One large room with a double bed and two lamps and an old wing-back chair and a half bath and no Mimi. I said, "Main house."

We slipped through the shadows to the main house, then along its base to an empty room at the front corner of the house. There were two windows and both windows were dark, though the door across the room was open and showed a dimly lit hall. I cut the bottom of the screen, reached through to unlatch the frame, then pulled myself up and went in.

The room had at one time been a child's bedroom. There were two little beds and a very old chest and a high shelf of toys that hadn't been touched in many years. Other people's toys. Torobuni had probably bought the place furnished and hadn't bothered changing the little bedroom. Maybe he had never even been in it. Pike handed up the shotgun, then came in and took the shotgun back. Standing in the dark I could hear voices, but the voices were far away.

We went out the door and along the dim hall, first me, then Pike. The dim hall opened onto a wider hall that ran toward the center of the house. There were a lot of old landscapes on the walls and a double door into what was probably a den or trophy room with antelope heads. Halfway down, a guy was sitting in a brown leather wingback chair, smoking a cigarette, and flipping through a *Life* magazine that had to be thirty years old. I took out the Dan Wesson, held it down at my side and a little bit behind, then stepped into the hall and walked toward him. When he looked up I gave him one of my best smiles. "Mr. Torobuni said there was a bathroom down here but I can't find it."

He said something in Japanese, then stood up and I hit him on the left temple with the Dan Wesson. It knocked him sideways into the chair and I caught him on the way down and dragged him back into the shadows. No one shouted and no one fired shots. The voices from the back of the house went on. Pike took him from me and said, "Go on. I'll catch up." His glasses shone catlike in the dark.

I said, "Joe."

He said, "I'll catch up." His voice was quiet, soft in the darkness. "You want the girl?"

We stood like that, both of us holding the man, and then I nodded and let Pike have him. I went back into the larger hall and followed it past the den and into the entry. When Pike caught up with me, there was a fine spray of blood across his sweatshirt.

The main entry was paneled and wide and open the way they made them in elegant old houses. To our right was the front door, and across from the front door there was a stair going up to the second floor. I said, "If they want her out of the way she'll be upstairs. Maybe the third floor. Old house, the servants' quarters were up under the roof."

We went up. There was an ornate landing and a long hall running the width of the house and no one sitting in chairs. At the west end of the hall there was another, narrower stair that went down to the kitchen and up to the third floor. Servants' stair. I said, "Check the rooms on this floor. I'll go up to three."

On the third floor, the walls were plain and the carpet was worn and it was still very warm from the summer sun. There was a rectangular landing with a tiny bath and two closed doors. I tried the first door. It was locked. I knocked lightly. "Mimi?"

Inside, Mimi Warren said, "Huh?"

I put my shoulder against the door and pushed hard and the old jamb gave. Mimi was sitting cross-legged and naked on a queen-sized bed with satin sheets. There were yellow roses in a vase by the bed. Her hair was brushed and her skin was bright and she was wearing a thin gold chain around her ankle. She didn't look scared and she didn't look crazy. She looked better than I had ever seen her. When she saw me, her whole body gave a jerk and her mouth opened. I touched my finger to my lips and said, "I'm going to get you out of here."

She screamed.

I ran to her and put my hand over her mouth and pulled her close to me. She made a sound like *uhn* and flailed and hit and tried to bite and the roses crashed to the floor. There was a tall skinny window in the room, open for air, and down on the terrace there were shouts and the sound of running men and then the heavy undeniable *boom!* of Pike's shotgun.

I let Mimi scream and took her around the waist and carried her down the stairs to the second floor. Pike was at the top of the main stair, firing down toward the front entry. I said, "Back here. Stairs down to the kitchen."

He fired off three quick rounds, then fell back, reloading as he came.

The servants' stair was long and steep, and a man with one eye appeared at the bottom when we were halfway down. I shot him once in the head and lifted Mimi over him and then we were off the stairs. We went through the laundry and across the kitchen and through a swinging door into the dining room just as Yuki Torobuni and the midget with stupid eyes and the three guys from Japan came in from the outside. Torobuni and the midget had guns. The guy from Japan with the pony tail had the Hagakure. The midget shouted something and Torobuni raised his gun and I shot him twice in the chest. He fell back into the guy with the ponytail, knocking free the Hagakure. The guy with the ponytail threw himself in front of the two older guys and pushed them outside as the midget jumped forward, firing crazily into the floor and walls. Pike's shotgun *boomed* again and the midget slammed backward into the wall, a crimson halo over what used to be his head.

We were halfway across the dining room when Eddie Tang came in through the French doors. He didn't have a gun. I pointed the Dan Wesson at him anyway. "Get out of our way."

That's when the door behind us opened and the guy with the nothing mustache put a High Standard .45 automatic against the back of Joe Pike's head. Eddie liked that a lot. "Man," he said, "what a coupla assholes."

35

Outside, cars were starting and there was more shooting and men running and then cars accelerating hard on the gravel drive.

The guy with the mustache took Pike's shotgun and .357 and my Dan Wesson. Eddie held out his hand toward Mimi and said, "Come on, Me. It's okay." Me.

He didn't snarl and he didn't sneer and he didn't treat her like a dumb kid he had used to get his way. He took off his jacket and put it around her. "You okay?"

"It's cold."

He rubbed her arms, cooing to her. He told her that he loved her, and he told her that they were going to be fine as soon as they got to Japan, and he told her everything was going to be just as he had promised. He said those things, and he meant them. Every word. It was not what I had expected, but then, things rarely were.

I said, "You didn't kill Ishida to get the book. You

killed him because he wanted the book so bad he was going to hurt the girl to get it." The yakuza hadn't taken Mimi from Asano's. She'd gone with them. Just like she'd gone with Eddie from the hotel.

Mimi said, "Why can't you leave me alone? Why do you have to keep finding me? We're going to Japan. We're going to be happy."

Eddie gave Mimi a little squeeze and tipped his head toward the Hagakure. "Get the book."

She padded over and picked it up and padded back. The jacket fell off and she was naked again, but she didn't seem to notice.

I said, "These people killed Asano, Mimi. Doesn't that tell you something?"

Mimi gave me the out-from-under look, and there was something angry in her face. "He thought he was my father. He thought he could boss me just like my father." Her eyes went red and strained. "I don't have a father."

Eddie said, "Shh," the way you calm a nervous dog. He snapped at the Mustache Man, pissed and wanting to know where everyone had gone, and the Mustache Man snapped back.

I said, "You're right, kid. You don't. He bled to death where you dropped him on Mulholland Drive."

Mimi's left eye ticked.

Eddie said, "Shut the hell up."

There was a heavy thud from the front of the house, and loud voices, then another car roared to life.

I said, "Hey, Eddie, you love her so much, how'd you help? You turn the crank? You say, 'What the hell, off the old bastard?'"

Eddie gave me uncertain eyes and I knew then that it had been Mimi. Just Mimi. Eddie probably hadn't even known. She'd gone off, maybe slipped away from him, just done it, then come back and told him, juiced and a little bit crazy. Blood simple. You could see it in his face. Eddie Tang, yakuza murder freak, even Eddie couldn't imagine killing his own father.

Mimi pulled at him. "Let's go, Eddie. I wanna go now."

I said, "She's sick, Eddie. She needs to go back and work with people who know what they're doing. If she doesn't, she'll never be right."

Mimi said, "No."

I said, "Leave her. I'll see she gets help."

Mimi said, *"No."*

The guy with the nothing mustache shouted something, wanting to finish it and go, but Eddie ignored him. Eddie knew there was something wrong, but he was fighting it. "She goes back, they'll put her in jail for killing her old man."

I shook my head. "They'll put her in a hospital. They'll work with her."

Outside, men crashed around the side of the house. Eddie barked something else in Japanese to the Mustache Man, then turned back through the French doors and yelled. Just as he did, a fat guy with no hair slammed out of the kitchen, waving a gun and screaming. Mustache Man looked, and when he did, Joe Pike took the High Standard out of his hand and shot the fat guy. I hit Mustache Man in the face with a roundhouse kick, and he went down, and then Eddie Tang was back in the house. It had taken maybe a third of a second.

I said, "That's it, Eddie." I picked up the Dan Wesson, then edged forward and pulled the girl toward me. She tried to jerk away, but she didn't try very hard. Maybe she was tired.

Eddie's face was dark. "Don't touch her, dude."

I pointed the gun at him. "Get out of the way."

Eddie put himself in the center of the door and shook his head. "You want the Hagakure, take it, but Mimi stays with me."

I looked at Pike. His glasses caught the light and showered it around the room.

"Make your brain work and think about this, Eddie. I'm going to see that she gets help. I'm going to see that she's made right."

Eddie Tang shook his head. "No." He took a step toward us. Me with the Dan Wesson, and Pike with the High Standard, and he took a step toward us.

I aimed the Dan Wesson at his forehead. "Eddie. Get real."

Eddie's shirt was wet and sticking to his skin. He yanked off the tie, and most of the shirt came with it. The tattoos writhed and glistened like living things. They crawled up his biceps, over his shoulders, and down across his chest and abdomen. Dragons roared and tigers leaped and samurai warriors locked swords in combat. Red, white, green, yellow, blue. Brilliant primary colors that made him look feral and monstrous and of the earth. He went down low and stared at us.

Pike's mouth twitched.

I said, "Joe. Not you, too?"

Joe Pike raised the High Standard level with Eddie's heart. "Your call."

Some days. I pushed Mimi to the side and put down the Dan Wesson and Pike dropped the High Standard and Eddie Tang launched two spin kicks so quickly that they were impossible to see. Mimi screamed. Pike rolled under the first kick and I pushed myself sideways and hit Eddie's back. Pike came up and snapped a roundhouse kick to the side of Eddie's head and punched him in the back of the neck and the kidneys. Eddie's body tightened like a single flexed muscle and he shook it off. I'd seen Pike crack boards with that kick.

Mimi screamed again and ran forward, scratching and hitting, and Pike pushed her down hard. She stayed there, holding the crumbling Hagakure to her breasts and watching with wide eyes.

We kept Eddie between us, moving on our toes and staying out of reach. Eddie was big and strong and knew the moves from a thousand tournaments, but tournaments weren't real. Real is different. If it wasn't, maybe we'd be dead.

Outside, there were no more shots and no more cars racing away. Voices came through the house and then faded and there was nothing. Maybe everyone was gone and we were all that was left, men alone in a dark wood, fighting.

We moved so that Eddie could never long face either of us. If he turned toward one, the other had his back. Pike would strike, and then me, and both of us worked to stay away from his hands and feet. He was faster than a big man was supposed to be, but having to work against two of us took away his timing. He couldn't get off the way you can get off one-on-one, and after a while he began to slow. We hit the big muscles in his back and his thighs and his shoulders, and he slowed still more. The certainty that had been in his eyes began to fade. It made me think of King Kong, fighting the little men for the woman he loved.

Far away, maybe on the other side of the lake, there were sirens. Something flickered on Eddie's face when he heard them, and he glanced at the girl. When the cops got here, she would go back, and he would go back, but they wouldn't go back together. He made a deep grunt and he tried to end it. He turned his back to Joe Pike and came at me. I backpedaled and Pike came in fast. Eddie ran me back against the doorjamb. He snapped a fist out and the fist hit the jamb and shattered wood and plaster. I rammed the heel of my hand up into the base of his nose and something cracked and blood spurted out and he grabbed me. Pike wrapped his hands around Eddie's face and dug his fingers into his eyes and pulled. Eddie let go and jerked an elbow back and you could hear Pike's ribs snap. I hit Eddie with two quick punches to the ear and followed them with another roundhouse kick that again snapped his head to the side. He staggered, but stayed up, and I said, "Shit."

The sirens howled closer and closer until the sound seemed to come from every direction, and then they were at the front of the house. Eddie was in the middle of the room, sucking air, with Pike and me on either side. Back where we started. Only now there was sweat and blood and cops at the door. Eddie looked from me to Pike to the girl, then lowered his hands and stood up out of his crouch as if someone had called time out. The girl said, "Eddie?"

He shook his head. There were tears coming down

his face, working into the blood. He had given it his best, but it hadn't been enough.

I said, "It's over, Eddie."

Eddie looked at me. "Not yet." When he said it, he looked old.

Eddie Tang stepped over the fat guy and pulled Joe's shotgun from beneath the Mustache Man. He looked at it and then he looked at Joe Pike. There were more voices outside and somebody yelled for somebody else to watch himself. Mimi said, "Shoot them, Eddie. Shoot them *now*."

Eddie said, "I love her, man." Then he tossed the gun to Joe, bared his teeth like something crazed and primal, and charged straight ahead with a series of power kicks that could knock down a wall. Joe Pike fired four rounds so quickly they might have been one. The 12-gauge blasts in the small room made my ears ring and the buckshot load carried Eddie Tang backward through the French doors and out into the night. The four spent shells bounced off the ceiling and hit the floor and spun like little tops, and outside a cop voice shouted, "Holy shit!"

When the shell casings stopped spinning there was silence.

For the longest time, Mimi Warren did not move, then she looked at me and said, "I don't feel anything."

I said, "Kid, you've had so much done to you that the part that feels went dead a long time ago." Maybe Carol Hillegas could fix it.

Mimi cocked her head the way a bird will, as if I'd said something curious, and smiled. "Is that what you think?"

I didn't move.

She said, "I'm such a liar. I make up stuff all the time."

I went to her, then, and put my arms around her, and she started to scream, flailing and thrashing and trying to get to Eddie, or maybe just trying to get away from me. I held on tight, and said, "It's all right. It's going to be all right."

I said it softly, and many times, but I don't think she heard me.

36

The mountain cops were pretty good about it. The sheriff was a guy in his forties who had put in some time with the Staties and knew he was in over his head when he saw the mess. His partner was a jumpy kid maybe twenty-one, twenty-two, and after enough gun-waving the sheriff told him to put it away and go get an extra pair of cuffs out of the cruiser.

They found some clothes for Mimi, then cuffed us and drove us down to the State Police substation in Crestline, about a thousand feet lower on the mountain. The Crestline doc got pulled out of bed to check us over and tape Pike's ribs. Mostly, he looked at Mimi and shook his head.

When the doctor was finished, a state cop named Clemmons took Pike's statement first, and then mine, all the while sucking on Pall Mall cigarettes and saying, "Then what?" as if he'd heard it a million times.

After I had gone through it, Clemmons sucked a double lungful of Pall Mall and blew it at me. "You knew the girl was in there, how come you didn't just call us?"

"Phone line was busy," I said.

He sucked more Pall Mall and blew that at me, too.

The jail was a very small building with two tiny holding cells, one for men and one for women, and from Clemmons's desk I watched Mimi. She sat and she stared and I wondered if she'd do that the rest of her life.

Clemmons called L.A. and got Charlie Griggs pulling a late tour. They stayed on the phone about twenty minutes, Clemmons giving Griggs a lot of detail. One of the Staties brought in the Hagakure and Clemmons waved him to put it on a stack of *Field & Stream* in the corner. Evidence. When Clemmons hung up he came over and took the cuffs off me and then went to the holding cell and did the same for Pike. "You guys sit tight for a while and have some coffee. We got some people coming up."

"What about the girl?" I said. Clemmons hadn't taken the cuffs off her.

"Let's just let her sit." He went back to his desk and got on the phone and called the San Bernardino County coroner.

I went over to the coffee urn and poured two cups and brought them to Mimi's cell. I said, "How about it?" I held out the cup but she did not look at me nor in any way respond, so I put it on the crossbar and stood there until long after the coffee was cold.

More Staties came and a couple of Feds from the San Bernardino office and they gave back our guns and let us go at a quarter after two that morning. I said, "What about the girl?"

Clemmons said, "A couple of our people are going to drive her back to L.A. in the morning. She's going to be arraigned for the murder of her father."

"Maybe I should stay," I said.

"Bubba," Clemmons said, "that ain't one of the options. Get your ass outta here."

A young kid with a double-starched uniform and a baleful stare drove us back up to Arrowhead Village and dropped us off by Pike's Jeep. It was cool in the high mountain air, and quiet, and very very dark, the way no city can ever know dark.

The McDonald's was lit from inside, but that was the only light in the village, and the Jeep was the only car in the parking lot. We stood beside it for a while, breathing the good air. Pike took off his glasses and looked up. It was too dark to see his eyes. "Milky Way," he said. "Can't see it from L.A."

There were crickets from the edge of the forest and sounds from the lake lapping at the boat slips.

Pike said, "What's wrong?"

"It wasn't the way I thought it was. Eddie loved her."

"Uh-huh."

"She wanted to stay with him. She hadn't been kidnapped. She wasn't going to be killed."

He nodded.

Something splashed near the shore. I took a deep slow breath and felt empty. "I assumed a lot of things that were wrong. I needed her to be a victim, so that's the way I saw her." I looked at Joe. "Maybe she wasn't." *I'm such a liar.*

Pike slipped on the glasses. "Bradley."

My throat was tight and raw and the empty place burned. "She made up so damn much. Maybe she made that part up, too. Maybe he never touched her. I needed a reason for it all, and she gave me that. Maybe I helped her kill him."

Joe Pike thought about that for a long time. Centuries. Then he said, "Someone had to bring her back."

"Sure."

"Whatever she did, she did because she's sick. That hasn't changed. She needs help."

I nodded. "Joe. Once you had the gun you could have wounded him."

"No."

"Why not?"

He didn't move for a time, as if the answer required a complete deliberation, then he went to the Jeep. When he came back he had the translation of the Hagakure. He held it respectfully. "This isn't just a book, Elvis. It's a way of life."

Tashiro had said that.

Pike said, "Eddie Tang was yakuza, but he killed Ishida for the girl. He committed himself to getting her to Japan, but we stopped him. He loved her, yet he was going to lose her. He had failed the yakuza and he had failed the girl and he had failed himself. He had nothing left."

I remembered the way Eddie Tang had looked at Joe Pike. Pike, and not me. "The way of the warrior is death."

A cool breeze came in off the lake. Something moved in the water and a light plane appeared in the sky past the McDonald's roofline, its red anti-collision light flashing. Pike put his hand on my shoulder and squeezed. "You got her," he said. "You got her safe. Don't think about anything else."

We climbed into the Jeep and took the long drive back to Los Angeles.

37

I spent most of the next day on the phone. I called Lou Poitras and found out that they would be holding Mimi at the L.A. County Correctional Medical Facility for an evaluation. I called Carol Hillegas and asked her to pay Mimi a visit and make sure Mimi had good people assigned to her. The black Fed Reese called me more than once, and so did the woman from the L.A. County district attorney's office. There'd been a lot of conference calling between L.A. and San Bernardino and Sacramento, but nobody was going to bring charges. Nobody was sure what the charges would be. Illegal rescue?

Terry Ito stopped by that evening and said he hoped he wasn't disturbing me. I said no and asked him in. He stood in my living room with a brown paper bag in his left hand and said, "Is the kid going to be okay?"

I said, "Maybe."

He nodded. "We heard somebody nailed Yuki Torobuni."

"Yeah. That happened."

He nodded again and put out his right hand. "Thanks."

We shook.

He opened the bag and took out a bottle of Glenlivet scotch and we drank some and then he left. By eight o'clock that night I had finished the bottle and fallen asleep on the couch. A couple of hours later I was awake again and sleep would not return.

The next day I watched TV and read and lay on the couch and stared at my high-vaulted ceiling. Just after noon I showered and shaved and dressed and took a drive over to the County Medical Facility and asked them if I could see Mimi. They said no. I left the front and went around back and tried to sneak in, but a seventy-five-year-old security guard with narrow shoulders and a wide butt caught me and raised hell. It goes like that sometimes.

I bought groceries and a couple of new books and went home to the couch and the staring and the feeling that it was not over. I thought about Traci Louise Fishman and I thought about what Mimi had said. *I make up stuff all the time.* Maybe it couldn't be over until I knew what was real and what wasn't. Some hero. I had brought Mimi back, but I hadn't saved her.

At a little after four that afternoon, the doorbell rang again, and this time it was Jillian Becker. She was wearing a loose Hawaiian top and tight Guess jeans and pink Reebok high-tops. She smelled of mint. It was the first time I had seen her in casual clothes. I stood in the door and stared at her, and she stared back. I said, "Would you like to come in?"

"If you don't mind."

I said not at all. I asked if she would like something to drink. She said some wine would be nice. I went into the kitchen and poured her a glass of wine and a glass of water for myself. She said, "I tried your office but I guess you haven't been in."

"Nope."

"Or checking your answering machine."

"Nope."

She sipped her wine. "You look tired."

"Uh-huh."

She sipped the wine again. "The police spoke with me, and so did Carol Hillegas. They told me what you had to do to get Mimi. It must have been awful."

I said, "How's Sheila?"

Shrug. "Her family has come here to be with her. I've been talking to her, and so have the doctors who've seen Mimi. She's going to join Mimi in therapy. She'll probably enter into therapy on her own, too."

"Have you seen Mimi?"

She shook her head. "No. I heard you tried."

I spread my hands.

Jillian put her wineglass down and said, "Is it always this hard?"

I stared out through the glass to the canyon and shook my head.

Jillian Becker sat quietly for a moment, swirling her wine and watching it move in the glass. Then she said, "Carol Hillegas agreed with me."

"What?"

"If the one who makes the pain stop is the one who loves them, then that's you."

I finished the water and put down the glass and looked out at the canyon some more. The cat door clacked and the cat came in from the kitchen. When he saw Jillian he growled, deep and warlike. I said, "Beat it."

The cat sprinted back into the kitchen and through his door. Jillian said, "What a nice cat."

I laughed then, and Jillian Becker laughed, too. She had a good, clear laugh. When the laughter faded, she looked at me. "I wanted to tell you that I'm leaving Los Angeles. There is no more Warren Investments. Even if there were, I would leave. I'm going to find a position back east."

Part of me felt small, and growing smaller.

"But I'm going to stay here in L.A. for another couple of weeks before I go. I wanted to tell you that, too."

"Why are you going to hang around?"

She looked at me steadily. "I thought I might spend some time with you."

We sat like that, me on the couch and Jillian on the chair, and then she put out her hand. I took it.

Outside, a red hawk floated high over the canyon, and was warm in the sun.

Please turn the page for
Robert Crais's latest
Elvis Cole and Joe Pike novel,

A DANGEROUS MAN

1.

Isabel Roland

Three tellers were working the morning Isabel Roland was kidnapped. Clark Davos, a sweet guy whose third baby had just been born; Dana Chin, who was funny and wore fabulous shoes; and Isabel, the youngest teller on duty. Isabel began working at the bank a little over a year ago, three months before her mother died. Five customers were in line, but more customers entered the bank every few seconds.

Mr. Ahbuti wanted bills in exchange for sixteen rolls of nickels, twelve rolls of dimes, and a bag filled with quarters. As Isabel ran coins through a counter, her cell phone buzzed with a text from her gardener. Sprinkler problems. Isabel felt sick. The little house she inherited from her mother was driving her crazy. The sprinklers, a leaky roof over the porch, roots in the pipes because of a stupid pepper tree, the ancient range that made scary popping noises every time she turned on the left front burner. Always a new problem, and problems cost money. Isabel had grown up in the house, and loved the old place, but her modest salary wasn't enough to keep it.

Isabel closed her eyes.

Why did you have to die?

Abigail George touched her arm, startling her. Abigail was the assistant branch manager.

"I need you to take an early lunch. Break at eleven, okay?"

Isabel had punched in at nine. It was now only ten forty-one, and Izzy had eaten an Egg McMuffin and hash browns on her way into work. She felt like a bloated whale.

"But it's almost eleven now. I just ate."

Abigail smiled at Mr. Ahbuti, and lowered her voice.

"Clark has to leave early. The baby again."

They both glanced at Clark. His baby had come early, and his wife wasn't doing so well.

Abigail shrugged apologetically.

"I'm sorry. Eleven, okay? *Please?*"

Abigail squeezed her arm, and hurried away.

Isabel gave Mr. Ahbuti his cash, and called for the next customer when Dana hissed from the adjoining station.

"*Iz.*"

Dana tipped her head toward the door and mouthed the words.

"*It's him.*"

Ms. Kleinman reached Izzy's window as the man joined the line. He was tall and dark, with ropey arms, a strong neck, and lean cheeks. Every time he came in, Dana went into heat.

"*Iz.*"

Dana finished with her customer, and whispered again.

"Studburger."

"Stop."

"Double meat. Extra sauce."

"Shh!"

Ms. Kleinman made a one-hundred-dollar cash withdrawal.

As Izzy processed the transaction, she snuck glances at the man. Gray sweatshirt with the sleeves cut off, faded jeans tight on his thighs, and dark glasses masking his eyes. Isabel stared at the bright red arrows tattooed high on his arms. She wanted to touch them.

Dana whispered.

"Manmeat on a stick."

Isabel counted out twenties.

As Ms. Kleinman walked away, Dana whispered again.

"Finger lickin' good."

Izzy cut her off by calling the next customer.

"Next, please."

The man was now third in line. Dana called for a customer, and the man was now second. Clark called, and the man was hers.

"*Iz*."

Dana.

"Ask him out."

"Sh!"

"You know you want to. Do it!"

Izzy said, "Next, please."

Dana hissed, "Do it!"

When he reached her window, Izzy smiled brightly.

"Good morning. How may I help you?"

He laid out three checks and a deposit slip. Two of the checks were made payable to Joe Pike, and the third to cash. They totaled a considerable amount.

Joe Pike said, "For deposit."

"You're Mr. Pike?"

She knew his name, and he probably knew she knew. He came in every three or four weeks.

"I've helped you before."

He nodded, but offered no other response. He didn't seem friendly or unfriendly. He didn't seem interested or uninterested. She couldn't read his expression.

Isabel fed the checks through a scanner. She wanted to say something clever, but felt stupid and awkward.

"And how's your day so far?"

"Good."

"It's such a pretty day, and here I am stuck in the bank."

Pike nodded.

"You're so tan, I'll bet you're outside a lot."

"Some."

Nods and one-word answers. He clearly wasn't interested. Isabel entered the transaction into her terminal, and gave him the deposit receipt.

The man said, "Thank you."

He walked away, and Isabel felt embarrassed, as if his lack of interest proved she was worthless.

"Iz!"

Dana leered across the divider.

"I saw you talking!"

"He thanked me. Saying thanks isn't talking."

"He never talks. He thinks you're *hot*."

"He didn't even see me."

"Shut *up*! He *wants* you!"

If only.

Isabel wondered if she could scrape together two hundred dollars for a new garden timer.

She glanced at her watch. Ten fifty-two. Eight minutes from a lunch she didn't want, and an event that would change her life.

2.

Karbo and Bender

Karbo and Bender missed her at home by ten minutes. Materials found inside gave them her place of employment, so now they waited at a meter six blocks from a bank near the Miracle Mile.

Karbo slumped in the passenger seat, sipping a café mocha.

"Ever kidnap anyone?"

Bender glanced away. Bender was the driver. Karbo was the smile. They had worked for Hicks before, but never together. Karbo and Bender met for the first time at four that morning outside a strip mall in Burbank. They would part in approximately two hours, and never meet again.

Karbo said, "Sorry. My mistake."

No questions allowed. They knew what they were supposed to do, how they were supposed to do it, and what was expected. Hicks prepped his people.

Bender gestured behind them.

"Here he comes."

Karbo lowered his window.

Hicks was a hard, pale dude in his forties. Nice-looking, not a giant, but broader than average. Nonthreatening, if you didn't look close. A nasty edge lurked in his eyes, but he hid it well. Karbo and Bender were nice-looking, nonthreatening guys, too. Especially Karbo.

Hicks had come from the bank.

"She's a teller. Figure on making the grab at lunch."

Bender arched his eyebrows.

"Why lunch?"

"People eat lunch. Employees park in back, but with all these little cafés, no way she'll drive. She'll probably exit the front, and give you a shot. You get the shot, take it."

Bender's eyebrows kissed in a frown.

"Wouldn't it make sense to wait at her house, grab her when she gets home?"

Hicks glanced left and right, relaxed, just looking around.

"Time is an issue. You want out, say so, and I'll get someone else."

Karbo changed the subject. He didn't want out. He wanted the money.

"I have a question. What if she goes out the back?"

"If she exits the rear, you're out of the play. If she isn't alone, say she comes out with a friend, you're out of the play. Maybe she won't even come out. Maybe she brought a sandwich. No way to know, right? You have one job, and only the one."

Karbo said, "The front."

People would be watching the rear, for sure, but this was how Hicks operated. Compartmentalization. Minimum information. If an element got popped, they had nothing to give. Karbo admired the tough, precise way Hicks did business.

Hicks rested his hand on the door.

"Picture."

Hicks had given them a five-by-seven photograph of a twenty-two-year-old woman. Having changed the play, he didn't want the picture in their possession. The picture was evidence.

Bender returned the picture, and Hicks offered a final look.

"Burn her face into your brains. We can't have a mistake."

A high school photo printed off the internet showed a young woman with short dark hair, glasses, and a smile with a crooked incisor.

Karbo said, "Burned."

Bender cleared his throat. Karbo sensed the man thought they were moving too fast, but the money was huge, and their involvement would end in minutes.

Bender said, "What's she wearing?"

"Pink shirt. Kinda dull, not bright. A pink shirt over a tan skirt. I couldn't see her shoes."

Hicks tucked the picture into his jacket.

"She'll be easy to spot, but if anything looks weird, drive away. Anyone with her, drive away. Am I clear?"

Karbo and Bender nodded.

"Clear."

"Go."

Hicks walked away and Bender eased from the curb.

Their ride was a dark gray Buick SUV owned by a leasing company in La Verne, California. Late model, low miles, the full option package. They had picked up the Buick at 4:22 that morning, specifically for use in the crime. After they delivered the girl, they would hand off the Buick, pick up their cars and money, and go their separate ways.

Karbo thought Bender was having second thoughts, but Bender surprised him.

"Beautiful day, isn't it? Lovely, lovely day."

Karbo studied the man for a moment. "Yeah."

"Gorgeous. A perfect day."

Bender hadn't said ten words all morning, even when they were searching the woman's house. Karbo figured he was nervous.

"I know we're not supposed to ask, but you've worked gigs before?"

Bender tapped the blinker and changed lanes. "Three or four."

"This will be easy. Hicks's gigs are always easy."

"Snatching a person in front of a bank in broad daylight can't make the top of the Easy list."

"You didn't have to say yes. You should've backed out."

"Right."

"I don't want to work with someone I can't trust."

"I'm concerned, is all. He's making this up on the fly."

"A lot of these gigs, this is what happens."

"You're not concerned? You don't see the risk here?"

Karbo saw the risk. He also saw the reward.

"Look at this face."

Karbo grinned and fingered his dimples.

"I'll have her in the car in ten seconds tops. No big scene, I promise. Five minutes later, she's out of our lives. What could be easier?"

"You may be a moron."

Karbo shrugged.

"True, but you get to stay in the car. I'm the guy who gets out."

Bender finally nodded.

"You're right. And if anything looks weird, we drive away."

"Damned right we do. Fast."

Bender seemed to relax, and found a spot at a meter with an eyes-forward view of the bank.

Karbo liked the location. A commercial street lined with single-story storefronts two blocks south of Olympic. A straight shot to the freeway if needed. The girl would turn toward or away from them when she left the bank, and either was fine. A lot of people were out and about, but this shouldn't matter if Karbo did his job quickly and well.

Karbo said, "You were right."

"About?"

"The day. It's a beautiful day in the neighborhood."

"You're a moron. A perfect day doesn't make this any less risky."

They watched the bank. They didn't pay attention to the people who went into the bank, or the men who came out. They watched for a twenty-two-year-old woman wearing a pink shirt over a tan skirt.

They paid no attention to the man wearing a sleeveless gray sweatshirt. They did not see the red arrows tattooed high on his arms, and barely noticed when he entered the bank. They paid even less attention when he emerged a few minutes later.

This was their mistake.

Their perfect day was about to turn bad.

3.

Isabel

Ten fifty-three.

Isabel helped her last customer, logged out of her terminal, and closed her station. She wasn't hungry, so she wondered if she had time to run home and catch the gardener.

Dana said, "Iz?"

Dana leered, and lowered her voice.

"We can look up his number. You can call, and tell him there was a problem with the transaction."

Isabel rolled her eyes, and left the bank at eleven-oh-two.

She didn't feel up to dealing with the gardener, so she decided to get a smoothie. She was debating between chocolate and chocolate-caramel when a shiny new SUV pulled to the curb ahead of her. A good-looking guy climbed out, opened the rear passenger door, and looked around as if he was confused. He saw her, and offered a tentative smile.

"Oh, hey, excuse me?"

Izzy returned his smile.

"Yes?"

He approached and touched her arm, exactly as Abigail had touched her arm moments before. His smile and manner were halfway between embarrassed and little-boy-charming.

"I'm supposed to return this gift, and I can't find the darned address. I'm totally lost."

He touched her toward the open door, his fingers a polite invitation to help with his problem.

Isabel went with him, and saw nothing inside but a clean backseat in the clean car beneath a clean blue sky. Another man sat at the wheel, and never looked at her.

Isabel didn't have time to turn, or ask which address he couldn't find. He shoved her hard, shoulder and hip, and drove her into the car. She grabbed at the edge of the roof, trying to save herself, but her grip broke free.

"Stop, what are you—stop!"

He dove in on top of her. The door slammed.

Isabel screamed, but his hand covered her mouth. She screamed as hard as she could, but her scream could not escape.

4.

Joe Pike

Upscale mid-city area: boutiques and pastry shops, a Tesla filling a loading zone, an older gentleman walking twin beagles, a homeless man splayed in the shade from a shopping cart heavy with plastic bags. Pike wasn't looking to save someone's life on the day he left the bank.

Pike's red Jeep Cherokee was parked across the street. He departed the bank at 10:54, and slid behind the wheel. He tucked the deposit receipt into the console, removed his .357 Magnum from beneath the front seat, and considered the two female tellers.

Dana and Isabel. Pike had noticed the expressive glances and whispered comments they traded. Their infatuation might have been welcome if they worked at a coffee shop or fitness center, but not at a job where they had access to his banking information. Pike's current business interests included a partnership in a detective agency, a custom gun shop in Culver City, and several rental properties. His former employers included the United States Marine Corps, the Los Angeles Police Department, and various private military contractors. During his contract years, his fees were paid by foreign governments approved by the United States, shell companies controlled by the CIA and NSA, and multinational corporations. This employment had been legal, but the transfer of funds from his employers had left a digital trail that a curious bank employee might question. Pike had maintained accounts at this particular bank for almost two years, and wondered if it was time to move on.

Pike was pondering this when Isabel's pink shirt caught his attention. She stepped from the bank, paused to put on a pair of sunglasses, and set off along the sidewalk. A dark gray SUV eased to the curb ahead of her. The driver's head turned as the vehicle passed, and something about the way he tracked her felt off.

Pike noticed details. The Marines had trained him to maintain situational awareness. Multiple tours in hot spots from Central America to Afghanistan had baked in his skills. The driver wasn't simply looking at Isabel; he seemed to be locked on a target.

A nice-looking man got out of the passenger seat, and opened the backseat door. Pike saw the man's head and shoulders across the roof. He turned, and Isabel smiled. They appeared to know each other, but Pike read a question in her body language.

The man touched her arm, and gestured toward the vehicle. Isabel went with him as the older gentleman with the beagles passed behind them. The older gentleman paid no attention.

Isabel and the man looked in the SUV, and disappeared so quickly the SUV might have swallowed them. In the instant she vanished, Pike saw a flash of shock in her eyes. Her fingers clutched the roof, and then she was gone. The blinker came on, and the SUV eased into traffic.

Pike wasn't sure what had happened. He watched the departing vehicle, and clocked the surroundings. The gentleman urged his beagles along, but a woman in a bright floral dress stood frozen. She gaped at the SUV as if she had seen something monstrous, but didn't know what to make of it. No one else stopped, or stared, or shouted for help.

The SUV put on its blinker, and turned at the next corner.

But the skin across Pike's back tingled as it had in the deserts and jungles. He started his Jeep, and followed.